A SLICE OF MURDER

A Shilpa Solanki Mystery

MARISSA DE LUNA

BLOODHOUND
— BOOKS —

www.bloodhoundbooks.com

Print ISBN 978-1-914614-88-0

For Jan and Bruce

Chapter One

Shilpa Solanki dropped the bloodstained knife. She couldn't just leave it there, so she threw it in the sink. There were several caterers around. One of them would wash it.

Her heart was beating like an Indian drum in a Bollywood wedding scene. Her mother made her watch those movies, hoping it would put her in touch with her culture, her roots. A little icing mishap should not have made her this jittery. But this was her first big commission, and she wanted to get it right.

'Shilpa, Shilpa darrrling,' the host called.

Shilpa spun around, wiping the perspiration from her upper lip and pushing her dark hair back behind her ears.

Mrs Drew, a woman of large stature who spoke with a plum in her mouth, was heading towards her, hands flapping, her billowing cream-and-pink dress fluttering around her. Shilpa clasped her shaking hands behind her back.

'You have everything you need?' Mrs Drew asked.

'You've changed, Marg!' a guest commented as they passed the kitchen.

Mrs Drew blushed, turning to her guest. 'I was a little too hot in that other thing.' She looked at Shilpa. 'So, dear?'

'I...' Shilpa hesitated. She cleared her throat. 'I was looking for a spatula.'

'Hmm, must be one around here. It is a kitchen. Have you looked in the drawers?'

Shilpa had looked everywhere, and there were several places to look. The Drews' house in South Devon was palatial, and their stunning kitchen with white marble worktops was bigger than Shilpa's combined living space. Failing to find a spatula she had contemplated using the back of a knife. It was how she had stumbled across the dirty implement.

Mrs Drew nodded politely to dismiss the guest who had commented on her attire. She turned back to Shilpa. 'I know where there's one. I borrowed it from Cook to open the drawer on the bureau. It always sticks in the heat. It must be in the study. Wait there; I'll only be a second.' She darted out of the kitchen, adjusting her pink hat as she went. She returned less than a minute later waving around a navy-and-metal spatula which matched perfectly with the kitchen units.

'Thank you,' Shilpa muttered, stepping towards the naked lemon cake. It was naked, but it still required frosting, which you had to apply and then scrape off to give it that exposed look. She had recently learnt the simple but effective technique. You had to put a lot of effort into making something look effortless, a lesson she had learned in her previous life.

The frosting on one of the tiers had smudged. Shilpa needed to correct it before she took it out into the heat of the marquee. Her hands shook, but she managed to do what was needed. The cake was perfect. It was ready to go. She was ready to go. As soon as the cake was placed on the centrepiece, she would leave quietly through the garden gate behind the Portaloos.

Mrs Drew watched, looking quite exhausted.

'Is everything okay?' Shilpa asked. Her host didn't seem her usual composed self, although Shilpa had only met her once. It had been Margery Drew who had called on her services, describing in detail what cake she required right down to the lemon curd filling and mint leaf and blueberry topping with yellow pansies. 'It's their colour,' she had said.

'Not quite, dear.' Mrs Drew was standing uncomfortably, shifting her weight from one leg to the other. 'Harriet took an absolute age to get ready. I've barely seen her at her own engagement party, and now it's Mason, my daughter's fiancé,' Mrs Drew said, wringing her hands together. 'I've looked everywhere for him. The thing is…'

'Go on,' Shilpa said.

'The thing is… Mason, well… he's missing.'

Chapter Two

Shilpa woke with a start and looked at her alarm clock. The luminous green digits flashed 5.59. One minute before her alarm sounded. It was Saturday. Market day.

Swinging her legs out of bed, she lifted herself up, allowing the duvet to fall to the floor. She heard her mother's voice telling her to make the bed, but she paid no attention to the commentary in her head. Instead, she turned her alarm off and padded over to the bathroom, the garish orange wallpaper startling her even though she had seen it countless times; another item on the list of things that needed fixing. She washed her face and pulled her long black hair into a knot above her head. That would do. She had just a couple of hours to make a batch of carrot-and-cardamom cupcakes.

Shilpa found her slippers and dressing gown and made her way to the kitchen. She glanced at the pineapple muffins and caraway spiced dinner rolls in their sealed containers and turned the oven on to 180 degrees. Taking the carrots, cardamom, brown sugar and other ingredients that she needed from the small pantry, she turned the Nespresso machine on and popped a purple capsule inside. Pressing the button, she waited for her morning fix, drumming her fingernails on the work surface. As the machine whirred into action, she had an uneasy feeling in the pit of her stomach. She swallowed it down moments later with a large sip of black coffee, wondering how she never had time to make a morning hot drink in her previous life.

In Devon, her coffee machine was getting good use. At least she could utilise one item from her past. The rest of her city possessions remained in large brown boxes littering every room of the house. She washed her hands and noticed the unease creeping up on her again. It was hard to get away from your own thoughts here. At six in the morning there was silence on the estuary. There were no sirens or drunks chattering as they made their way back to wherever they slept. Here it was just the occasional seagull squawking and a gentle breeze as the tide came in or out depending on what the moon was doing.

She looked through the large bi-fold doors and her shoulders relaxed. She hadn't yet tired of the view of the serene water filling the estuary and the picture-perfect fields on the other side. She didn't think she ever would.

She walked over to the sitting room and opened a window, taking a deep breath and letting the fresh salt-laced air fill her lungs. The two-bedroom house she had inherited was beautiful. Barely visible from the main road, it was built into the cliffside, which meant there were a few steps from the front door down to the sitting room and open-plan kitchen, and then further along there were two bedrooms and a bathroom. The loft stood half a storey above ground level. There was a balcony outside the sitting room's bi-fold doors with stairs that led to the garden full of various herbs, sweet-smelling lavender, red valerian and blue agapanthus, which were in full bloom in the summer sun. Past the garden a makeshift wooden ladder led to the slipway.

She loved the old house despite the list of repairs. Her uncle's inheritance had come at the right time and had saved her from another life.

She walked back to the kitchen, allowing her mind to drift as she beat the sugar, oil and eggs together. She had made these carrot cupcakes so many times she could do it in her sleep. Her father's favourites. His only consolation for having an unmarried daughter, her mother had casually pointed out. But it wasn't her marital status making her uncomfortable. She was used to her mother droning on about that. It was what she had seen yesterday – the knife.

Harriet and Mason's engagement party had been her first big event. She wasn't sure how she had managed to secure the Drews as her first clients, but she had, and it was a big deal. They knew people. They knew the whole town of Otter's Reach; probably owned it, she had joked when she told her mother about the event. She didn't want to screw it up. And yet somehow, she felt she had, because she had seen a blood-stained knife the same day that Mason had gone missing, and she hadn't said anything about it.

After her naked lemon cake had been placed in the marquee, she had wanted to sneak out, but she had been caught in the commotion that had ensued as soon as Mrs Drew had expressed her concerns for her missing son-in-law-to-be.

'Probably taking a leak,' one of the guests had said. He had a red nose and ruddy cheeks and was swaying slightly.

Mrs Drew ignored him. 'I've looked for him everywhere. And Harriet too,' she said, perching on the end of a wooden chair, dabbing her perspiring face with a pale-pink handkerchief.

'He wouldn't just disappear,' said a tall woman with dark hair, who wore an emerald-green cocktail dress and deep-red lipstick. Someone had called her Izzy. She had a polished look about her that gave her an air of celebrity. Her eyes shone; her sun-kissed skin glowed. The woman placed a comforting hand on Mrs Drew's shoulder, but it must have felt as awkward as it looked, because she quickly removed it. 'I'll take another look in the barn,' she said, and left the marquee.

'I've checked the garages again,' another man said.

Shilpa had wanted to leave. She had things to do at home, namely baking for the market stall today. At the time, she hadn't considered that the knife she had casually thrown into the Drews' sink had anything to do with Mason's disappearance, assuming it had just been used to cut a piece of meat. But the more she thought about it, the more she believed the knife was significant.

She slipped the filled cupcake tins into the oven and started to beat the cream cheese with the icing sugar, silently cursing herself for not saying anything yesterday. She had joined the search party, checking the pool house and in the shrubbery. She had even peered in the photinia red robin hedge and had nearly fallen into it.

The guests looking for the missing fiancé assumed he had either got cold feet and had run off, or that he was drunk in a ditch. Shilpa had listened to all the theorising and had agreed with one lady that he probably had an urgent errand to run.

Shilpa put the mixing bowl down and found the marzipan carrots she had made previously. Yesterday evening, after hours of searching, she had finally managed to slip out of the party only to bump into Mr Drew as she was getting into her car. He was pulling into the drive as she was about to leave, and he was going to block her in. She had no choice but to approach him and ask him to move his vehicle.

'Ah, the cake lady,' he said after he had blocked in someone else's car. 'Do pop by another time – with cakes, of course,' he added. 'By tomorrow we may have located that blasted man.' There was no love lost there then. But fathers could be protective of their daughters. Her own father certainly was when her mother let him. And she had heard two of the cooks saying that Mr Drew didn't approve of Harriet's choice of husband, something about him being an under-achiever. A typical dad comment.

Shilpa felt weary. In less than an hour, she would have to drag herself and her baked goods to the square to set up her stall. She had looked forward to the last couple of market days, but today she just didn't feel like it. She walked back to the sitting room and picked up the remote. She turned on the television, averting her eyes from the summer rain that had started to fall. Her eyes glazed over as images flashed on the screen, but then something caught her eye and her heart skipped a beat. Her cup of coffee fell to the floor as she raised her hands to her mouth.

A body had been found at the Drew house, and there was no doubt in Shilpa's mind that it was Mason Connolly.

Chapter Three

Alison Bishop turned off the television. Her hands trembled as she placed the remote down, lining it up with the edge of the coffee table.

They would soon come for her. Standing up, she paced around her living room, then she stopped and peered out of the window. The lady across the road was tending to her hanging baskets again. The woman was obsessed, although she couldn't talk.

Mason. It had started with a crush, turned into a relationship of sorts, became an obsession and ended... ended like this. It couldn't be, and yet it had. It was over. A part of her felt relieved, like a weight had been lifted from her shoulders; but somewhere at the back of her mind there was a gnawing foreboding that her actions over the last twelve months were going to catch up with her.

She opened her laptop and went to the local news page. There was a bird's-eye-view photograph of the Drew house. She could clearly see their drive and the apartment over the garage where she had, only yesterday, stood outside and screamed at Mason one last time. And if she looked really closely, she could see the tyre marks on the road outside. How long would it take the police to put it all together? To match those skid marks with her little white Nissan Micra. She should never have gone to the Drews'. It was Mason's day – his day with Harriet – and yet she couldn't help herself. She hadn't received an invite to their engagement party. Izzy had.

When she was sunk down in the driver's seat, discreetly taking photos, waiting to see Mason, Izzy had arrived. She had sashayed into the house as if she owned it. *Urgh*, the thought of that woman made her feel sick. Izzy had stopped by the entrance of the house and had turned, looking towards Alison's white car, her dark eyes and red lips full of life. Alison had quickly taken a photo before Izzy looked away.

Alison had felt pathetic in her pale-blue summer dress with little yellow birds on it. She was bland and nondescript, like her car. She didn't even buy the happy couple a gift. Izzy would have gone over the top. There had probably been something magnificent in the large gift bag she had been carrying. Izzy thought Alison was pitiable. She never said it out loud, but she didn't have to. It was clear from the look she gave her every time she saw her. Alison hated the way Izzy made her feel. She should have died as well.

A shiver ran down her spine. The dress was heaped on a sheet of plastic by her washing machine. She had considered washing it. A hot wash and a scoop of Vanish might have got the stains out, but she didn't think it was worth it. She would never be able to wear that dress again.

Izzy was right. She was pathetic. No wonder Mason had left her.

'This isn't working,' he had said, just over eighteen months ago on the 15th of November. She knew the date well. It had been a thundery day, and rain had mixed with her tears as she walked home from their last date in the café. Alison had written down in her diary every date that they had, every place they had been to together; how she felt in the morning and before bed. Her therapist had advised her to keep a diary, telling her it would help her organise her thoughts. But all it did was fuel her desire to relive the moments that she had spent with Mason.

Alison closed her eyes. She recalled walking up the drive to the Drew house. She had picked a quiet moment. All the other guests – the invited guests – had arrived. She stepped behind the large topiary to the side of the house when she heard voices, and then she waited. Waited for what seemed like forever, but she had watched him long enough. She was certain Mason would go to his bolthole. And when he did, she would speak to him, reason with him.

Eventually she saw him leave through the front door, telling his overprotective mother that he just needed some fresh air. He stepped out with a taller man.

'Evan,' he said. 'The best man won.' Mason slapped his friend on his back.

Evan smiled. But it looked more like a sneer to Alison. She took a step closer and peered through the hornbeam hedging. Evan's hands were balled into fists in his pockets; she could tell by the way he flexed the muscles in his forearms. He was a foot taller than Mason and stronger by the looks of it. They didn't like each other.

'Glad you could come though,' Mason said, adjusting his thick-framed black glasses and touching the side of his nose. 'Good to see you here.' He didn't mean it. Alison could tell by the way the tone of his voice changed, the way he narrowed his eyes ever so slightly. Evan nodded and walked back into the house.

She had waited for a further five minutes after Mason started walking towards the garage. She was patient, even her mother had said so. Her mother's comments had often been laced with sarcasm, but Alison knew that good things came to those who waited. Another five minutes wouldn't kill her. She had looked around, listened for distant voices and then as quietly as she could she made her way to the front of the annex.

Chapter Four

'So, you were there? At the party?' Leoni asked, wiping her hands on her apron and handing Shilpa her fourth coffee of the morning. She leaned in, expecting the gossip. She wanted to know first-hand what had happened; whose body had been found at the Drews'.

Shilpa gave her a half nod. She wasn't going to be the one to tell Mrs Blabbermouth. She should never have told her about her big event in the first place. She had to learn to be more discreet. Although she was slowly coming to realise being inconspicuous in a small town like Otter's Reach wasn't an option. It didn't matter if you told people your business or not; they found out anyway.

Another customer attracted the barista's attention, and Shilpa slid away to a seat at the back of the coffee shop. She usually sat by the window people-watching, but today she wanted to just blend into the background.

It was only eleven o'clock, but she had sold out of baked goods already. It was only the fifth market she had attended since moving to sleepy Otter's Reach and already she was gaining a reputation. The money she made from the stall wasn't great, but then she wasn't maximising her potential, as her father would scold. She could bake more and charge more. The stall hadn't been something she had wanted to do. It was her uncle who had had a stall selling jams and chutneys and Shilpa had sort of inherited it from him along with the house.

'Once a month in the low season and weekly in the summer,' Kelly, who ran the market, had said in a squeaky voice. She had a desolate look about her, and Shilpa had wondered whether it was because Kelly was having difficulty finding another stallholder or if that was just her look. 'It'll give you a name around here, and you could display pictures of your occasion cakes. You know what they say – the best way to get business is through word of mouth.'

Shilpa had smiled and agreed, more because she didn't want to let Kelly down than anything else. Kelly had beamed at her for just a second before her gloomy look returned. She didn't feel the need to tell her she had been a brand executive in London and knew exactly what marketing tricks to employ to sell her cakes. Instead she had offered the kind lady some tea and a slice of her flourless orange-and-saffron cake, which Kelly still mentioned every market day.

She checked the news application on her phone. A local news station had set up camp outside the Drews'. They didn't have any further information, just that a body had been found. They didn't say whether there were any suspicious circumstances surrounding the death; nor did they say that the body was that of Mason Connolly. She was desperate to know if the knife had been found. It must have, but had it been washed up and put away or discarded before the police arrived? She had failed to speak up last night, but now that there was a body, she had to say something to someone.

She stood up decisively, but then doubt crept in. If they had found the knife, it was likely her prints would be on it.

She sat back down and chewed a fingernail. She checked the news application again. Nothing. It was no good just sitting around, waiting for information. There had to be a way for her to find out more.

Hadn't Mr Drew asked her to pop around with some baked goods? Could she legitimately do that now? The family would be grieving; there would be police. From the pictures on the news this morning, it looked like the place was swarming with forensics in those white coveralls. They would all be hungry, she reasoned. She could take them cake; cake always made people feel better. It was one of the reasons she liked baking. She would tell them about the knife too, because the longer she kept that to herself, the more guilt she felt.

It was only just past eleven. Enough time to go home, have a shower and bake. Bake what? What cakes were appropriate for a family in mourning and a hungry police force?

Shilpa parked up outside the large stone villa with its arched windows and ornate lights. It was one of the few houses on the exclusive Honeywell Drive at the top of Otter's Reach. It dominated the vista if you looked back towards the town from the estuary. From where she was parked, the house should have been hidden by its large hedge, but the mouth of the gravel driveway was wide, and despite the gates there was a clear view of the house and granny annex above the garages. As she pulled the key out of the ignition, she noticed that her hands were shaking. She wasn't quite sure if it was from her coffee binge this morning or if it was just nerves. She certainly felt anxious as she got out of the car and opened the boot to retrieve her freshly baked goods. She had decided on a batch of scones and a tray of crumble cake, which she had neatly sliced into handheld pieces.

She carried her containers up towards the gates of the house, grateful she had put on a pair of French Sole flats before leaving the house, and not a pair of heels. She stood a foot shorter than the policeman at the entrance.

'You can't enter, miss,' he said. 'There's a police investigation going on at present. You'll have to come back another time.'

'Why?' she asked, feigning ignorance. 'What's happened?'

The policeman ignored her.

'Is it a crime scene?' she ventured. She peered through the gates towards the pillared porch that framed the front door. The large house looked serene in the afternoon sun. It certainly didn't look like a crime had been committed there. She couldn't see a single soul. The buzz of activity from the morning television report must have died down. She turned towards the road; the news van was still positioned outside. She wondered if they would be interested in her presence. She hoped not and quickly looked back at the policeman again.

'I know the family,' she said. It was a half-truth.

'But you're not family,' he responded.

She agreed that she wasn't. She wanted to say she had cake. That seemed to work with most people when she wanted something. People could never say no to freshly baked cake. But she had never tried it with the police before. She opened her mouth, but the words wouldn't come. It was a childish and insolent assumption, and she was neither of those things. Perhaps it was better to lead with the truth.

'I was here yesterday,' she said.

The policeman looked at her, waiting for her to say something else. She didn't want to. The silence was awkward. Shilpa hated awkward silences. She always took responsibility for them.

'I might have some information relating to the body that was found,' she said, whispering the last part. The policeman looked away from her, spoke into his radio and waited. She heard the white noise of the device, a crackle, and then someone spoke. The officer looked down at her and her Tupperware, then he opened the gate.

'Follow me,' he said.

Chapter Five

Shilpa looked around the gardenia-painted interview room
in Glass Bay Police Station. There was an alarm strip at
waist height along each wall and a fluorescent tube light which
had a large crack in its casing. The room contained nothing
more than a desk and two chairs.

The window opposite her looked out onto the rear of the
police station. Police cars in white, yellow and blue littered the
car park. How had she got herself into this situation? It was a
mess, and she knew exactly who to blame. It was her uncle.
Her dead uncle.

On his recommendation, her parents had been persuaded
to move from Delhi to Goa and finally to Tooting Broadway in
search of a better life. Shilpa's mother had been pregnant with
her when they put roots down in England. When her uncle
decided to move to Devon, her mother refused to move again.
Her mother had always likened her brother to Shilpa because
they were both single. Shilpa didn't mind ending up like
Dipesh. It seemed to her that he had a good life, living in a
quaint town in a house overlooking Otter's Reach Estuary. He
had run a small fishing store and spent most of his time doing

what he loved best: making jam. But it still came as a surprise when he left her his house. It was a nice surprise though, because her inheritance came at a time when she needed it the most.

She had a great career, one her friends envied, but what else did she have? And with each passing year it dawned on her that her life was going nowhere, even though she was repeatedly told she had it all. At thirty-five, she took a closer look. She lived in central London, but she rented a shoebox. She had a great job, but you were only as good as your last advertising campaign. The grind was continual, the hours long. The directors remembered your mistakes, never your successes. But it wasn't all doom and gloom. She loved the life London gave her – the nights out, the healthy pay cheque each month. She had Instagram-worthy holidays and a cupboard full of Louboutins.

But she was still single. Despite her protests about an arranged marriage, her mother had set up several suitors. 'He comes from a good family,' her mother would say. 'This one is a surgeon. What can you find wrong with a surgeon?' 'This one's family is wealthy.'

None were a match. Shilpa turned down a dozen. The rest had rejected her. The rejections stung even though she had no desire to date any of them. It was especially painful when she had already labelled them as no-hopers. She didn't dwell too much on what they must have thought of her; she couldn't. It hurt too much.

'They're threatened by your job,' her mother would say. 'You should quit.'

So much for feminism. 'Why work when you can be a homemaker?' her mother would say. Shilpa rarely dignified her questions with a response. Her mother would never change.

When Shilpa turned thirty-five, it was as if an invisible line had been crossed and there was no going back. Her married friends were having children. Her single friends were settling down. When Tanvi, their group's equivalent to Samantha from *Sex and the City*, announced her engagement just a week after her uncle died, Shilpa knew something had to change.

'How long?' she asked.

'Three months,' Tanvi had replied.

'Three months? I've owned shoes for longer than that which I'm not committed to. Why didn't you tell me?' she asked, taking on a more serious tone.

'You were busy,' Tanvi said. That was true. Her uncle's death had brought with it a plane full of overbearing relatives from India, and her mother had ordered her to be a good host. The late evenings and early mornings helping her mother in the kitchen, frying pakoras and making large vats of daal, enough to feed a small nation, meant she had ended up commuting from Tooting to work every day. She had been busy.

'And I was busy,' Tanvi said. 'Work, Jason. You know.'

Jason – what kind of eighties name was that? Shilpa had thought, ignoring the fact that she had been born in the same decade. Shilpa, who usually told Tanvi exactly how she felt, kept her thoughts on her fiancé's name to herself. Her strong opinions were another reason her mother had cited for her numerous matrimonial rejections. Things between her and Tanvi were already changing, and her friend hadn't even said 'I do'.

That night Shilpa went to sleep with a strange feeling. Tanvi was always free for an impromptu city break; Tanvi was always up for a night out. But now she was alone. Truly alone. She found she couldn't sleep. Something in her life wasn't quite right. Somewhere along the line she had taken a wrong turn, or perhaps she had been so focused on having a great career and wearing the latest shoes that she had completely missed a turn somewhere.

At thirty-five, she was single, without enough money to buy her own place. All she had to show for her high-flying career was a wardrobe of shoes to sit down in. Unlike her idol Carrie Bradshaw, she had no Mr Big to rescue her. She had no one.

No sooner had Tanvi publicised her engagement than Shilpa discovered that her uncle had left her his house in Devon.

'I'm keeping Uncle Dipesh's house,' she announced two weeks after she discovered her inheritance. She had visited Otter's Reach only once, but that was enough to know that she wanted to give the small town a go. As she drove along Estuary Road towards the house on the top of the cliff, she passed a small flea market bustling with people. The tide was coming in, and boats and small craft bobbed along with the incoming water; the gulls were squawking overhead, and the Easter tourists were milling about eating fish and chips from paper packets along the quayside. The air smelled clean, fresh and wholesome, something she couldn't say about London. Lush trees and shrubs lined the road, giving privacy to the large houses on either side. New contemporary houses with their expanses of glass sat in harmony with the older properties – a mix of Victorian mansions and seventies' apartment blocks. Every few metres, benches and flower beds exploding with purples, pinks, oranges and yellows had been installed. Shilpa hadn't yet stepped out of her car but she could see that the town exuded a community spirit.

'Whaaaat?' her mother asked, her mouth full of omelette. She wiped the greasy residue from her face with the edge of her dupatta.

'I've made up my mind and you can't change it.'

'Good, good. I can help with the inheritance tax,' her father said. 'Rent it out.'

Shilpa shook her head. 'I'm going to live there,' she said.

For the first time in her life, her mother was shocked into silence. Her brother laughed.

Now, at the police station in Glass Bay, she reflected that had it not been for her uncle's decision to move the family to England, she wouldn't be here, perspiring in the airless room and waiting to be questioned about the death of a man she believed to be Mason Connolly. Blaming her uncle was a stretch, but she wanted to blame someone.

Chapter Six

Detective Inspector Scott Drayton walked into the interview room and put a powder-blue folder on the table. He sat down and looked at Shilpa. She smiled and examined her hands. Her fingerprints and a DNA swab had been taken from her as she was checked in at the station. It was voluntary, they said, but seeing as she had nothing to hide, she complied. She had assumed they would make her press her fingers into black ink to take her prints, but she had been mistaken. Things had moved on from her days of watching reruns of *The Bill*. It had all been done electronically and there was no black residue on her fingers to remind her of her ordeal.

'I have your statement here,' DI Drayton said, pulling a sheet of paper from the folder. He was tall and skinny, with icy blue eyes and a kink in his nose. She wondered if someone had punched him in the face in the line of duty or if that was just the shape of his nose. She tilted her head and looked at him as he glanced over her statement. Maybe a jilted lover had caused the misshapenness, she decided.

He passed the paper over to her. 'Read it, make sure you're happy with what it says, then sign and date it,' he instructed.

No small talk then. She nodded. She had hoped for a jovial detective. One she could joke with about how naïve she had been in picking up the knife and then not mentioning it. Drayton, with his dark-grey suit and frosty gaze, just made her feel like an ignorant child. He didn't have a sense of humour, so she could hardly tell him that her first thought when she had seen the knife was that it had been used to cut a bloody bit of beef. A sign from her gods, no doubt prayed for by her mother, that she should not be indulging in the flesh of a sacred animal. Beef, and in particular steak, was one of her favourite meals, and she had enjoyed a steak dinner the night before the party.

Shilpa read through her statement. It was devoid of emotion. She would have peppered it with a few more adjectives. She looked up at Drayton and decided not to share her useless comment with him.

'It's fine,' she said. 'It gives you all the facts.'

'If this gets to court, we may rely on this statement, and you may need to testify to it.'

She nodded. 'So, what happens now?'

Drayton looked towards the door. 'You're free to go. But stick around, yeah.'

She stood up, her chair scraping the floor as she pushed it back. The noise setting her teeth on edge. No 'thank you' then. She wondered why she had bothered. Oh yes, because her fingerprints were all over the murder weapon. Well, that was if the knife was the murder weapon. Drayton wouldn't give anything away in that regard. As she stepped out of the station, the fresh air hit her. In any event, she had done the right thing, and it felt good.

'Shilpa.' She heard her name and turned.

'Thought it was you,' said a man with a familiar face. 'It's Danny.'

She quickly tried to place him but failed.

'Sheffield,' he said.

She looked at him blankly.

'University.'

'Daniel Richards?' she said, staring at him. He looked so different. Her housemate Lena had had a crush on him. She had struggled to see what her friend saw in him, but now she could see an attraction. He was a good foot shorter than she was, but he still had that thick brown hair. It wasn't long anymore but cropped, and it suited him much better.

'I didn't make a lasting impression on you then?' he said.

Shilpa laughed. 'What are you doing here?' she asked, looking at the station behind him.

'I work here,' he said. He didn't ask what she was doing at the station. She recalled that Danny had been thoughtful like that. She put her own lack of consideration down to inheriting her mother's genes. Danny had been doing a degree in geography or something like that when they were in university together. He lived in the flat above hers, and they used to meet in the pub at the end of their road for boozy Friday nights and hungover roasts on a Sunday. That was nearly fifteen years now; she had forgotten about Lena and Danny – and most of her university friends for that matter. It wasn't by design. They had just drifted apart, and when they met up, they found they had little in common.

'So, you live here?' she asked, suddenly missing a good night out.

'Been here ten years now.'

Shilpa looked at his left hand. No ring. 'Maybe we could catch up over drinks,' she said. 'I've just moved to Otter's Reach. It would be good to get some local insight.'

'Sure thing. I know Otter's Reach,' he said. He looked at

his watch. 'Look, I've got to be somewhere.' He pulled his mobile phone out of his pocket, swiped the screen and passed it to her. 'Give us your number. I'll message you and we can get together.'

Shilpa did as he asked and then waved as he headed towards his car. It would be good to catch up with an old friend. She looked at the station and recalled the detective inspector's parting words. It would be handy to have a friend in the police force too.

Shilpa put on a pair of shorts and made herself a glass of iced tea before walking down the lichen-stained steps from her balcony to the garden. She stopped to smell the lavender and then walked along the slipway. One day she would have a boat for still summer days like today when she needed to unwind. There was nothing like being on the water to still the soul, she thought, remembering a carefree winter holiday in Barbados after a stressful fortnight at work. Devon wasn't Barbados, but it had its charm. It was why she was still here three months later. This southern English seaside town was slowly beginning to feel like home. She could see why her uncle was so drawn to this place.

The tide was going out slowly, and there was a gentle breeze blowing. At this time of year, the estuary was busy with tourists on chartered RIBs going between Salcombe and Otter's Reach. But whenever the tide was out, apart from a tourist or two who didn't understand the estuary, it was once again still. She sat cross-legged on the old concrete slipway and waved to John and Graham on their catamaran, which was tied to her mooring. She hoped they didn't take her presence as a sign to come over and talk to her. She wasn't in the mood for talking. She needed some quiet time to think about what had happened today, because something was niggling at her, and she wasn't quite sure what it was.

Detective Drayton hadn't exactly given much away at their interview. He took her statement without so much as confirming whether anyone had been murdered. But it was clear from that morning's news report that a body had been found, and she had seen with her own eyes that Mason Connolly had been missing at his own engagement party. Nor could she deny the distress on Mrs Drew's face when she had visited the house with her condolence cakes.

After she had gained access to the Drew house earlier, she had been ushered into the drawing room by another police-man, where she was made to wait while he fetched the detec-tive. She was told not to leave the room, and she had obeyed, taking it as an opportunity to have a good look around. She couldn't help it. Another trait inherited from her mother. The room was opulent, with a high moulded ceiling and a gold-and-crystal chandelier hanging in the middle. Heavy navy box-pleated curtains adorned the tall windows. One wall was covered in photos – mainly of the Drews, their happy family. It appeared that Harriet was their only child. A spoiled child. Each Christmas and birthday photo showed a mountain of presents next to her as a child and then teenager. A large picture of Harriet and Mason hung at the end of the wall. It was slightly skewed, and Shilpa touched it to straighten it. It was then that she noticed that the wallpaper surrounding the picture was slightly darker than the rest of the wall. The picture had recently replaced another one which had been in a slightly bigger frame; she could tell because the sun hadn't bleached the paper. She looked carefully at the other pictures, but none of the others seemed to have been replaced.

After half an hour of waiting, she looked at her watch, but there was no sign of anyone coming to retrieve her. She had hoped to see the family, express her deepest sympathy and of course, tell the police about the knife. Now she wondered if they had forgotten her.

She was about to leave when she heard a voice. She looked up and noticed there was an air vent in the wall above where the pictures hung.

'I never go into this office. It's not my domain. I certainly couldn't tell you what he keeps in there.' It was Mrs Drew. 'It's his space,' she said. She sounded tearful.

'So, you didn't enter the study that day?' another voice said. Another police officer, Shilpa guessed.

'I was busy with the party. Making sure our guests had drinks and that the canapés were being served. You know what these waitresses can be like. Too busy standing round gossiping about what they got up to the evening before. You have to be on at them all the time to make sure you get good service. You'd think that after all the parties I've thrown the caterers would only send their best staff, but no. It's a constant string of students looking to make some easy money. I was very busy,' she said. Another sob. 'I saw the cake lady come in; ask her. At around midday I popped into the kitchen to see her. Check everything was all right.'

'We will,' said another deep voice. On reflection, that voice belonged to Drayton. There was a clattering, and after that Shilpa could no longer hear the voices. She assumed they had gone to investigate what the noise was. Her palms began to sweat, and she felt the knot in her stomach tighten. Mrs Drew had retrieved the spatula from her husband's office the day of the party in a matter of seconds. A spatula she used to open the bureau drawer. It was a throwaway comment that Shilpa would not have retained had a body not been discovered at the house later that day. Maybe Mrs Drew had forgotten about the spatula altogether. Nevertheless, it was clear that Margery knew her husband's study quite well, so why was she lying?

Chapter Seven

Detective Drayton never questioned Shilpa about Mrs Drew and her husband's office, so she didn't say anything. She could hardly say she had been eavesdropping while waiting in the drawing room. As it was, she had to confess to picking up the bloodstained knife in the first place.

Shilpa heard a familiar noise of shoes on the estuary shingle.

Graham was walking towards her with two glasses. He held one out to her as he approached. 'Gin?' he offered.

She smiled, put her glass of iced tea down and took it.

'Now, John told me to leave you alone with your thoughts, but you looked ever so worried about something, so I thought I'd make you a drink, and I needed to give you this.' Graham fished a key from his pocket, passing it to her.

Shilpa took it and studied it.

'It's a key to your front door,' he said. 'I completely forgot we had it; a spare Dipesh had given us to hold on to just in case of emergencies, you know, like if he locked himself out, that sort of thing.'

'Thanks,' Shilpa said, pocketing the key. She would probably give it back to Graham a month from now. She would need someone local to keep a key for her 'just in case', but she hadn't thought about it yet, so it could keep. She tried the drink Graham had made her. It was strong.

'Salcombe Gin,' he said. 'It's local. With Indian Slimline and a sprig of rosemary. Rosemary I stole from your garden yesterday. Sorry about that. Dipesh didn't mind.'

Shilpa tapped the concrete next to her, offering Graham a seat.

He sat next to her in silence for a minute before he spoke. 'You miss your uncle?'

She nodded. Now that she lived in his house, he was always in her thoughts. She missed his jovial demeanour and his *joie de vivre*. He was her kindred spirit, her mother always said, even if she had meant his bachelor status, but she did feel his loss.

'He was a lovely man, your uncle; so kind and generous. I never knew he had a heart problem.'

'Neither did I,' Shilpa said. 'But he did. My mother said he kept it quiet. She said he had it coming, too.'

Graham gave Shilpa a look.

'My mother doesn't mince her words,' she said with a small laugh. 'His hobby of making jams probably didn't help either. There was something about his salt intake in the coroner's report as well, so I think she thought she was justified in her assumptions.'

'John and I had asked your uncle to spend the day with us on the boat the day he died, but he was busy. Maybe he sensed something and wanted to rest. It had been a cold but sunny day, and we decided to go for a ride out towards Salcombe for fish and chips. Dipesh didn't come, and I regret that John and I didn't see that he was unwell. It's terrible that we didn't even know about his heart.'

Shilpa let out a breath, and Graham put a comforting arm

around her. 'I think he had a good life though. It wasn't a long life, but a good one. It's awful that you've had to deal with your uncle's death and now this,' Graham said.

It was Shilpa's turn to give Graham a look.

'Leoni told me,' he said quickly. 'I hear you were at the party.'

'I only delivered the cake,' she said. 'I didn't know the Drews.'

'You don't need to have known the deceased to be affected by death, especially a murder.'

'They've confirmed it?' Shilpa asked.

'They?'

'The police. They wouldn't tell me anything. Not who died or how they were killed. All I know was that a body was found at the house, just from what I saw on the news. But it must be murder, because they wouldn't have a police detail at the Drew house if it wasn't suspicious, would they?'

'Young Mason, Harriet's partner, was murdered. I didn't hear it from the police, but Mr Drew told me when I was there an hour ago.'

'You were at the house?'

Graham nodded. 'I tend to their garden. It's been so hot these last few days, I thought I would go and water the plants once the police had left. It's not something they need to concern themselves with, with everything else that's going on. I didn't expect to see anyone, let alone talk to any of them. The Drews like their staff to be invisible. I can't remember the last time one of them actually went out of their way to speak to me, but today Mr Drew did. He marched out of his house like he had something important to say. I could see him through the glass doors, and I considered making a quick exit. You see, I thought he was going to tell me off for coming to the house under the circumstances.'

'But he didn't.'

Graham shook his head. 'He told me that Mason's body had been found in the flat above the double garage to the front of the house. It sounded like he was desperate to talk to someone about it.'

Shilpa took another sip of her drink. She had been right. Mason Connolly was dead.

'Did Mr Drew say how he died?' she asked, holding her glass a little tighter. Had no one checked the annex in all that time they were looking for the missing fiancé?

Graham looked into the distance towards the fields across the estuary, where rapeseed was growing. 'Said there was blood everywhere. He was the one who had found him. Well, their dog found him when Steven went to check the annex. Came running into the kitchen, blood all over his paws. Mr Drew followed the prints and found the body,' Graham said, as if reading her mind.

'Oh, how terrible,' Shilpa said. She had never met Mason Connolly, but she was sure he didn't deserve that end. 'Poor Mr Drew. I can't imagine what it must have been like to find his future son-in-law like that, in his home.' She was certain now that the knife she had found had been used in the attack. What else could have caused all the blood? It explained why the DI had asked her so many questions about it. If Mason had been shot, they wouldn't have been interested in the knife.

Graham laughed. 'You haven't been in Otter's Reach long at all, have you?'

She gave him a quizzical look.

'Mr Drew was probably more upset about the décor of their granny annex than the death of Mason.'

Shilpa stared at Graham. She had overheard the cook at the Drews' say that there was no love lost between Mason and Mr Drew. She had assumed they were just indifferent to one another, but now she wondered if there was more to it than that.

Graham drained his drink. 'The Drews have a chequered history in Otter's Reach. Would love to tell you more, but I need a refill. Why don't you join John and me on the boat for dinner? We can fill you in then.'

Chapter Eight

'We miss your uncle,' Graham said as he cleared their plates away. The evening was pleasant, and the tide was in, so they ate a simple supper of crab linguine with a bottle of Pecorino on deck. Graham returned from the galley with a chocolate mousse and three bowls.

'I miss him too,' Shilpa said. She didn't mention the guilt she felt for having seen so little of him in the run-up to his demise.

'Have you had a chance to go through his things?'

Shilpa shook her head. 'It's all in boxes in the garage,' she said. Several of her relatives who had arrived in England soon after his death had taken it upon themselves to clear his house. They had started moving all his clothes and ornaments (the ones they chose not to take) into boxes. But the do-gooder relatives had stopped their task as soon as they heard his house had been left to his spinster niece.

'*Tche*,' she heard one of her aunts say, wrinkling her nose like she had just smelled something bad. 'That Shilpa must be the same type as him.'

'Poor thing,' another had said. 'At least she has a house if she has no one in her life. A house is better than nothing. We must not deny her that also.'

At the time, Shilpa had bitten her tongue and stayed quiet. Now she wished she had said something. It was time that she looked through her uncle's things too. For a start, it would help clear some of the space in the house and allow her to settle in properly – unpack the boxes piled up in every room and make the house her own before her mother arrived and asserted her presence. And perhaps there was something amongst his things that she could pass to Graham and John. They spoke so fondly of him that she wanted them to have something of his – that's if her relatives had left anything decent.

'Dipesh used to let us shower in his house,' Graham said.

'And when it was miserable and cold, we often stayed over after a bottle or two of Pinot Noir,' John reminisced. 'That's not to say we're expecting you to extend the invitation,' he quickly added.

'No, not at all,' Graham said. 'Oh, I hope you don't think that. I guess we're just trying to say that your uncle was a good man, a kind man.'

John topped up their wine glasses. 'Graham said you want to know more about the Drews.'

'I'm curious, that's all,' she said. 'They sound interesting, and Mason's death has certainly got me thinking.' She decided not to tell the couple that she was probably a suspect in his death, given her prints were on the knife, but she reminded them that she had been there when Mason went missing.

'Don't turn detective on us,' John said. 'It's far too dangerous to go snooping. Isn't it, Graham?' he said, turning to his partner. 'You're Dipesh's niece. We need to look after you.'

Shilpa assured them she wouldn't. But she didn't quite believe her own words.

'Good,' Graham said, patting her shoulder and helping himself to pudding.

'Well,' John said. 'Mrs Drew was desperate for children, but she only had Harriet. It's common knowledge this, not just hearsay. Ask her yourself,' he said as he explained that Harriet was a spoilt only child. 'She couldn't do anything wrong in the eyes of her parents. And with their money, she got everything she wanted. And she wanted things, that young girl.'

'One year when she was little, Mr Drew bought her a top-of-the-range trampoline. Harrods, I think he ordered it from,' Graham said, scooping up his chocolate mousse with a spoon and holding it close to his lips. 'She wasn't happy though, was she, John?'

'It wasn't pink,' John said. 'It was black. She didn't like that. Of course, daddy dearest replaced it within twenty-four hours for his precious daughter.'

'I haven't met Harriet, not properly,' Shilpa said. 'Her mother ordered the cake.'

'She would, wouldn't she. Her mother's like her PA,' John said. He stood up, taking the empty Pecorino bottle inside. He returned minutes later with a fresh bottle and topped up their glasses.

Shilpa laughed. She was quite tipsy and was enjoying John and Graham's company. She could see why her uncle had made them firm friends.

'Didn't you meet her at her own engagement party? You did the cake – and a good job, from what I've heard. You mean to say she didn't even say thank you?'

Shilpa waved her hand in front of her face. 'Oh, she was busy. She's newly engaged, and I know what it's like,' she said. Although she didn't. She didn't even know what it was like to have a long-term boyfriend. She reached for her glass and took a big sip, swallowing down the feeling of inadequacy.

'That's not the point,' Graham said. 'Manners don't cost a thing. These Drews, they're too busy for their own good.'

John gave Graham a sideways glance. 'It's just Harriet. She's too self-important.'

'I barely saw her at the start of the day. Her mother complained she was taking an age to get ready. I later saw her frantically looking for Mason. She didn't look very pleased with her fiancé disappearing like that.'

'If he wasn't dead already, she would probably be plotting it now,' John said. 'No one leaves Harriet Drew. Did you see Harriet when they first noticed Mason was gone?' John asked.

Shilpa shook her head. She thought back. She was so preoccupied with the cake she hadn't paid much notice to what was happening around her, but she had wondered where the bride-to-be was, thinking it was strange that neither Harriet nor Mason were mingling with their guests.

Graham playfully hit John on his shoulder. 'You're terrible,' he said with a mock scowl. 'Tell her.'

'Tell me what?'

'Harriet's a black widow,' John said, leaning in towards Shilpa as he spoke.

'I'm not following,' she said, suddenly uneasy. She looked out over the water and the light from the boat reflecting on the liquid surface. The water was calm, and she tried to absorb some of its tranquillity, but it was no use. Tension bubbled up within her, a low-level anxiety making her fingers drum the base of her glass.

'She's been engaged before,' Graham said, lowering his voice as an RIB sped past, carrying late-night revellers from the pub to their holiday cottages. Shilpa had to strain her ears to hear him.

'A young man called Finley,' John added. He wiped the remnants of chocolate mousse from his bowl with his finger and put it in his mouth. 'Delicious,' he said.

'He died,' Graham said.

'Are you serious?' Shilpa asked.

'Deadly,' said Graham. 'It was investigated and everything. It was an accident.'

'He was abroad at the time, on his stag do. Turkey, I think it was.'

Shilpa enquired when it happened. John told her it was a couple of years ago and that the whole town felt sorry for her.

'They really did,' Graham added. 'But now this has happened. She's either very unlucky or something's going on.'

Shilpa looked at her right hand, recalling the weight of the knife she had found at the Drews'. 'It's not like she had reason to murder her fiancé, is it?' she added.

Graham shook his head. 'I don't think she did. I mean, she wasn't even in the same country as poor Finley when he died. I think it was a genuine accident.'

'And like you say,' John added. 'What's her motive for knocking off Finley – or Mason for that matter? I could under-stand if they were married and she wanted rid, but her fiancés both died before the big day.'

'Maybe she wanted to break up with them but couldn't find the right words,' Graham said.

John made a face and laughed. Shilpa was silent. She hadn't met Harriet, but she had heard about women who liked the idea of being engaged, of being wanted, but didn't actually want the men who had proposed. At the same time, these women didn't want their lovers to be anyone else's. Murder would be the perfect solution to that kind of problem. Could Harriet be one of those women? She shook away the thought. She was getting ahead of herself.

'It's more likely that it was her dad that did it – Mr Drew,' John said.

'John,' Graham scolded. 'You can't say that. He pays my wages.'

'Shilpa's not going to tell anyone. Anyway, these are just my observations, love. You know that,' John added.

Shilpa nodded. 'Why do you say it could be Mr Drew?'

'You know dads and their daughters,' Graham said. 'No one's ever good enough for their princesses.'

'It's not just that though, is it?' John said, shifting in his seat. Shilpa noticed Graham narrowing his eyes at his partner. There was an awkward silence before Graham turned to Shilpa. 'Look, all this talk is just that. Talk. I hope you aren't taking anything said here seriously.'

'Oh no,' Shilpa said.

Graham leaned back in his chair and laughed. 'Good. Anyway, like you said, it's not like you are looking into who killed Mason.'

Shilpa smiled, but it wasn't that convincing. John suddenly looked concerned. 'You aren't seriously looking into this, are you?' he asked.

She explained how she had found the knife, that she couldn't get the image of it out of her head. Of course she wasn't going to investigate, she said eventually, when neither Graham nor John looked convinced. She was just interested, that's all, given she was in all likelihood there when it had happened. And there was an element of truth in that.

Shilpa was just about to make her excuses to leave when she felt her phone vibrate in her handbag. She pulled it out and looked at the message. It was Danny. She read the message and smiled.

'Boyfriend?' Graham asked.

'No, nothing like that,' Shilpa said, despite the heat in her cheeks. Danny wanted to meet up. He was in town if she was awake and up for a few drinks, he had messaged. Shilpa drained the contents of her glass and made her excuses. She stood up and said her farewells to John and Graham, thanking them for the lovely meal and all the wine they had plied her with.

Graham kissed her on both cheeks. 'Mind that table,'

Graham said as she followed John towards the tender. 'It's lethal. We really need to get those corners rounded.'

Shilpa stepped around the small but solid coffee table on the deck with razor sharp edges. As she got into the tender with John, she wondered if it was the water making her feel dizzy or all the wine she had consumed.

As John rowed Shilpa the few metres to her slipway, he said, 'If you're interested in Mason Connolly's death, you need to speak to Leoni. She'll tell you what we don't know. Not much gets past Mrs Blabbermouth. If she doesn't know it, it's probably not worth knowing.'

Chapter Nine

Steven Drew closed the door on the detective inspector and retreated to his study, his place of solitude. It was the only part of the house where he could get any peace and quiet now that his home was a crime scene. Even in death, Mason Connolly was making a nuisance of himself.

When he had first called in the murder, he had expected an incompetent detective sergeant to attend. It was, after all, a Friday evening, but instead Detective Inspector Drayton had turned up, ordering about his family and party guests, or at least what remained of them. Drayton was no fool, and he wondered now if he should have lied about his whereabouts that day. The key to a good lie was to tell a half-truth. Just change one or two details; that way it was easier to remember the fabrication, and it was always more believable, but he had no choice. He couldn't pick and choose what to include this time.

Steven had been in Otter's Reach for years. After taking over his father's small accountancy firm on the High Street, he had grown the business. It was now the go-to accountancy firm in the South Hams. There wasn't a High Street without a

Drew Accountancy presence, and that sloppy Mason Connolly, that young upstart, was never going to get his grubby little hands on the company he had taken years, not to mention countless risks, to develop.

Why did his daughter always pick such failures? Hadn't he shown her what a little bit of determination and work could do? He had been exemplary, working hard for most of his life. Harriet should have chosen her life partner accordingly, but no. That was far too simple for her. Maybe it wasn't Harriet, he reasoned, never wanting to attribute sole blame to his only daughter. Maybe it was just young men these days. They wanted things handed to them with benefits and flexi-time. He had heard about that in the Dartmouth office just last week. 'So, if I come in at 8.30, can I leave earlier?' he had overheard a graduate asking. He didn't wait to hear the reply; he was already stressed, and he could hear the voice of his lover gently reminding him of his heart condition. The thought of her instantly calmed him, and he had quickly gathered the papers he had gone to the office for and had made a quick exit.

The young didn't understand the meaning of hard work; perhaps he just had to accept that. Harriet's first fiancé, Finley, had a degree in media studies, which in his opinion wasn't a legitimate subject. The first time he met Finley, he had been wearing an ill-fitting suit and had an idea that he was going to change the world with the invention of a new kind of hand dryer that sounded very similar to Dyson's. It seemed to him that Finley liked the idea of being an entrepreneur, but he had no intention of actually doing any work to get what he wanted. He wondered what his daughter had seen in him.

Finley was a loser, but he did have some things going for him – a passion for water sports and travel – and of course, he didn't have much money to his name. After some digging, Steven discovered that the boy's family didn't appear to have much either. It hadn't taken too much to make the boy disappear, even if things hadn't gone exactly to plan. Mason was a different matter. The Connollys were a well-established family in South Devon with more wealth than the Drews, although Steven would never admit that publicly.

Mason had a degree in economics paid for by Connolly Senior. Although rumour had it his father kept him on a tight leash where money was concerned after his older brother had squandered thousands after marrying a waitress he had met in a strip bar in Vegas. It was clichéd but true, and the patriarch of the family wasn't going to let that happen again.

Harriet's choice of husband wouldn't have been so bad if Mason had a plan of his own; a plan to start his own business, or to take a role in his father's company. He just needed to show some ambition to prove worthy of his daughter's hand. Mason wasn't ready to take on *too much* work, as he had put it over a light lunch one Friday. He went to his father's office each day, to show willing and receive a handsome pay cheque at the end of each month from Connolly Shipbuilders, but it was all for show. Nevertheless, Harriet was taken with him from the start.

'Mummy, he's so divine,' he heard her say as he retrieved his toast one morning.

His wife passed him the marmalade as she turned to her daughter. 'What is it you like about him?' she had asked.

'Everything. He's just so clever and he knows things and people. He knows the best people. We're going to the Wolseley for brunch next weekend with Lottie and Donald. They own a vineyard in the South of France. I hope I like them. We could go there this summer. Tie it in with St Tropez. Mason's parents have a place there…' her daughter said, gushing as she spoke. It turned his stomach slightly, and he told both his wife and his daughter that he would be taking his breakfast in his study. Finley hadn't been dead in the ground five minutes and already Harriet had found another useless article to date.

Mason was tricky to get around but not impossible. Steven had seen the cracks. Like his investigative accounting, he knew where to look, he knew what to look for, and when he found the flaw, he used it to his advantage. It was how the game was played, and it wasn't often that Steven Drew lost.

Chapter Ten

The shrill sound of her ringing phone woke Shilpa from her slumber. She looked towards the noise. She had left her phone on her dresser when she got home last night. It wasn't within her grasp. She turned towards her alarm clock and rubbed her temples. She had drunk far more than she should have. Eight o'clock on a Sunday. Who was ringing so early? It wasn't her mother. She had allocated a special ringtone for her, because her mother always called at the worst moment to ask her all manner of awkward questions she deemed urgent – like when she was going to get married when she was in the middle of a date, or if she wanted to be a geriatric mother when she was having lunch with friends. Eight on a Sunday morning was too early, even for Mrs Solanki.

The telephone stopped ringing, and Shilpa pulled the duvet over her head. Then it started again. She grunted before pulling the duvet back and padding over to her dresser. She caught a glimpse of her room in the mirror. It was a mess. Clothes from last night were scattered on the floor, moving boxes were open in the corner; a patent toe and the corner of a vintage Chanel bag peeped out of one of the boxes. There was no place for Manolos and Chanel in Otter's Reach. She adjusted her satin pyjamas and slipped her feet into a pair of Uggs, then she looked at her phone. A number she didn't recognise. She answered it. Her personal line was the same number she had put on her Sweet Treat flyers.

'Hello, Sweet Treats. Shilpa speaking,' she said into the handset.

There was a silence followed by a cough. For a moment Shilpa thought it was a hoax call, someone having a joke at her expense, but then she heard a small voice.

Two hours later, Shilpa had swallowed a mug of black coffee with two paracetamol and had showered and dressed. It was a cool day, and she had chosen a long cream cardigan to wear over her jeans and T-shirt. The doorbell rang at exactly ten o'clock.

Shilpa opened the door to a woman in her sixties, dressed head to toe in beige, who looked like she had an affinity for cake.

She stuck her hand out in a businesslike manner, but Shilpa could see that the woman had been crying from her red-rimmed eyes. 'June Connolly,' she said. 'Mason's mother.' And on saying his name, her eyes welled up and fat tears stained her cheeks.

'Come in,' Shilpa said, putting a comforting arm around her and ushering her into the house. Once she was seated, she offered her a slice of coffee-and-walnut cake and a cup of tea.

'He was all I had,' June said. 'He was everything to me.' She dabbed her eyes with a tissue Shilpa had given her. 'You must think me a fool, because Mason was a grown man, and he hadn't lived under my roof for so long. I had time to get on with my life, but he was my only son, my only child. I gave up my career when I had him. My whole world revolved around him. Some mothers do that, you know. There are no board meetings and business trips when you are a stay-at-home mum. Your day revolves around football practice and birthday parties. Do you have children?' she asked. She didn't wait for an answer. Looking directly at Shilpa, she said, 'No, you're too young. Don't leave it too long, mind. It's hard work having a little one, and it doesn't get any easier.'

Shilpa smiled, the same smile she reserved for nosy aunties that enquired after her fertility. She looked through the bi-fold doors towards the estuary and towards Graham and John's catamaran, wondering how much they'd had to drink after she had left. She had seen John eyeing up the half-empty bottle of Amaretto as she followed him to the tender. John and Graham had been so good to her since her arrival in Otter's Reach. They had welcomed her, often popping over in those early days to check she was settling in okay. They had truly made her feel at home. She pursed her lips. She couldn't blame John and Graham entirely for her hangover. Guilt stirred in the pit of her stomach. It was coming back to her now. Danny had messaged and she had met him. One drink had turned into… she couldn't remember. Nothing happened between them. Danny was the perfect gentleman, which made him all the more attractive. But there was definitely a chemistry; she could tell. And she was never wrong when it came to chemistry. Well, almost never.

'Thank you for seeing me on a Sunday,' June said, wiping a crumb of cake with the edge of her napkin. She lifted the cup of tea to her lips and took a sip, leaving pink lipstick marks on the rim.

Shilpa waved her comment away. 'Not at all. After what happened, it's the least I can do.'

A tear escaped down June's cheek. 'It's such a tragedy. My poor boy. My poor, poor boy.'

Shilpa went over to June. She wasn't the best with words, but she did her best to comfort Mason's mother. She wanted to say that Mason would be missed, that for the brief time that she knew him, he had made an impression on her. But she couldn't, because she hadn't even met the man. Instead she said, 'It must be a great loss to you and your husband.'

'Mr Connolly isn't here. He's away on business.'

'Oh,' Shilpa said.

'You haven't said the wrong thing, dear. I'm used to that reaction. To go away now and leave when this... this is happening, it just shows what kind of a person he is. He wasn't even here for his only son's engagement.' June looked away, her fingers to her lips. 'Sorry, I shouldn't have said that. It just came out.' She looked back at Shilpa. 'You won't repeat it, will you, dear? It's a small community and...'

Shilpa put a finger to her lips and returned to her seat. 'Tell me how I can help,' she said.

'It feels quite nice to talk to someone, someone who wasn't born and bred in Otter's Reach, or in Devon for that matter. You probably already know that everyone here knows everyone's business. It was a terrible shame Mason and Harriet got together, a terrible shame. I thought with both of them growing up in a small town that they would want to spread their wings – marry out of their existing community. I thought that Mason would have fallen for someone in London. But I was wrong. I suppose familiarity breeds love.' June took another sip of her tea and adjusted her suit jacket, which was pulled taut over her thick waist.

'So, they were childhood sweethearts?' Shilpa asked.

'Oh, nothing like that. They weren't close growing up. It was only recently that they found each other. Mason had his fair share of young ladies running after him before Harriet. There were several women who would have accepted a proposal from him. One had fiery red hair; I know Mason had a soft spot for her. I never got to meet many of his girlfriends, but I met this one quite early on. I was meeting Mason for lunch in London at the time. He was there on business and he had a free hour, so I agreed to meet him, and she was with him. I was delighted. Mason wasn't a secretive boy, but he was shy when it came to women.' June smiled at the memory.

'That meeting told me that my Mason was serious about this lady. He never liked me meeting his girlfriends. Said I asked too many questions.'

Shilpa smiled. So, her mother wasn't the only one then.

'She was a lovely girl,' June said.

'So, what happened?' Shilpa asked, but June didn't know.

'It wasn't long before Harriet was on the scene. And she certainly didn't want any of Mason's exes at the engagement party. I would have liked to meet the redhead again. She didn't mind any of my questions.' June looked up at Shilpa. 'I wasn't too intrusive. I held my tongue. I only asked her about work and her future plans. It's important to know about these things.'

Shilpa smiled. June sounded just like her mother.

'Although I can't blame Harriet for not wanting her fiancé's ex at their engagement party. It's not like she could invite hers,' June said.

'Did you know Harriet before Mason started dating her?' Shilpa asked. The paracetamol had started to take effect, and she was feeling better. Not great, but better. June had sparked her curiosity into Mason's past. Everyone she had spoken to so far was keen to tell her about Harriet. Harriet, with her black widow status, was starting to look like a prime suspect, but what about Mason? He had a past, and it was likely that the person who used that kitchen knife on him was part of his past. Could a scorned ex-lover have killed him? A frenzied knife attack certainly fitted the bill for a crime of passion.

'I knew of Harriet. Everyone knows of the Drews. They're

a big family here. But I can't say I knew the girl. It wasn't that long after they started dating that I met her. You see, they were together less than a year before they got engaged. I didn't think Mason was ready to settle down. Between you and me, when Mason first told me, I thought she was pregnant.' Tears trickled down June's face. 'I was angry at the time, but now it would have been a blessing if it were true. I'll never have a grand-child. Nothing to remember my Mason by.'

Shilpa padded over to June and put a reassuring arm around her.

'Look at you, dear. You're so tiny. How do you keep so slim?' June asked, although she didn't give Shilpa the time to answer. 'Anyway, the reason for my visit,' she said, hurriedly now. 'I didn't think I could explain over the phone. Not in my state. I want you to do the catering for Mason's funeral.'

Chapter Eleven

Alison put the tiny figure on her white windowsill and took a picture. This one would make her at least a fiver after her costs were paid. She poured herself a large tumbler of gin as a reward for her accomplishment. The tiny needle-felted leopard looked back at her as she leaned back and took a large gulp of her drink, letting the alcohol do its thing. The sighting of a leopard a few years ago by an old man with more whisky in his veins than blood had, surprisingly, been taken seriously, and a shaky video taken soon after by a computer geek with thick-rimmed glasses sealed the deal. The Otter's Reach Leopard was born.

The tourist board saw it as an opportunity, and after the hysteria of worried parents died down, the Otter's Reach Leopard became a local legend. Alison had overheard an old granny telling a supermarket checkout assistant that wild cats were all the rage in the sixties and that Harrods had sold them willy-nilly back then. She had assumed that the local leopard was a descendent of such a purchase by one of the rich families in the area.

'The animals were wild, and when people realised their new pet wasn't a friendly thing, they released them on the Moors,' the granny had said, looking in the direction of Bovey Tracey.

Alison had laughed behind the woman's back, but a quick online search confirmed that the old woman had by no means lost her marbles and most of what she had said had some truth in it. It was then that she had an idea of turning her failing needle-felt crafting business around using the Otter's Reach Leopard as her cash cow. Needle felting had always been her passion. There was something about creating tiny woodland animals that you could hold in the palm of your hand that she found quite satisfying, and of course, they looked so adorable.

Alison had turned her love for felting into a business when her parents had died. They had left her a large inheritance, which meant she didn't have to work too hard, but she needed some income, because even she knew that her inheritance was finite. After she had paid for her apartment, she had rather large expenses, especially with all the travel she had done of late.

Alison looked away from the tiny leopard and poured herself another glass of gin, this time with a splash of tonic, and picked up her phone, scrolling through her pictures. She stopped at a selfie of her and Mason outside the Shard. You couldn't really see the full profile of the building in the picture, just a part of the steel and glass. It was a rare day they had spent together, just them, no one else. She continued to scroll.

Another picture of her holding a big chimpanzee stuffed toy in Hamleys. Mason must have taken that one. He hadn't wanted to enter the store, claiming he wasn't five years old, but she had pulled him in, and he had been in awe of the Lego displays and train sets. She saw a flash of nostalgia in his eyes as he picked up a wooden train and set it down again. She was good for Mason; she knew it. His mother knew it too, she mused as she stopped on a photo of Mason and his mother. She was just like Mason. Her soft brown eyes and thick hair. She had been so eager to question Alison about her hopes and dreams. From the short time she had spent with her, she could tell that June Connolly liked her.

Mason, of course, had been angry that she had bumped into them like that. He hadn't wanted her to meet his mother. He had been clear about that. But it wasn't her fault that she just happened to be at the same restaurant that he and his mother were meeting at for lunch.

'It's not like I've been stalking you,' she had whispered to him, putting her hand on his shoulder. She looked towards his mother, who was beaming at her.

'I didn't say that,' Mason mumbled. Alison looked at him for a moment and smiled.

As she reminisced, her thumb over the screen of her phone, ready to scroll on, she wondered if that meeting had been the beginning of the end for her. She had to meet his mother to have any sort of chance with him. Alison had assumed, by the way he spoke to his mother on the phone most lunchtimes, that he valued her opinion. But she realised she had been wrong, because it turned out he didn't value his mother's opinion whatsoever when it came to his choice of bride.

It wasn't long after she had met June that she had been cast aside like a used napkin. She looked at the photo again, at Mason's suspicious eyes. He wasn't looking directly at her lens but at her. There was something there she hadn't noticed before. Had he realised what she had done? It would explain why his calls became less frequent after their lunch. Did she know then that she was obsessed with him? Was that why he broke it off with her and not because he met Harriet like she had always assumed?

She hadn't been obsessed with him, not then. And anyway,

even afterwards, she wouldn't have called it an obsession. Maybe a small infatuation where she had followed him to various destinations as he travelled around the country on apparent business. It wasn't criminal to buy a train ticket and sit in an adjacent carriage to someone or to sit in a coffee shop opposite their workplace. She had become the master of disguise, hiding her mop of electric red hair under a wig – she had a beautiful selection of them. She wasn't a stalker. It's just that she liked being close to him, and her work allowed her to spend time away from her craft in the day, because she could always catch up at night. Plus, spending time in cafés and on trains when Mason wasn't visible allowed her to sketch. She had come up with a whole series of needle-felted foxes on one particular rainy day in a Starbucks, and they had been a hit with her customers, so really she needed the time away from her desk to get her creative juices flowing.

Mason didn't know that she had followed him that day to the restaurant he often frequented for lunch, the same way he didn't know she had the key code to the apartment Mason used at the Drews. A code she often used when she needed some time away from home to sketch and meditate – or at least try and meditate. Meditation was a hard task when she saw Mason every time she closed her eyes. The last time she had used that code she had worn gloves, but there were countless times before that she hadn't been so careful. Would her fingerprints still be imprinted on the keypad? She let the thought go. They had a cleaner, after all. Under normal circumstances she would have been worried – a fear would grip her insides, turning them to liquid – but today she didn't feel that way. Today she felt invincible, because she didn't have a police record. No prints for the police to compare hers against. The only way they could track her to the Drews was if someone had seen her the day Mason had been killed, or if someone mentioned her to the police. Like Izzy said, she was a nobody. There was a slim possibility that Izzy had seen her in her car as she watched the house that day, but Izzy wasn't going to say anything to the police. She was certain of that.

Alison lifted her drink to her lips and swallowed the contents, quickly pouring herself another. She scrolled past the photo of Mason and his mother. There was a beautiful profile shot of Mason in the distance. The sight of it made her heart lurch.

Perhaps she would make a photo book. She had enough pictures, and it would be a nice way to commemorate him, the time she had spent with him and without him. Alison continued to scroll, tears filling her eyes, knowing she would never see Mason again. The gin was clouding her mind. Then she stopped on a photograph that made her fling her glass at the wall. Why did she have a picture on her phone of Mason with his arm around Harriet? She stared at his eyes, so full of life in this shot, so full of love compared to the one she had taken of him that day she had lunched with him and his mother. She swallowed the bitter taste of bile rising up in her throat. Then she saw it, the reason why she had kept the heart-breaking photo. If the police ever caught up with her, then this photo might just save her.

Alison put her phone down and took a deep breath. She needed something else to concentrate on, to take her mind away from Mason and his terrible demise. It was the only thing that seemed to occupy her thoughts at the moment, and it wasn't healthy. Even she knew that. Her mother, if she were still alive, would have been proud, would have given her a gold star for making progress. 'Very good, Alison,' she would have said. 'You really are becoming more self-aware.'

She opened her laptop and did a quick Google search to find the website she was after. She had overheard at Leoni's that someone was poking their nose where they shouldn't have been. The homepage for the site she had called up appeared on her screen. She smiled. It was about time she had a new subject.

Chapter Twelve

Why on Earth had she agreed to cater for a funeral? She made cakes, not canapés, yet Shilpa had readily accepted the proposal. June Connolly wasn't the pushy sort, not at all like Mrs Drew. She didn't throw her weight around, she didn't make demands, and yet she had managed to convince Shilpa, when she didn't have the first idea how to go about it.

'Don't worry, dear,' she had said. 'It will only be a few guests. Let's presume one hundred and fifty.'

Shilpa looked at her wide-eyed.

'You think that's too few to cater for?' she asked. 'Should you be taking this down? Although your memory is probably much better than mine.'

Shilpa, who wasn't often speechless, picked up a notepad and pencil that lay on the coffee table beside her and started making notes. Ten minutes later, when June had paused for breath, Shilpa found her voice. 'I don't really do catering,' she said. 'Just cakes. Occasion cakes.'

June Connolly didn't appear to hear her, or if she did, she had conveniently ignored her plea. 'It's just you did the cake for the engagement party,' she said, holding a tissue to her right eye. 'You knew Mason.'

Shilpa had tried to correct her, saying she hadn't met Mason, that Mrs Drew had arranged the whole thing, but this too fell on deaf ears. Shilpa asked after the engagement party caterers, to which June replied, 'You're such a lovely girl for taking this on.' Shilpa silently nodded, thereby sealing the deal. So, it wasn't just Indian mothers who knew how to get their way by conveniently ignoring what they didn't want to hear. Shilpa had only herself to blame. After all, she had years of experience dealing with her own mum. But June had just lost her son, her only son. She couldn't say no.

Shilpa pulled her mobile phone from her bag and started typing a message to Olivia. Her brown leather Mulberry bag banged against her hip as she strode towards Leoni's, past the pink thrift and sweet-smelling wild carrot growing along the perimeter of a picnic spot on Estuary Road. Today only a few benches were taken up by families in Devon for the summer holidays. The children sat eating their pastries, buckets and bacon in netted pouches by their sides, eagerly anticipating a day's crabbing. Shilpa turned her attention back to her phone. Olivia was a fellow market stallholder who specialised in savoury nibbles. She hoped she was free and could help her get out of this mess she had found herself in. Pressing send, she slipped the phone back into her bag and turned her thoughts towards the cake she had agreed to make for the funeral. 'A simple cake,' June had said, before adding that she wanted something different. 'Something to be remembered.' Shilpa mentioned an Earl Grey-and-lemon cake she had once tried, and June nodded appreciatively. It was settled then – Earl Grey and lemon it was.

∾

'I'll be with you in a minute, luv,' Leoni said, wiping her hands on her apron and rushing back into the kitchen. She appeared a moment later, sweeping away a strand of hair from her brow with the back of her hand. 'What's in that banana bread, eh? They've been going crazy for it,' she said, motioning to the customers seated in the café.

Shilpa touched her nose. 'That's a secret,' she said.

'Your usual?' Leoni said, turning towards the coffee machine. 'It's been a mad morning.' She turned and handed Shilpa a cup. She stepped out from behind the counter and looked Shilpa up and down. 'This becoming a uniform?' she asked.

Shilpa looked down at what she was wearing: black velvet French Sole Hefner slippers with vibrant blue butterflies on the toe, grey chinos and a navy-and-white T-shirt. Now that she couldn't indulge in Louboutins anymore, she found herself drawn to the simple Breton. Looking for a new stripy T-shirt was how she whiled away her spare time, and she had quite a bit of that. Her lack of things to do in Otter's Reach was part of the reason she had found herself drawn to the Connolly case. That and the knife she had seen the day Mason had been murdered. She looked at Leoni and then back at her garments. She was building quite a collection.

'Looks like it,' she said, and sighed at the loss of her once on-trend style.

They seated themselves in the corner of the coffee shop and Shilpa took a large sip of her double macchiato. It instantly perked her up as she felt the coffee slide down her throat. It wasn't long before Leoni brought up the subject of Mason Connolly's death, or 'that terrible business', as she referred to it.

'His mother wants me to cater for the funeral,' Shilpa confessed.

'Poor thing,' Leoni said. 'He didn't have a chance, not with

Harriet's history.' Leoni explained how it wasn't just Harriet whose black widow reputation made her a suspect in Mason's murder.

'Her dad tried to pay off her previous fiancé Finley. I don't know how much,' Leoni said. 'The boy didn't take it though. He said no.'

Shilpa considered this. She had never been in love enough to ever have to weigh up the fantastical notion that someone would offer her a large sum of money to step away from her one true love. 'How do you know?' she asked.

'There was a big fuss at the time. Finley told Harriet what her dad had done, and she wasn't happy, she made that known. The staff at the Drews' were talking. There'd been fights between father and daughter, Harriet brought forward their wedding date, and then funnily enough the poor lad died abroad just before the wedding. Finley wasn't good enough for Steven Drew's daughter, and neither was Mason,' Leoni said. 'Drew has money, so he can make things happen,' she added.

Shilpa ignored her last comment. 'Mason came from a good family – a wealthy family from what I've heard. Surely that made a difference,' she said, playing devil's advocate.

Leoni finished her mug of tea. She looked up as a man in a blue T-shirt walked into the coffee shop and selected a baguette from the chilled unit and passed it to the cashier. Leoni agreed that Mason had wealth and was better-looking than Finley, but she was confident that it was his womanising that had put him on the back foot with Steven Drew.

'He had this one girl that I occasionally saw him with before Harriet. Izzy was her name, and my, she was beautiful. Don't get me wrong, Harriet's a looker too. But there was something about this Izzy that just turned heads. You know, dark hair, olive complexion. She has a reputation for not letting anyone or anything get in her way. She was certainly something, but I think she got a better offer, because she dumped the poor chap – or so went the rumour.'

'I saw someone matching that description at the engagement party,' Shilpa said, remembering a beautiful woman of similar type with a polished look.

Leoni leaned in conspiratorially. 'Was the woman you saw in green?' she asked.

'She was.'

'Well then,' she said with a smile, happy to have learned something new to gossip about. 'Always wears green, that one; they even refer to her as the Green Goddess. I remember overhearing a bunch of girls in here bitching about her, and that stood out. No idea why.'

'It suited her, I suppose,' Shilpa said, noting that Izzy was a woman other women felt insecure around. Once again, she looked at her Breton top and chinos. 'If you feel good in something, it makes sense to keep wearing it.'

'Izzy moved to someplace near Mermaid Point a few years ago, so I never really kept up with her. Maybe she and Harriet were friends, because why would Harriet allow one of Mason's exes to her engagement party? Especially a better-looking ex.' Leoni threw her head back and laughed. 'Ooh, it must have been some party.'

It was clear that June hadn't known about Izzy, because she'd said that none of Mason's exes were invited. Harriet must have known though.

'Who knows what really happened to poor Mason,' Leoni said. 'What's certain is that Mason died that day in the Drew house, and everyone is talking foul play. Steven Drew has form, doesn't he? I'm just putting two and two together. Those police at Glass Bay keep a tight lid on things. It's a shame they aren't based here, because if they were, I'm sure I'd know a darned sight more about the case.'

If Leoni was right about the pay-off, then Steven Drew

could have paid to have Finley killed. If it had been that easy, then maybe he had done the same with Mason. But in his house? On his property? Had he just wanted to protect his daughter, or had he enjoyed the power? It was plausible that Steven could have killed Mason at home to test the boundaries, to see if he could evade capture once again. Or perhaps he wanted to get caught, the guilt of Finley's death weighing him down.

Shilpa was mulling over whether Steven Drew was a murderer when Leoni spoke again. 'Harriet didn't wait long before she found another victim.' Leoni was a gossip who was rarely wrong, or so people said. But this was a stretch too far. Surely Harriet wasn't dating already.

'What do you mean?' she asked. But as the words left her mouth, the door to the coffee shop opened and Harriet walked in with a tall man with dark hair and broad shoulders. The man ordered an espresso to go. Leoni kicked Shilpa under the table and Shilpa looked away. She noticed a few locals had stopped their conversations to stare at the couple.

Leoni was on her feet immediately. 'Oh, pet,' she said. 'How are you holding up?'

Harriet tilted her head to one side and put her hand on her chest. 'It has been difficult,' she said a little too dramatically. 'A shock, really.'

'Terrible,' Leoni said. 'I'm glad to see you're out and about.'

'Evan has been a wonderful support,' Harriet said, her perfectly manicured red nails giving his shoulder a squeeze. She was either oblivious to what people were saying about her or she didn't care. Leoni wished Harriet well and sat back down. Harriet looked towards her and Shilpa smiled, but Harriet blanked her. She didn't recognise her then as the woman who'd spent a good part of twenty-four hours making her engagement cake. Or maybe she had recalled her but didn't like to acknowledge the staff.

'That was Evan White,' Leoni whispered as soon as the couple left the shop. 'A college sweetheart. The two have dated on and off for years. They are each other's backup plans,' Leoni said, adding that they would be engaged before summer was out on account of Harriet wanting to be married before she hit thirty.

Shilpa finished her macchiato. She was thirty-five with no sign of a husband on the horizon. She understood how Harriet felt, but she would never just settle. She thanked Leoni for the coffee and the chat and stood up.

'It's ginger syrup and cardamom,' she said.

'Sorry?'

'In the banana bread.' Just the thought of her grandmother's recipe gave her a warm feeling inside. She was glad she wasn't the only one who loved it.

Chapter Thirteen

'I'm surprised at her, that's all,' Margery said, looking towards the photo of Harriet and Mason hanging on the wall. 'And I do feel bad for her, for this to happen a second time. She doesn't deserve such bad luck.'

'She doesn't, but then she's better off for it,' Mr Drew said.

'Oh, for goodness' sake,' his wife said in a whisper. 'Lower your voice.'

'Why? There are no police around,' Steven said even louder. He picked up the post from the table and sifted through it before putting it back down. This was the last conversation he wanted after a long day at work. What had Margery been doing all day? Nothing, except for conjuring up reasons why someone would want both their daughter's fiancés dead. It wasn't going to help anyone, certainly not him.

'Harriet's home; she might hear you. You must be more sensitive. We all know you didn't like Finley or Mason, but for all our sakes you must at least pretend that you did, especially now.'

You're the one questioning how our daughter managed to move on so quickly, Steven wanted to say. He looked at his wife. He wanted to ask why, but not because he wanted to know why. He knew the reason. He just wanted to see her squirm. He opened his mouth and then quickly closed it again. Sport wasn't a good enough reason to discuss this any further. Instead Steven nodded and smiled, concealing a bitterness in his clenched fists, which were now safely hidden in his pockets.

'Where were you?' Margery asked, looking away from him and into her empty teacup for the umpteenth time.

'I popped to the office. I wanted to–'

'Not just now,' she interrupted. 'At Harriet and Mason's engagement party.'

'I was here,' Steven said. Once again, he picked up the post and flicked through the unopened envelopes, avoiding her gaze.

'Not for all of it. You went somewhere. And when you returned you were wearing something different.'

He looked up at his wife. 'What are you on about?' he asked.

'You were wearing the salmon-pink shirt for the engagement party. You put it on that morning, and I noted the pink because you don't usually wear that colour and you should. It suits you. Don't you remember? Then later when I saw you again after the search for Mason had commenced you were in a white shirt. The creases hadn't even been ironed out. You went somewhere and you changed.' Margery whispered these last words.

He accused her of being delusional then and walked out of the drawing room and into the study. Once inside, he turned to close the door, but Margery was right behind him. He considered telling her where he had been the day of the party. That would really shock her. Then he decided against it.

'You know you're not to come in here,' he said.

She gave him a wounded look and left.

Once the door was safely closed, he padded over to the

bureau. With some effort, he opened the drawer he was after and emptied out the contents. He could feel his blood pressure rising. Mason hadn't just been an under-achiever; he had been something else, something much worse. He had wanted to put a stop to what he was doing, because no one told Steven Drew what to do. No one forced his hand before he was ready. No one had extorted money from him before, and no one would ever again.

He took a deep breath and restored the drawer and its contents safely back inside the bureau. Then he walked over to the drinks cabinet, poured himself a large whisky and downed it in one.

Chapter Fourteen

Shilpa wondered if it was plausible to claim she was just passing if she lingered outside the police station long enough, waiting for Danny to finally appear. Unlikely story. He would see right through her, especially as the police station was in a cul-de-sac in Glass Bay, miles from Otter's Reach. She rubbed her hands together and stepped out from behind her stall to get a hot chocolate from the neighbouring stallholder. The morning still had a chill in the air, and she didn't really want to be there. She could tell it was going to be a slow one. It was supposed to be scorching later on, so she imagined the tourists were up and out early, choosing to breakfast at the cafés at Blackpool Sands or Slapton before their day at the beach. The Otter's Reach locals hadn't yet woken up.

'These Saturday mornings come around quick, don't they,' Derek said in a West Country accent as he ladled hot chocolate into a Styrofoam cup. She nodded, handed him two pounds and took the drink from him. The hot liquid relaxed her as it slipped down her throat. She thanked Derek and realised that he was the first person she had spoken to since she had woken up. She wondered if she was lonely. Was that why she was becoming increasingly fixated on Danny? Was she just allevi-ating boredom, or did she really fancy him? She decided to pick the latter. This was no time for a poor-me pity party. She had known it was going to be tough uprooting and moving to Devon; leaving her best friends behind to start over in a small town. But today it felt like hard work. She looked back at her stall and the two customers that had just entered the market square. They were heading towards a stall selling flowers, so she walked over to Olivia's.

'So, did you get a date with that chap you're stalking then?' Olivia asked, before she even said hello.

Shilpa grinned. 'Not yet,' she said. On a particularly wet afternoon last week at Leoni's she had shared her feelings for Danny with Olivia. She had kept the details to a minimum, only sharing that she had her eye on someone that she quite liked. She knew what gossip could do to a relationship, espe-cially in a small place like Otter's Reach. If Olivia knew who she was after then Leoni would soon know, and it would get back to Danny, and who knew what would happen. Although would that be such a bad thing? If Danny knew she liked him would he look at her differently?

Shilpa asked Olivia if she was ready for the funeral and thanked her again for helping out. Olivia waved her comments aside and pushed a few stray blonde curls away from her face.

'I'm glad I could help. It's so sad. I've never heard of a murder happening around here. And at a party too. I went to school with Mason.' Shilpa was surprised that Mason hadn't been privately educated, but Olivia informed her that his father thought he would be better rounded if he stuck it out with the local kids.

'Mason was a charmer,' Olivia continued. 'A bit angular, but he had a dark, brooding look that caught girls' attention.'

Shilpa glanced back at her stall and then turned towards Olivia.

'And have you heard Harriet is now dating Evan White?' Olivia said. She didn't wait for a response before giving Shilpa the low-down on Harriet's new boyfriend. According to Olivia, he was a quiet introvert but better-looking than Mason, and he owned White Water, the stand-up paddle-boarding empire in Devon. 'A self-made man. Much better suited for the daughter of Steven Drew,' Olivia said.

'Harriet had an interest in Evan even before he made his money,' Olivia said. 'Which is saying something. I'm surprised they didn't get together sooner. I spotted them last night in the bar at the top of the hill. There she was, Harriet, all legs and red lips. Evan had his hand on the small of her back and was whispering something in her ear. It looked quite intimate. And to think Mason isn't in the ground yet. I don't know how that woman gets away with it.'

Shilpa didn't say anything about her conversation with Leoni or that she had seen Evan and Harriet together at the café. She looked back towards her stall again. Two customers had stopped to talk to Derek. They would be at her stall next, but then again, Derek could talk. She reckoned she had at least five minutes.

'So, who do you think bumped off Mason Connolly?' Olivia asked, offering Shilpa a mini sausage roll.

Shilpa shrugged.

Olivia smiled. 'Keeping quiet on who you think it is, I see. Everyone has a suspect in mind. It's the most exciting thing that's happened here. My money's on Harriet. She didn't love him and wanted to be with Evan. Goodbye, Mason.'

'She could have just called it off with Mason. To have two fiancés die isn't something anyone wants.'

'Unless the death of one gave you the taste to get rid of the second,' Olivia said. 'I know a copper at Glass Bay. My brother-in-law. It's not his department. He's keeping tight-lipped about the whole thing, but I bet he knows a thing or two.'

Shilpa considered asking Olivia if she knew Danny but then thought better of it.

'Do you think Evan could've done it?' Shilpa said, throwing her empty cup in a bin close to Olivia's stall. It wouldn't be the first time someone had killed out of jealousy.

Olivia didn't think so, even though she knew he had been at the engagement party. She had grown up with Evan and couldn't believe he would do something like that. 'He's got a brain,' she said. 'And he uses it. He's never been the sort to use his fists.'

There's always a first time, Shilpa thought as she walked towards her stall. She knew from her own experience with a possessive ex that the rich liked getting their way. They were not good at rejection. They usually got whatever they wanted no matter who they hurt in the process. Shilpa dug her hands into her pockets. It was a big generalisation. And she liked Olivia. The woman was warm and genuine. She trusted her opinion. If she thought Evan was innocent, then maybe he was.

Chapter Fifteen

As it turned out, it wasn't a wasted morning. Olivia had to leave early to pick up her boys from football practice, so Shilpa had a box of savoury pastries to take home, and an hour after that, Danny had turned up to buy a chocolate brownie.

'Heard they're legendary,' he said.

Her cheeks coloured as she picked up two brownies with her tongs and put them in a brown bag for him.

'How much?' he had asked.

'Nothing,' she said with a grin.

'You won't make any money that way,' Danny said. 'How's about I take you for a coffee then. I don't need to get back for another hour.' He looked at his watch. She had closed her stall early, and they had headed to Magdalena's café on the High Street for a tea. Danny had suggested Leoni's, but Shilpa felt like keeping her morning date quiet. Leoni said she didn't know any of the police at Glass Bay, and she could see the café owner wanting to befriend Danny just so that she had a contact there.

Once seated, Danny ordered an espresso and she decided

on a herbal tea. Shilpa laughed at something inane Danny had said as they waited for their drinks. What Danny had said wasn't funny, but she assumed her subconscious was telling her to start flirting. She would need to do something to take their casual friendship to another level if that's what she wanted. If that's what he wanted. She tried asking about his personal life, but Danny didn't give her a direct answer. She couldn't blame him. Her questions were vague. She decided to try a different tack.

'Do you know much about the Mason Connolly case?' she asked. 'There's a rumour going around that his fiancée has already moved on.'

'You shouldn't believe everything you hear around here,' Danny said. 'Otter's Reach is a small town, and people love to gossip.'

Shilpa grimaced. 'That didn't come out right,' she said. 'I mean, if something like that were to happen to me, I think I'd have holed myself up somewhere, probably at my parents' house. There wouldn't be room for any rumours.'

Danny looked at her blankly. She continued, 'I don't have any significant other, so I guess the chances of something like this happening to me are quite slim. You?' she asked. She looked up at the waitress as she brought over their drinks, willing her to spill them – anything to remove her from this awkward conversation.

'Chances of something similar happening to anyone are quite low,' he said. 'It's a strange one.'

Shilpa nodded. Back in London, she excelled at her job. With brand management came a huge communication role. She thrived on putting presentations together, paying attention to detail, of getting what she wanted from her team. Her communication skills were applauded in her annual appraisal, and yet she failed miserably at speaking to members of the opposite sex when she fancied them.

She saw her chance to remove herself from the hole she had been digging herself into. 'You're right. It's an odd case.'

'You've been following it?' he asked.

'I made the cake for the party. I was there.'

'Ah, so that's why you were at the station the other day. Met our DI then?'

Shilpa nodded. 'Are you working on the case?' she asked, raising her cup of peppermint tea to her lips.

'That would be telling,' he said, giving her a sideways glance. Then he smiled. 'I'm doing a bit of work for the DI. I'm not in the criminal investigation department, but you hear things, and around these parts you occasionally get dragged into cases not necessarily in your area.'

'There's been talk of his fiancée…' Shilpa trailed off.

'I know what you're going to say, but I think Harriet's innocent. People around here have preconceived ideas of her. She's not a bad girl, really, just misunderstood.'

'You know her?' Shilpa asked.

Danny didn't respond, and Shilpa felt something stir inside her. 'How is she misunderstood?' she asked.

'She's had to deal with the Drew family name and what that brings. Like most of us, she's just trying to do the right thing. Wants to make her parents proud. Wants to settle down and have a family.'

'Is that your professional or personal opinion?' Shilpa asked. Danny smiled, and she noticed the corners of his eyes creased when he did. She caught herself staring and quickly looked away, concentrating on pouring herself another cup of tea from the green-and-white-spotted teapot the waitress had brought over with her cup. Then she asked him about other suspects. She could think of a few. Harriet, her dad and her new boyfriend Evan. Then there was Mason's ex-girlfriends – the redhead and Izzy.

Danny shrugged. Either he was too professional to

comment or he didn't know. He looked at his watch. 'I gotta be making tracks,' he said. He stood up abruptly. 'Rain check?' he said, putting a tenner on the table and turning to leave.

'Sure,' Shilpa said, a little taken aback, and before she could even say goodbye, he was gone. She looked into her cup and wondered what had just happened. She finished her tea and placed the cup back on its saucer. 'Nice,' she said out loud. Why had she brought up the Connolly case? Of course he wouldn't want to be interrogated about his work outside of work. He hadn't asked her any questions about the perfect bake. *Good one, Shilpa*, she thought to herself sarcastically. He did say rain check though. Every cloud and all that.

Shilpa stood up and grabbed her bag. Then she paused and looked around at the other customers, as she had a sense that she was being watched. An old gentleman concentrated on his scone, and a lone woman with dark hair was staring intently at her magazine. The woman briefly looked up. Shilpa noticed she had the most amazing bone structure set off by a vibrant green scarf. She sighed. She was being paranoid. No one looked the least bit interested in her. She shook off the feeling and stepped out into the summer day.

Chapter Sixteen

'Mum, I'm going to be late,' Shilpa said into her mobile as she slammed shut her car door. She usually used this line when her mother started lecturing her about something or other, but this time she was actually going to be late.

'But he's a nice boy,' her mother said.

'I don't really have time for this.' Shilpa turned the key in the ignition, but the engine wouldn't start. She hit the dashboard and tried again.

'I gave him your address,' her mother said sharply.

'You did what?' Shilpa asked incredulously as she turned the key again and again.

'I gave him–'

'I heard you. Why would you give some complete stranger my address?'

'Didn't you hear me? He isn't a stranger. He's Bippu Aunty's nephew.'

Shilpa gritted her teeth. She didn't even know who Bippu Aunty was. 'Fine,' she said, hurrying her mother along. She tried the ignition again. The car started, and she breathed a sigh of relief. She didn't want to know any more details about this prospective new man. She could always pretend not to be in when he turned up. Shilpa said goodbye, disconnected the call, put her phone on silent and glanced over to the boot. The Earl Grey-and-lemon cake had turned out okay after all. She had done two large cakes to feed the guests, and she reckoned it would be enough. The lemon frosting, with just a hint of yellow so it wasn't too garish, was pretty good too. 'Fitting,' she'd said to herself as she loaded the cakes into the car. Her choice of cake was perfect for a funeral.

'So, you made it then,' Olivia said to Shilpa as she walked in with a cake in each hand, her handbag slung over her shoulder. Shilpa smiled. She had made it to the wake, but not the church service. She just didn't have time. The first batch of frosting she had made wasn't right, so she had to start again. Then she had to find something black and appropriate to wear, which had been a trial in itself. She eventually found an old Vivienne Westwood dress in the last packing box she had decided to open which fitted the bill. And then of course there had been the phone call from her mother and her car ignition playing up. It had been doing that for some time, and she had meant to get it looked at before she got stuck somewhere. Another thing for her never-ending list. She shoved the thought to the back of her mind.

It was a shame she'd missed the church service because she'd wanted to check out the guests. See how well Harriet played the grieving fiancée and if Evan White would have the nerve to show up. She also wanted to observe Harriet's parents. Her dad, Steven Drew, didn't think much of Mason and was rumoured to have attempted to pay off Harriet's previous fiancé. Her mother Margery wasn't innocent either. She had told the police that she never went into her husband's study when Shilpa knew she had been in there. At the party Margery had told her quite clearly she had used the spatula to jimmy open the old bureau drawer. What was in that drawer? Whatever it was, she was sure the Drews would have disposed of it by now, as soon as the police had left their home.

'You didn't miss much at the funeral,' Olivia said. 'Harriet shed some obligatory crocodile tears. She wore a beautiful black veil under a pillbox hat, very fifties and glam; not what you expect for your local town funeral. Evan was there too. Stood on the other side as they were lowering Mason into the ground; kept looking at Harriet. I like Evan, but it was a little disrespectful.'

Shilpa had placed the cakes on the table near the cheese puffs and was now looking at the open front door as the guests started to filter through. A petite lady with pale skin and electric-red hair walked in alone. Large bug-eyed sunglasses covered most of her face. She looked lost, alone, like a nervous graduate at a business networking lunch. By the colour of her hair, Shilpa assumed this redhead was the ex-girlfriend June had mentioned.

'Her name's Alison. One of Mason's exes,' Olivia said, confirming her suspicions. 'She's a bit cuckoo if you ask me. A custard short of a pudding. I overheard her telling her mates that Mason was going to marry her. But that was before Izzy, let alone Harriet, so if you ask me, it was all in her head.'

'Overheard?'

'In a bar,' Olivia said, arching her eyebrow. 'I do go out sometimes, despite three kids. It was a rare night off. Anyways, I'm not that much older than her, and there are only two bars in this town. Two bars, two cafés, one pub and a couple of restaurants. It's how everyone knows everything. She could have done it.'

'She's tiny,' Shilpa said, watching the red-haired woman. 'Can't see her being able to overpower a grown man.'

Olivia suggested that Mason could have been drugged. It was a good point. Shilpa knew so little about the case. Danny wasn't proving useful either. Maybe once they were closer things would be different. But then again, it would probably be a long time before that happened. She sighed. Right now, Danny seemed as far out of her grasp as finding out who killed Mason Connolly. She sliced the cakes and then pulled her phone out of her bag, following Olivia into the kitchen. Before she could think about it and stop herself, she sent Danny a text asking if he wanted to meet later in the week.

She instantly received a reply, bringing a smile to her lips. He suggested a game of tennis on Monday afternoon. Tennis wasn't really her thing, but why not. She sent him a thumbs-up emoji in response and considered whether she had any suitable sportswear before slipping her phone back into her bag.

From the kitchen, with the door open, she had a good view of the guests. She watched Alison. Her skin was almost translucent. Alison was good-looking in an ethereal kind of way, and she had a quirky sense of style with her ruched deep-red velvet gown and black lace-up boots. Shilpa watched as she helped herself to a large gin and a cheese puff, which she picked at like a bird. She hadn't seen Alison at the engagement party, but then if Olivia was right, there was probably a good reason she hadn't been invited. June had said no exes were invited, but Izzy, the good-looking ex with the dark hair, had been at the party.

She watched Harriet now as people walked up to her, offering her their condolences, telling her anecdotes that involved Mason. Every so often Harriet would wipe a tear from her eye. When she saw Alison, the two women stared at each other for just a moment, and although she couldn't see Alison's face, Harriet's expression was one of pure hatred.

'Shilpa, dear, you must come and join us celebrating Mason's life. You're as much a guest here as the others,' June said, handing Shilpa a glass of prosecco and steering her by her elbow towards the living room. 'Oh look,' June said. 'My dear friend Steven.'

Shilpa watched as Steven Drew offered his condolences and then passed on those of his wife. 'She couldn't make it. She isn't feeling well,' he said with regret, although the blink-and-you'd-miss-it roll of his eyes betrayed his words.

'Oh, that's a shame,' June said. 'It's a hard time for all of us.' June cleared her throat and looked away. Her voice caught as she introduced Shilpa to Steven.

'We've met,' Steven said, offering Shilpa his hand.

'Yes, silly me. Of course you have,' June said, her eyes watching Steven Drew. 'Shilpa made Harriet and my Mason's engagement cake.' Her voice caught again, and Steven put a reassuring hand on her arm. June leaned in towards him for a moment and then pulled away. 'It's just such a sad, sad time,' she said.

'And Bernard?' Steven said. 'He's here, yes?'

'Yes,' June said. She looked towards Shilpa. 'My husband,' she said by way of explanation. 'He's over there.' She pointed towards the large bay window at the front of the house. A tall balding man was stooped in the window, wearing an ill-fitting suit and holding a plate full of canapés close to his chest. He didn't fit the image of a shipping magnate that Shilpa had imagined.

'I must go and say hello,' Steven said. 'Please excuse me.'

'Before you do, Steven,' June said, her voice soft, 'you must employ Shilpa for your event next week. What is it again?'

'It's a launch for our new digital chat service.' Steven looked at Shilpa. 'It's what the younger clients want. You know what these millennials are like. No one actually wants to physically speak to someone these days. The event is just a small thing,' he said. He looked Shilpa up and down. Then he abruptly took out a business card from the top pocket of his suit and scribbled a number on the back. 'We wanted to cancel it with what has happened, but…' He trailed off, leaving Shilpa wondering if Mr Drew, who was known not to have cared much for his future son-in-law, was struggling to believe the boy's death was a good enough reason to cancel his event. 'This Tuesday,' he continued. 'The event starts at four. We're expecting fifty people and need something appropriate.'

Shilpa was shocked into silence by his abrupt manner, but then Steven Drew held out his hand. 'Think you can manage that?' he said with a smile which softened his features. And although she wanted to say she would check her diary, that she would give it some consideration, she didn't. Instead, she found herself agreeing and suggesting fifty cupcakes with the Drew Accounting logo and fifty with the digital chat icon. Business was business, after all.

'Simple, branded,' he said, and she nodded, thinking it was an easy bake as well.

'That sounds lovely,' June said, and winked at Shilpa before she walked off.

'Call my office,' Mr Drew said. 'Ask for Loretta. I've put her details on the back. Send your invoice to her after. Now, if you'll excuse me, I've got to talk to that chap. He really should tidy himself up a bit,' he mumbled, and with that Steven Drew walked in the direction of Bernard Connolly.

Chapter Seventeen

'Interesting, don't you think, that he missed his son's engagement,' Olivia said, walking up behind Shilpa. 'He couldn't have approved of the match. And look at him. If I was worth half of what he's worth I wouldn't be dressing like that.'

'He's just lost his son.'

'He always dresses like that,' Olivia said. 'Even when Mason was alive.'

'Zero dress sense; a little like Steve Jobs – and look at Bill Gates. What is interesting though is, like you say, he missed his son's engagement.'

'Some deal with China, apparently,' a voice said from behind them.

'Oh Danny, love, you gave me a fright,' Olivia said.

'You two know each other?' Shilpa asked, looking at Danny curiously.

'Yes, we go back,' Danny said, kissing Olivia on her cheek.

'Shilpa, this is the copper I was telling you about. My brother-in-law. Married to my sister,' Olivia said. 'But how do you two know each other?'

Shilpa stood motionless in the middle of Mason Connolly's

wake, feeling like she had just been hit by a bus. She wanted to say something. She wanted to ask Danny why he hadn't mentioned that he was married.

'We went to university together,' Danny said. 'Bumped into each other just the other day.'

'You need to introduce her to Theo,' Olivia said. She turned to Shilpa. 'He's a detective sergeant on the case.' She turned back to Danny. 'Did you know she was the one to find the bloodstained knife at the Drews'? How creepy.'

'Theo won't be able to tell you anything. He's all right though. Moved this way a couple of years ago,' Danny said with a shrug. 'Very sure of himself. Might be why he's still single.'

Olivia scowled at him. 'He's a fine lad. Danny's just a bit narked that this guy has come in from another force and is a sergeant. Not to mention at least a foot taller and better-looking,' Olivia said playfully, squeezing her brother-in-law's shoulder.

'Oh, give over,' Danny said with a forced laugh.

'He's a charmer, this one,' Olivia said, looking at Danny with affection. 'So, tell me. Did you see him again?'

Shilpa stared at Olivia, her mind in a fog. 'Who?'

'The man you're after.' Olivia turned to Danny. 'She's after someone.'

'Oh,' Shilpa said, trying to sound nonchalant. 'We met. It didn't work out.'

'You decided that pretty quick,' Olivia said. 'Just yesterday–'

'It went downhill from there,' Shilpa said, cutting her off. Her mouth was dry. She downed her glass of prosecco.

'Careful with that,' Olivia said, looking at her glass. Shilpa scanned the room for the waiter to offer her a refill.

Danny smiled. Not a malicious smile, not a know-it-all smile, but a genuine smile which told her he had never been interested in her in the first place. 'We're meeting for tennis tomorrow. How about we make it doubles, and I'll bring Theo too if he's free. I didn't realise you were in the dating game,' Danny said.

'I'm not really in the dating game,' Shilpa said, her cheeks colouring.

'Oh, get out of it,' Olivia said. 'You're a gorgeous young single woman and without the burden of children. You're most definitely on the lookout.'

Shilpa couldn't help but nod. It must have been the shock.

'Lo can't make tennis, silly. Not with the problems she's had and that swollen belly. She's about to pop,' Olivia said, turning to Shilpa. Shilpa wanted to cry. 'But I could give it a go. The kids have their own things on tomorrow.'

'That's settled then,' Danny said. 'I'll give Theo a call.'

'You know,' Shilpa said, plastering a smile on her face, 'I'm just going to check on the cake.' She quickly walked away from Danny and Olivia. She closed her eyes and rubbed her temples. She had thought Danny had been flirting with her. She had been mistaken – his wife was pregnant. Olivia said that her brother-in-law worked at Glass Bay. Why didn't she mention Danny then? Was it possible that Danny genuinely liked her? She shook her head. It wasn't. She had been stupid, and even if he was planning on cheating on his heavily pregnant wife, she wanted no part in it.

Shilpa adjusted her handbag and walked towards the patio doors. She could easily escape through them without having to pass Olivia and Danny again. She walked quickly, her head bowed, until she bumped into someone. She looked up. The woman in front of her was stunning. She wore a forest-green bodycon dress, entirely inappropriate for a funeral, but nevertheless she carried it off somehow. She was sure the woman with her dark curls and sparkling eyes was Izzy – dressed in signature green, as Leoni had mentioned.

She had definitely seen her at Mason and Harriet's engagement party.

~

Shilpa looked up to the darkening sky as she got into her red Fiat. She tried the key in the ignition, but it wouldn't start. Her car wasn't old. It shouldn't have been playing up like this. She hit the dashboard and tried again.

'Come on,' she shouted.

Nothing.

Five minutes later, with no joy in getting her car to start, she decided she would walk. Remembering she had a duty as caterer to clear up after the guests, she quickly sent Olivia a message asking the favour of her. She made an excuse of feeling a little unwell. Olivia's response was instantaneous. She would clear up, and she told her to get a good night's rest ahead of their tennis game – only if she was up to it, of course.

As Shilpa pulled the key out of the ignition, a fat drop of rain landed on the windscreen. She looked back at the house she had just snuck out of and then at her shoes. She had worn heels. Not Louboutin 3.94 inches but a respectable three inches. After months of living in Devon, she had pretty much forgotten how to walk in heels. She was close to punching the steering wheel when she remembered she had a spare pair of flats in the rear passenger seat. Finally, something was going her way.

She reached behind her, changed her shoes and stepped out of the car. The red love hearts on the toes of her black pumps jeered at her. Fat chance she was ever going to fall in love.

By the time Shilpa reached her house, she was soaking wet. The light summer evening was much darker than she'd anticipated. The sensor light to the front of the house wasn't working. Of course it wasn't. She wanted to scream. She rummaged around in her bag and several minutes later found her keys and walked towards her front door. Despite the rain, she heard a clicking noise coming from the garage directly behind her. She thought she had heard the noise as she walked the mile and a half home from the Connollys' house, but she had turned around a couple of times and there had been no one behind her. Now an eerie feeling came over her, the same one she had felt in the coffee shop yesterday. She shivered in her wet clothes, took a breath and decided to investigate. She hardly went into the garage, because it just contained more boxes of Uncle Dipesh's possessions that she needed to sort out, and out of sight was out of mind.

She tried the garage door, but it was locked; of course it was. She didn't have the key on her key ring. It was in the boiler cupboard in her kitchen. She closed her eyes. She was being dramatic. There wasn't someone in the garage. How likely was it that someone would have followed her home and then snuck into her garage in the time it took her to find her house keys in her bag? It wasn't, and in any event, who would want to follow her? She was being ridiculous, and she blamed Mason Connolly. His death was making her paranoid.

No one knew she was taking a keen interest in the Connolly death, she reasoned as she walked back to her front door and opened it. Well, maybe John and Graham, Leoni, Olivia – and Danny, sort of. Oh, Danny. She didn't want to think about him tonight. So, maybe quite a few people knew about her amateur sleuthing, but no one would be bothered by it, would they? It wasn't as if she was making much progress. She had asked a few friends for their opinions, that was all. She was hardly Miss Marple, but she definitely was a Miss. The thought of ending up as a little old lady with nothing to occupy her time but being an armchair detective made her heart sink a little further.

Shilpa let herself in, took her shoes off and locked the door behind her. She went to the bathroom, changed into her jogging bottoms and an old T-shirt and grabbed a towel from the radiator. It was warm to the touch, and she dried her hair with it. She needed a hot shower too, but she wanted to check something first. Shilpa padded into the kitchen and opened the boiler cupboard. She took a sharp intake of breath. The garage keys were missing. She tried to think of when she had last seen them. She couldn't remember. It must have been sometime in the last month, definitely before Mason's death. Or was it? Had she seen them in the last couple of weeks? No one had been in her home recently. Only June Connolly, and she was hardly a suspect. Plus, she had kept an eye on the grieving mother and hadn't left her for even a moment. Anyway, what would June Connolly want with the keys to her garage? Come to think of it, why would anyone want the keys to her garage, whether or not they were a suspect in Mason's death?

Shilpa shook her head. Everything always seemed worse at night. She was making something out of nothing. She took herself to the bathroom and had a hot shower, changing into her pyjamas. In a desperate attempt not to replay her humiliation, she decided to watch a movie. She was just about to make a hot chocolate when she heard a noise. Shilpa looked up the stairs towards the front door and then made her way towards it. A note had been pushed through the letter box. Had it been there when she first arrived home? She didn't think so. It was probably some flyer from a new takeaway or something. She pulled it from the letter box and was about to open it when she heard a knock at the door. It made her jump. Once she composed herself, she looked through the spyhole. The rain was still coming down fast, and it was now pitch black outside. She cleared her throat.

'Who's there?' she asked, pushing the flyer into her dressing-gown pocket. There was no response. She tried a little louder, but she felt foolish. She put her foot a little away from the door so that if the person behind the door tried to force it she could use her foot to stop them. She needed a chain across the door. Another thing for the list.

She opened the door a fraction, but she couldn't see anything. She opened it a little wider and saw a silhouette standing to the right of her front door. Then she screamed.

Chapter Eighteen

'Tanvi. Oh my days!' Shilpa cried. 'What are you doing here?'

'Don't just stand there. Let me in,' Tanvi said. 'I'm drowning out here.'

Shilpa stood aside. Drama queen. She was hardly wet at all. 'Come in. I just can't believe it. I was standing at the door wondering if it was an axe murderer, but it's you.'

'What's to say I'm not dangerous,' Tanvi said with a smile. She pushed her way through the front door and dropped her holdall on the mat. She took off her shoes and bounded down the stairs, sinking into the sofa like it was home. It brought a smile to Shilpa's face. Just when she thought nothing could lift her mood, her best friend had shown up. Maybe the gods were looking out for her. 'I told you I was coming up.'

'I didn't realise you were coming up today. Weren't you flying to Marbella this afternoon?' Shilpa said.

'Check your messages,' Tanvi said and Shilpa did. There had been a few missed calls and several messages. They were all from Tanvi. She had been so busy thinking about the Connolly case she hadn't even looked at her phone, which she had put on silent for the wake. The last time she had checked it was when she had messaged Olivia telling her she wasn't feeling so great.

'So, this is what Devon living is all about?' Tanvi said, looking at the Netflix homepage on Shilpa's television. 'Pyjamas and bed by eleven.'

'Rock and roll.'

'What's wrong?' Tanvi asked, taking on a more serious tone.

'Nothing,' Shilpa said. She didn't want to burden Tanvi with her problems just yet.

'You didn't really think there was a knife-wielding lunatic at your door, did you? Here? I don't think crazy murderers come out this far.'

Shilpa laughed. 'Of course not. It's just… Oh, don't worry. I'll explain later. Look at your curls, Tanvi,' Shilpa said, making her way down the stairs. She found a towel for her friend and made her a hot chocolate, joining her on the sofa.

'What's this?' Tanvi said, looking at the mug. 'Oh no.' Tanvi stood up. 'I didn't take two trains and a god-awful taxi journey through the pouring rain and through those hair-raising narrow lanes to have a blinking hot chocolate with you.' She walked over to the fridge and peered inside. 'Now,' she said, taking out a bottle of Tesco's Finest Gavi. 'This is more like it. Glasses?'

Shilpa pointed to the top cupboard to the right of the refrigerator and waited while Tanvi poured two large glasses of wine. Tanvi walked back to the sofa with the towel draped around her shoulders and passed Shilpa a glass.

'Spill,' she said. 'You moved here to get away from it all, but you don't half look miserable. Tell me what's going on. I wanna know.'

Shilpa studied her friend's face. 'You first,' she said.

'What d'you mean?'

'Your mascara has run, and it's not from the rain. I can see your eyes are red-rimmed. Plus, you didn't take two trains and make it to the back of beyond just on a sixth sense that something was going on in my life, did you?'

'I wanted to see you, that's all. Can't friends meet like old times?'

'Without checking I was home before jumping on a train?'

'We're not strangers. When did we ever call before dropping in on each other?'

'We always did. No one wants to make a wasted trip, even if it is only down the stairs,' Shilpa said, recalling the year they both lived in the same apartment building in London.

'Whatever,' Tanvi said, drinking half the contents of her glass. She looked at Shilpa. 'Do I look that pathetic?'

Shilpa nodded.

'Jason is basically two-timing scum,' Tanvi said, draining her second glass. 'Molly,' she added cryptically.

'Molly?' Shilpa asked.

'Oh yeah, I forgot you left us all in London and three months later you don't know who's who. Molly was new to the firm. Young graduate, pert bum, tight skirts. Typical, clichéd. It happened to me.'

'Oh, Tanvi. I'm so sorry. That's the worst luck.'

'Do you think it's karma?'

Shilpa scrunched her nose. 'No,' she said. Although it was possible. Tanvi was ruthless in her younger years. She didn't care whose boyfriend she slept with. 'It takes two,' she always said, or something like, 'I'm doing her a favour' or 'If he's tempted now, it's better they find out before they get hitched.' She did have some boundaries. Married men were strictly off-limits. But that was about it, and it didn't count if she didn't know they were married when they approached her. They always approached her. Credit where it was due though, she dropped them as soon as she found out they were cheating on their wives. The first time she found out, she unleashed hell on the unsuspecting man and swiftly sent his wife a comprehensive email detailing her partner's unfaithfulness. It didn't go down well. His wife blamed her completely, saying she snared her faithful husband like a siren, and she hounded Tanvi at every opportunity. She ended up having to change her email address and telephone number. After that, she left the wives alone. Not that there were many. Only about three in her history that Shilpa knew about.

'So, perhaps I haven't been the best person. I have a past. Who doesn't?' Tanvi said, but she didn't pause long enough for an answer. 'You, I suppose, Miss goody two-shoes. But Molly? I mean, really? It's so humiliating and degrading. *Urghhh.*' Tanvi stood up and walked to the kitchen. She returned with the bottle of wine and filled Shilpa's glass and her own. She placed the bottle on the coffee table and sank back into the sofa.

'You loved him, didn't you?' Shilpa asked.

Tanvi was silent. Shilpa had expected this. Tanvi never used words like love and commitment. She was a free spirit, that was her thing – until Jason.

'It's okay,' Shilpa said. 'You don't have to say it. I get it. So, what's the story? A fling, or is it something serious?'

'He's sleeping with her. I asked him this morning before he went for his morning run.'

'And?'

'Blatantly denied it. But he came back with cinnamon buns and coffee.'

Shilpa squinted at her friend. 'That's a sure sign of guilt,' she said.

'Don't joke,' Tanvi said. 'Why would he stop for cinnamon buns? Usually he gets me coffee, never buns. It was like a sweetener, literally. It was guilt. I don't need any other evidence.'

'Hmm,' Shilpa said. She wished she had someone to bring

her coffee and pastries on a Sunday morning. Instead, she was making pastries for the whole of Otter's Reach. 'So, apart from the buns, how do you know he was cheating?'

'Late nights at the office; two of them, pretty soon after Miss Pert Bottom started. I checked the log, and Molly worked those two evenings as well.'

'So, they were legitimately working if they were both logged on the system?'

'Whatever,' Tanvi said. 'He's started wearing more after-shave than usual.'

'Okay,' Shilpa said, putting her glass on the table. She lifted her feet up onto the sofa and pulled her dressing gown around her. She heard the flyer she had picked up earlier crumple in her pocket. She reached in and pulled it out.

'And then there were the new clothes,' Tanvi said. 'I mean, not just a new shirt, but several new shirts. I asked him what the sudden rush on new clothes was about.'

'And?' Shilpa asked.

'He said that they were on sale.'

'Right,' Shilpa said. 'Could be telling the truth.'

'Could be a lie.'

'You checked?' she asked. She knew the answer before she responded. Tanvi would have checked. Who wouldn't? It wasn't as if a quick internet search was an effort. 'And that's it? That's your evidence?'

'What more do you want?' Tanvi said. 'I was willing to… I was willing to commit,' she said, spitting out the last word. 'I've never done something like this before. I won't be made a fool of.' Tears started to fall down Tanvi's cheeks. 'I loved him,' she said after a few heaving sobs. 'I really did.' Tanvi fell into Shilpa, who wrapped her arms around her. Shilpa held on to the flyer in her hand and soothed her friend.

'You don't think that perhaps you're looking for something to go wrong with Jason because you're scared of commitment?'

Shilpa asked gently. She knew it was the wrong thing to say as the words left her mouth. But when in the history of their thirty-year friendship had they ever pussyfooted around each other? They said it like it was, and maybe Tanvi just needed to hear it. She couldn't say for sure, but she had met Jason, and he was smitten with her friend. He didn't seem the sort to be attracted by a pert bottom and tight skirt. But what did she know about men? It wasn't as if she could even get herself a date lately. She let her friend cry into her chest, and after several minutes wondering if Tanvi was ever going to stop, she opened the flyer behind her back. She was expecting to be tempted with a variety of fried wontons and spring rolls on a home-printed leaflet for Asia Gardens, but what she saw chilled her to the bone.

Chapter Nineteen

Last night Shilpa had helped Tanvi into her double bed – the guest room wasn't up to visitors – and she had lain beside her wondering what to make of the letter she had received. It was a simple note, but it had churned her stomach. It said:

If you want to know who killed Mason, meet me Saturday evening at seven at the Old Cinema. I have something to show you.

It wasn't signed. It wasn't dated. She had been awake for most of the night wondering who had sent it. Someone who knew she was interested in Mason's death. But if they knew who had killed Mason, why hadn't they gone straight to the police? She had no authority, but then again, that could be the very reason this person wanted to speak to her. Shilpa had barely slept for worry. Finally, at eight in the morning, Tanvi had woken, and after two cups of coffee, Shilpa had told her all about Mason's death, exactly what she knew and her humiliation with Danny.

'A pregnant wife?' Tanvi said, sitting at the breakfast bar in the small open-plan kitchen.

'That's what you're interested in?' Shilpa said. 'I've just told you that my life could be at risk.'

'Risk? How? He or she wants to give you information and doesn't want to be seen. Anyway, you said everyone knows everyone's business in Otter's Reach. It isn't a huge place. Half the town probably knows where you live. And you don't have to go.' Tanvi held her third cup of coffee to her lips and then looked up at her friend. 'You're going to go, aren't you?'

'How long are you staying for?' Shilpa asked. She picked up her phone and sent a message to Leoni asking if she knew anyone who could take a look at her car.

'Charming.'

'You could cover me? Keep your distance, take photos, that sort of thing. Call the police if I don't come out in say half an hour of meeting whoever it is.'

'We're not Scott and Bailey.'

Shilpa put her phone down and looked at her. 'After my humiliation with Danny, I need some sort of distraction,' she said with pleading eyes.

Tanvi tilted her head and looked at her watch. 'I am on leave for two weeks. Right about now I would have been drinking a margarita on Nikki beach.'

'The time difference between here and Spain isn't that big.'

Tanvi smiled. 'When on holiday… Jason is such a slime-ball,' Tanvi said and looked away. Shilpa could see her eyes filling. 'Never again. I told him to clear his stuff from my apartment by the time I got back.' She sighed. 'Fine, I'll be your Bonnie.'

Shilpa looked at her blankly.

'You know, Bonnie and Clyde.'

'Yeah, sure,' Shilpa said. Her pulse quickened. There was

something about the note that had unnerved her, but she was too inquisitive to ignore it.

'This is much nicer,' Tanvi said as the ferry pulled into Salcombe Harbour.

'Thanks, Tanvi,' Shilpa said. She had dropped her car keys off at Leoni's before they had boarded the ferry. The café owner said she knew someone who could take a look at her car. Shilpa hoped she would get it back in time for the Drews' launch party tomorrow. It was one thing having to walk everywhere, but another having to lug her cakes around without her own transport.

'Otter's Reach is pretty good though. You're not in the thick of it there, are you?'

'Stop digging,' Shilpa said as they stepped off the ferry and walked along the main road to a restaurant overlooking South Sands. Shilpa had called and reserved a table that morning, so she wasn't expecting a prime table in the window, but that was where they were seated. It was a beautiful summer's day, and the sun glimmered on the brilliant blue waters. Sailboats studded the sea and children were laughing and shrieking in the distance. Shilpa took a breath and soaked up the atmosphere. They could easily be in the Mediterranean with this view, not just somewhere in the British Isles. That was Devon for you. They ordered a bottle of Sancerre and a variety of seafood and talked about London, reminiscing about their young and carefree days, sipping wine as they waited for their food to arrive.

'And you found the bloodstained knife?' Tanvi asked as she checked her lipstick and hair in her compact. 'More exciting than London.'

'Are you trying to make up for calling Devon a backwater earlier?'

'I didn't say backwater,' Tanvi said, looking through the window out at the sea. 'It's beautiful, and I'm quite jealous. Look what you've got on your doorstep.' Tanvi picked up her phone and scrolled a little before placing it back on the white tablecloth.

'There isn't much of an update online,' she said. 'They've confirmed the death as murder and that they're holding someone for questioning.' Tanvi smiled as the waitress placed a seafood platter before them.

Tanvi nodded. 'Isn't there someone you can ask about the case? Doesn't Danny know anything?'

Shilpa smarted at the name. 'They've set up this tennis match later with one of Danny's colleagues. They're trying to set me up. I'm not sure I can face them though.'

'Why? Danny didn't even know you were coming onto him by the sounds of it,' Tanvi said. She held a black shell containing a plump mussel close to her lips.

'Still,' Shilpa said. 'I know what I felt.'

'Take a look around,' Tanvi said as a family walked through the door of the restaurant. 'I would meet whoever you can.'

'And what will you do while I'm out?'

'Has Otter's Reach got a spa?'

Shilpa nodded.

'Well then, that's exactly what I'll be doing. I'm looking forward to it already. So, who's this mystery man?'

'A man called Theo. He works in CID at Glass Bay, or so Olivia said. He lives near Mermaid Point and only moved there two years ago. It's good, as not too many people around here will know about him, so there will be less talk. I doubt he'll tell me anything of interest though.'

'You never know,' Tanvi said. 'He might if you turn on the

charm. So, who do you think did the deed?' she asked, picking up a whelk.

'On the limited information I have, any one of them could be the murderer. Gosh, that word sounds so foreign.' Shilpa speared a pink prawn on her fork and dipped it in the seafood sauce.

'His fiancée Harriet has form from what you've said. She's pretty obvious though. Same goes for her dad. Do you think it's possible they could be in on it together? And the mother is hiding something, you say?'

'A murderous family?' Shilpa gave her friend a look.

'Could be.'

'Why would Harriet want to kill her fiancé? I get that her dad may have wanted rid of him, but the black widow stuff, I'm not sure I buy it.' Shilpa took a sip of her wine. It was starting to make her feel light-headed. She tore off a piece of baguette and popped it in her mouth.

'Have you spoken to her at all?'

'No,' said Shilpa.

'You can't rule her out yet then. Maybe you could arrange to bump into her with her new beau. We both could.'

'So, you do fancy playing detective for a couple of weeks then?'

'You could twist my arm,' Tanvi said.

'You can help with the baking as well. If I recall, you were pretty good at icing, and I think we have the perfect opportunity to meet Harriet and possibly Evan too.' Shilpa heard her phone ring and bent down to retrieve it from her bag. She looked at the number, smiled and then answered. Minutes later after a few gushing thank yous she disconnected.

'What was that all about?' Tanvi asked.

'That was Graham. The couple who live on the catamaran I was telling you about. They sorted out my car. Graham said that John looked at it and it's pretty much sorted,' Shilpa said, beaming. 'He's put the keys through my letterbox.'

'What was wrong with it?' Tanvi asked.

Shilpa shrugged. 'Graham didn't really say. He muttered something about knowing about boats better than cars and who am I to judge.'

'People are kind around here. Remember our old neighbours in London? I don't think any of them would retrieve a broken-down car for us, never mind get it going again.'

Shilpa smiled. 'It is rather friendly in Devon.'

'So, tell me,' Tanvi said, soaking up the last of the sauce on her plate with a piece of bread. 'What's this perfect opportunity to snoop that you mentioned?'

'Ah, that. Harriet's dad's digital chat service launch is tomorrow. I'm doing the cakes. I need to make fifty cupcakes at some point today. I was thinking a sweet lime flavour. I have several sweet limes in the fridge, and I need to use them. It was such an effort to source them, but I wanted to add something a little different to the Drews' engagement cake. In the end I didn't use them because Mrs Drew was so specific about what she wanted.'

'Digital chat?' Tanvi asked, with an eyebrow raised.

'Where's your mind? Pull it out of the gutter. He runs an accountancy firm.'

'Things really are all straight-laced around here. I'll help as long as you don't order me around like my mum.'

Shilpa put on her best Indian accent. '*Beta*, ice those cakes now. What are you looking at on your phone? Always on your phone. Phone, shmone. You'll never find a husband on that device. What is it you're looking at; Tinder? You need a Jatinder.'

Tanvi laughed. She coughed and spluttered. 'You've spent too much time in the kitchen with my mum.'

'She taught me how to make *gulab jamun* and *gajar ka halwa*.'

'And how are those Indian sweets going down with the Devon crowd?' Tanvi asked.

'I haven't tried them, yet. But I'm getting there.'

'You're right about one thing though. I'll never be wife material,' Tanvi said, looking at her phone again. She put her knife and fork together on her plate and leaned back. 'I'm stuffed. Couldn't eat another morsel.'

'I was mimicking your mum. Your mum, my mum, they all say the same thing. Is that Jason messaging you?'

'Bet he's taken Molly on our vacation.'

Her friend was always so dramatic. She was about to say so when someone caught her eye.

'Right…' Tanvi said, but then trailed off. She followed her friend's eyes, which were fixated in the distance behind her. 'What?' Tanvi said, turning around.

'The woman who walked in,' she whispered. 'She was Mason's ex.'

'The one his mother met?'

Shilpa shook her head as Izzy and her friend were seated behind Shilpa and Tanvi's table. The waitress came over to clear their plates.

'We'll take a look at the dessert menu, thanks,' Shilpa said.

Tanvi frowned. 'You're paying for my liposuction.'

'Okay, but on my new wages, I'll probably only be able to afford one buttock.'

Tanvi laughed.

'This is too good an opportunity to pass up.'

'In that case, maybe another glass of wine,' Tanvi said as the waitress returned with their menus. They each ordered a panna cotta. 'I–' Tanvi started but Shilpa cut her off.

'Shh,' she said, placing a finger on her lips.

'What?' Tanvi whispered.

'I can't believe he's dead,' Izzy's friend with blonde hair and perfectly manicured nails said. 'And I can't believe she was hanging around and shouting at him at his own party; that's crazy. Was she even invited?'

Tanvi leaned in towards Shilpa. 'How do you know they're talking about…'

Shilpa put her head down and listened closely. They must have been talking about Mason. How many dead people could there be around here? It wasn't long before Izzy mentioned who the screaming woman was. 'Alison wasn't invited. She was lurking around outside when I approached the house,' she told her friend.

Bingo, thought Shilpa. They were talking about the engagement party, and Alison had been there. Shilpa had heard an altercation between two lovers when she had been fretting about the cake. She had assumed they were guests, not the groom and his ex-girlfriend. How could she have missed Alison with her electric red mop? Unless she hadn't wanted to be seen. That made sense, as June hadn't seen her either.

'Oh, what did you wear, by the way?' the blonde asked Izzy.

'The green Matthew Williamson,' Izzy answered with a smile.

'Good choice,' Tanvi whispered. Shilpa made a face as their panna cottas arrived, and they tried to look like they were having their own conversation. As soon as the waitress left, silence descended on their table again, and Shilpa strained her ears to hear.

'Who else could have or would have wanted him dead?' Izzy said. 'At school she was always picking legs off spiders. That's not normal behaviour. It's a sign. I've been reading up on killers now we have one in our midst. Alison wasn't popular at all. You could say she was a loner, and we all know how those turn out.'

Shilpa felt a slight irritation towards Izzy. *Not everyone was instantly popular at school*, she thought, recalling her own painfully shy childhood. She wouldn't have put it past Izzy to have been Alison's school bully. Alison probably wasn't a loner by choice. The spider legs though, that was another matter. The blonde woman asked Izzy what exactly Alison was shouting at Mason about just as Tanvi started talking to her about handbags. Shilpa gave her friend a stern look.

'I couldn't quite catch it,' Izzy was saying. 'She was hardly articulate. Something about him being her first true love. There were a lot of tears, mascara running down her face. She was wearing a hideous blue-and-yellow dress though, so it didn't really ruin anything for her.'

'And how did you get an invite?' her friend asked.

'I made a friend of Harriet. She throws some great parties,' Izzy said.

Cunning, thought Shilpa. Leoni was right. Izzy was one of those women who didn't let anything get in her way.

'Alison has got to be your main suspect,' Tanvi whispered.

Shilpa leaned in across the table towards her friend. 'Or she,' she said, pointing towards Izzy, her finger low, 'is making it up.'

'Why would she do that?'

'I don't know yet.'

'Have the police questioned you?' Izzy's friend asked.

Izzy was silent, and Shilpa craned her neck to take a better look at her. As she did, the blonde-haired woman looked up from her crab and avocado starter.

Shilpa immediately started laughing. 'Tanvi, you're so funny. I can't believe you said that.'

Tanvi rolled her eyes. 'Isn't your play date soon?'

Shilpa looked at her watch. 'It is. Hurry up,' she ordered her friend. She raised her hand to get the waitress's attention and asked for the bill.

'I didn't tell the police about Alison,' Shilpa heard Izzy say.

She stopped rooting around in her bag for her wallet and listened.

'Why ever not?' her friend asked. 'That doesn't make sense.'

No, thought Shilpa, *it doesn't make sense.* But she didn't get a chance to hear her response. The waitress arrived with the bill and started asking Tanvi about her hat. She couldn't hear anything, and by the time the bill was settled, Izzy and her friend were talking about Brazilian waxes.

Chapter Twenty

Evan sat in the drawing room of the Drews' house looking at the family photos that adorned the walls. The picture of Harriet and Mason still hung at the end of the second row. It wasn't long ago that an image of Harriet and Finley had hung in that very spot. *Maybe,* he thought, *the fiancés should have a picture wall of their own. The has-been wall.* He chuckled at his own joke. He would soon be standing tall next to Harriet, and their photo would be in that very spot, but unlike the rest of them, he would marry Harriet.

Harriet's father had called Evan this morning and asked him if he'd pop over. He had expected Margery and Harriet to be at home too, but when he asked their maid Rosa as to their whereabouts, she told them that the two women were out. Shopping, apparently. So, what did Steven want with him? He had already kept him waiting a half hour, and Evan detested having to wait for anything or anyone. Except Harriet. Harriet was always the exception.

He and Harriet had dated on and off for years but for one reason or another Harriet would never commit. Evan told himself it was because he was the one, that she would come home to him when she was ready to settle down but every time he believed she was ready it turned out that she wasn't. First it was Finley. A pathetic excuse of a man but Harriet had been taken in by his charms until the poor chap met his maker. Evan should have seen his opportunity but he had stupidly dithered, too confident for his own good. Harriet had been calling and messaging him. He thought he had the upper hand.

But one evening after a meal out together, Harriet had confided in Evan, telling him about Mason's advances, which had made his blood thicken. Harriet hadn't said that she was remotely interested in the man, but Evan should have known better. He had been lulled into a false sense of security as they laughed at Mason and his ambition, or lack of it. Harriet had even confessed that her father thought he was hopeless.

Two days after their evening out together Harriet found out that two beautiful women, Izzy and Alison, had fallen for Mason and suddenly Mason Connolly seemed much more appealing. Evan had to admit Mason knew how to charm a woman. He said the right thing, held doors open and always picked up the tab. Of course he did; he had stacks of his father's cash.

Evan didn't know much about Izzy, but she, like Alison, appeared to be a woman with a mission. Her mission was to marry for money. She soon set her sights on Mason – an easy catch, she had thought – but it wasn't to be. Izzy took rejection badly, judging by her behaviour at his friend's pub not so long after the break-up. Of course, Izzy said it had been an accident. That she was taking the wine glass back to the bar and hadn't set out to break it and use a shard of it to pierce her ex's skin. But no one believed her unlikely story of stumbling with the makeshift weapon and falling directly on the one person she had reason to hurt.

It was probably that knowledge that made Evan keep his distance from the dark-haired vixen. They could have helped each other out, but instead he had been left to his own devices. He had spoken to Izzy once, but she had been so insincere he knew that she wasn't the woman for him.

There was no denying that Izzy was beautiful – stunning, in fact – but she only ever paid attention to people with money. She had pretty much ignored Evan when he tried chatting to her one day in the pub. He was wearing his usual uniform of board shorts and vest. By his own admission he looked like a beach bum. Maybe she knew of him; she went to a school a couple of towns away and every so often the schools used to combine efforts for events like hockey for the girls, football for the boys and the occasional school disco. But, then again, maybe she didn't. He had kept a low profile with his company White Water, avoiding any sort of publicity that involved him personally, and although most people in the town knew what he did, only a few knew just how successful he was.

Izzy had given him a look that said, 'don't even think about speaking to me', but he liked good sport.

'You from around here?' he asked, wondering if she did remember him from school or not. Evan had put on a strong Somerset accent. The barman gave him a look, and he winked.

'Perhaps,' Izzy said.

'Can I get you a drink?' he asked.

'Sparkling, maybe,' she said, trying to put him off.

'Oh yes,' he said. 'You must be from around here if you know they do a mean cider.' The barman laughed.

'Sorry,' Izzy said, her eyes wide. 'I really must be going…' She trailed off, looking him up and down. Evan was keen to get to know her better, make his own decisions. 'I'm about to meet a friend…' she started.

The barman leaned in. 'Don't let his appearance put you off,' he said. 'Let me introduce you to Evan White. This man is self-made.'

Izzy turned to the barman and looked at him as if to accuse him of lying.

'He owns the stand-up paddleboard company White Water,' the bartender continued, giving Izzy a wink.

Evan noticed then that Izzy couldn't help but smile at him now. It was a glamorous smile, and those eyes captivated him. She touched her neck and looked at him, really looked at him, making the hairs on the back of his neck stand on end.

Evan stood up. 'I'll see you around,' he said in his normal voice and walked off. He was on a mission too, and that mission was Harriet. Izzy would have been fine for a one-night stand, but he couldn't afford something more than that. The way she was looking at him meant she was ready to dig her nails in.

It wasn't long after that that Evan found out that Harriet was victorious and thrilled with her conquest when Mason chose her over Alison and Izzy.

'Darling, you know you'll always have a place in my heart,' Harriet had said to him not long after she and Mason were engaged. 'Now is just not the right time for us.' Her words implied that there would be a right time, which was a little hypocritical given that she had just become someone else's fiancée.

Evan had considered dating Izzy to make Harriet jealous. Harriet enjoyed making others hurt. It was why she had invited Izzy to her and Mason's engagement party. Alison was too much of a liability, everyone knew that; but Izzy's presence would have satisfied Harriet's need to feel triumphant. Evan knew that dating Izzy would have given Harriet a taste of her own medicine.

Evan had tried to move on from Harriet, but he couldn't. He knew his destiny. She had kept him waiting, and he had allowed it. He couldn't wait around much longer though. He had no choice but to move things along a little.

Chapter Twenty-One

'This is Theo,' Danny said flatly.

Olivia winked at Shilpa from behind her brother-in-law. 'And this is Shilpa,' she said. 'Just moved to Otter's Reach, and she used to be Danny's university mate. Now she bakes cakes, don't you? Although I shouldn't just say bakes cakes. She makes the most amazing occasion cakes. She left the bright lights of London for this little place.'

'Oli,' Danny said. 'You're waffling.'

Not bad, thought Shilpa as she stretched out her hand to take Theo's. She could hear Tanvi's voice in her head applauding his good looks. He was tall, with dark hair and chocolate-brown eyes. He had an aquiline nose and a charming smile.

'Shilpa,' she said as he shook her hand.

Tanvi had picked the shortest khaki shorts for Shilpa to wear on her tennis date and a white racer back. Given the bottle of wine they had shared just a couple of hours ago, Shilpa had agreed to wear them. As she walked down from her house to the courts at the back of the town, she felt uncomfortable. She regretted her decision and felt quite exposed. She looked down at her blue Converses, the closest thing she had to trainers, and swung the old racket by her side as she took her position on the court.

'I hear you made quite the impression with the cakes you delivered to the Drews',' Theo said.

Shilpa blushed. 'Oh yes, that. Well, I just thought…' She trailed off, not knowing how to explain what she had done without sounding like an idiot.

Theo smiled. 'It was good of you to come forward about the knife,' he said as they took their positions on the court. His eyes softened, and although Theo had barely said anything, Shilpa felt the heat in her cheeks.

'I wasn't sure if I'd done the right thing, but I had to do something,' she said. 'So, murder. That must be an interesting day job.' Shilpa tried to steer the conversation away from her involvement. It made her feel uneasy whenever she thought about it, and now Theo had mentioned the knife she was pretty sure that it was the murder weapon.

'You could say,' Theo said. He lifted his head up to take a sip of his water, and she noticed his strong jawline. How was this man still single?

'The trouble is you can't just leave your work at the office. It follows you everywhere,' he continued. 'When there's a murderer at large, an unsolved case, you get little sleep until it's solved. This is a rare hour out for me. Danny convinced me I needed a break. Said I was lucky there was only one murderer on the loose.' Theo laughed. He adjusted his wristband and looked at his watch. 'After this I'm heading back to the station.' He looked up and fixed his eyes on her. 'Sorry,' he said. 'I shouldn't joke about killers and victims. We get so used to dealing with death and its ugly and often brutal causes that we try and make light of it. Keeps us sane. I hope you don't think I'm callous. We take our job quite seriously.'

Shilpa shook her head. 'Not at all,' she said, looking away

from the intensity of his stare. Danny was right: Theo was self-assured. Usually, this would have irked her. She didn't normally go for the alpha male, but perhaps it was time to make an exception. 'I've seen *Broadchurch*.'

'Ha!' he said, looking towards Danny and Olivia. 'This is slightly different to how they do it on television.'

Shilpa saw her opportunity. 'You're holding someone in relation to Mason's murder. I read about it on the news. So, doesn't that mean you can sleep easy tonight?'

Theo didn't respond immediately. 'Don't believe everything you read online,' he said eventually.

'Come on, you two,' Danny said from across the court as he bounced a tennis ball in front of his poised racket. 'Stop chatting so we can get on with our game.'

'You can be such a grump, can't you, Danny boy,' Theo said. He turned to Shilpa and grinned. He gently touched her forearm, and a small electric current passed through her. They took their places on the court, and in less than twenty seconds she saw a ball hurtling towards her. She swung her racket. The game had started.

Shilpa was exhausted by the time the match finished. She wasn't the best at tennis, but she wasn't as bad as she had expected, and Theo said she had a mean serve.

'Back to the station for me,' Theo said, picking up his towel from the edge of the court and wiping his face. Shilpa turned to see Danny and Olivia heading towards them.

'I don't suppose you fancy dinner one evening this week – if you can tear yourself away from the case, that is?' she asked.

'I'd like that,' Theo said. He picked up his phone and unlocked it before handing it to her. She tapped in her number and handed it back. He gave her a missed call and slipped the phone into his pocket. 'See you later then,' he said with a wry smile. He turned towards Danny, who had just reached them. 'Come on, mate,' he said. 'Back to the office.' The two men started walking away.

'Sorry, pet,' Olivia said to Shilpa. 'I've got to get the kids, so I can't stay and talk, but tell me quickly, what d'you think?'

'Yeah,' Shilpa said, trying to sound nonchalant. 'He seems all right.'

'He's a catch. Anyway, I've gotta go. Speak later, okay?'

Shilpa nodded as Olivia started running, racket in hand, in the direction of the car park.

As Shilpa walked home, she wondered what had come over her, asking Theo out like that. Yes, he was good-looking and they had got on well, but she wasn't normally so forward, and she didn't know the first thing about him. This probably happened to him regularly. No wonder he didn't stutter when he agreed to the date. She should have looked into Danny a little more before pursuing him, and then she wouldn't have felt so foolish when she found out he had a wife. She doubted Olivia and Danny would set her up with a married man though. She smiled as her phone buzzed and looked at her screen. It was a message from Theo saying he would be free tonight if she wanted that dinner. She responded with a yes.

As she approached the house, she noticed that the door was open and Tanvi was standing there with what looked like a photograph album in her hand. She had forgotten all about Tanvi. She couldn't just go off on her date tonight, especially when Tanvi had just broken up with Jason. She would text Theo and ask to rearrange. It was probably for the best, given she had fifty cupcakes to make for Steven Drew's party tomorrow.

'What have you found?' she said as she approached the house. The spa had been fully booked, so she had left her friend with the task of going through some of Dipesh's old possessions and making piles of charity shop, bin and keep items. She had only recently discovered a couple of boxes of his in the guest room when Tanvi came to stay and had tasked her friend with having a clear-out so that the room could be used. The rest of her uncle's stuff was in the garage. She still hadn't found the key, and just thinking about it sent a shiver down her spine. Something about that missing key felt off. Especially after the noise she had heard coming from inside the garage last night.

'You know how your mum always said that you and Dipesh were kindred spirits?'

'Yeah. Single to the end. That's my epitaph.'

'Dipesh wasn't as single as we thought.'

'Mum would have known if he had a significant other,' Shilpa said.

'You may want to take a look at this,' Tanvi said, opening the photo album in her hand.

Chapter Twenty-Two

'Glad you made it,' Steven said as he entered the room.

'No problem, sir,' Evan said, although he didn't mean it. Steven had kept him waiting for over forty minutes. He stood up and extended his hand to his future father-in-law. 'It's a terrible time for you all. I was hoping that Harriet would be here, and Margery. I haven't seen her since the party.'

Steven waved away Evan's comments. 'They're both out,' he said. 'Please sit. Did Rosa offer you a drink?'

Evan nodded and pointed to the glass of water on the coffee table.

'You need something stronger than that,' Steven said. 'Come on. You may as well come to my study.'

Evan suppressed a smile as he followed Mr Drew. Only a select few were allowed into this man's study. He wondered if Mason or Finley had made it through the door. He straightened his back as he strode through.

Steven poured two glasses of whisky and motioned for Evan to sit on the large Chesterfield. 'It's no secret that I wasn't the biggest fan of Mason Connolly. Harriet could've done better.' There was a long pause while Steven stared at Evan as if gauging his reaction. 'I'm not saying I would want any harm to come to the boy, but Mason Connolly wasn't all that he appeared.'

'How so?' said Evan.

'Well,' said Steven, a little flustered, as if he hadn't antici-pated any questions. 'He was a sneak.' Steven downed his drink. 'It sounds heartless of me, I know, and so soon after the event, but Mason Connolly's no longer with us, and it's time to think of our future.'

'Our future?' Evan said.

'Harriet doesn't like being alone. Never has done. Even as a child she always wanted someone around. We were lucky she took to Rosa. We should have given her a sibling, I suppose, but it wasn't to be, and it was probably for the best. I shouldn't admit this, but parenting wasn't really our forte.' There was an awkward silence before Steven spoke again.

'Harriet likes you, and from what I've heard, I'd say that you like her too. Am I right, Evan?'

Evan felt the room get a little warmer. Perhaps he didn't know where this conversation was going. He pulled at his shirt collar and looked at his drink. The glass of cold water he had left in the drawing room would have been a welcome relief as opposed to the warm liquid he now brought to his lips.

'I'm fond of Harriet,' he said.

'And you're self-made, Evan. The last two years have been very successful for White Water. You're ambitious, despite what you like to portray to others,' Steven said, looking Evan up and down.

'Excuse me?' Evan said.

'I know you keep a low profile,' Steven said, 'but you're ambitious, and you have the mind of an entrepreneur. You wouldn't have the kind of turnover you do otherwise.' Steven didn't pause long enough for Evan to respond. Evan wasn't sure whether to admire or be offended by Steven's manner and blatant admission of checking his company accounts.

'Devon is ripe and ready for people like you. People who want to make something of themselves. There is opportunity here, unlike other places, where everything you can think of has been done to death. You just have to have some determination and a little know-how, which you have.'

'So, what're you saying?' Evan said. It was well known in Otter's Reach that Steven Drew despised the young of today, branding them snowflakes within his own workforce. Harriet was lucky enough to be born into wealth. He loved Harriet, but he did wonder what Steven thought of his daughter's ambitions, because Harriet didn't have a job. Like Mason, she worked for her dad, taking a healthy salary, and frittered her time in the boutiques and lunch spots in and around Salcombe. 'Working is just so dull,' she often complained to him, not that he had ever witnessed her do any. Just thinking about her brought a smile to his lips. She didn't pretend to be something she was not, which was what he liked about her. Steven was a little two-faced. It was one rule for his family, another for everyone else.

But Steven, for all his flaws, was right about Mason. The man was underhanded. He had taken Harriet from under his nose and did everything he could to have an easy life. Harriet had been attracted to him only because she thought she had got one up on Alison and Izzy, but in reality she didn't love him. Evan knew it. He just did.

Mason got what was coming to him, and Evan was glad. He cast his mind back to the day of the party. The knife had felt heavy in his hand at first but took on a lightness that fateful day. Now there was nothing standing between him and Harriet, and judging by the direction this conversation was headed, he would say it wouldn't be too long before Harriet Drew was his.

'You like my daughter and my daughter likes you. It's fairly simple,' Steven continued, looking down at Evan. 'I have an event tomorrow, and I'd like you to be there.'

Chapter Twenty-Three

Tanvi held a bottle of red wine and scowled at Shilpa. 'Marbella would have been much better than this,' she said.

'You said you didn't mind helping.'

'Last night I was icing blinking cupcakes in green and white. Talk about showing a friend a good time,' she said, grinning. 'Now all of a sudden I'm a drinks waiter as well. I haven't done any waitressing since my college days.'

'It shows,' Shilpa said. 'Go on, get out there and mingle while I arrange these cakes.'

'I get all the best jobs.'

'Perhaps you should have said you weren't a waitress when that woman asked you to serve the wine.'

'"Get a move on and serve the wine", is what she said,' Tanvi corrected her. 'Well, I am dressed all in black like the other waiters, even if my trousers are Donna Karan.' Tanvi laughed. 'At least this way I can eavesdrop so you can talk to the right people. Remember, you're here to get the word out about Sweet Treats, so put your PR hat on. You were so good at all that in London. Here you seem to be more interested in solving a crime that has nothing to do with you! The sea air has done something to your brain.' Tanvi scanned around the room. 'Although I must admit, playing detective is more fun than promoting occasion cakes. Saint Laurent shoes at twelve o'clock,' she said. 'That must be our femme fatale, Harriet.'

Shilpa strained to look and then quickly turned as Harriet looked in her direction. 'Go on then, Tan. She looks like she favours a glass of red.' Tanvi didn't need to be asked twice. She headed in Harriet's direction. Shilpa started taking the iced cupcakes out of the boxes and carefully arranging them on a stand. It had been a late night for them yesterday. After Tanvi found her uncle's photo albums, they had searched through the remaining boxes in the house. They hadn't found much else, but that one album had uncovered a life he had kept hidden from her family.

Dipesh had a partner, a whole life she knew nothing about. The album Tanvi had found was full of photos taken in exotic locations and on city breaks around the Mediterranean. In most of the photos, the same man was present – someone, it was clear, he loved very much. So why hadn't he shared this with her? Perhaps he thought her parents were too antiquated, that they wouldn't understand his sexuality.

But she had spent most of last night thinking about it, and she came to the conclusion that her parents already knew. There were so many hushed conversations between her mum and dad after her uncle's death, and now those cutting remarks her aunts had made after his passing about the way he was made sense. But if her parents knew, why didn't they share it with her and her brother?

She had called her brother at two this morning to ask him if he had known. He wasn't best pleased she had woken him up, but he was as surprised as she was. Were her parents that close-minded that they wanted it hushed up even where their kids were involved?

The thought made her see red, which was why she had told her brother not to mention anything to her parents before she did. She would do some digging around on her own first before she confronted them. Who was the man in her uncle's life, and why had she never met him? More to the point, where was he now? Surely they lived with one another. Yet there was no trace of him in the house, and that album had been squirrelled away at the bottom of a dusty old box of books, almost like it had been forgotten under the pile of Danielle Steels.

Her uncle had lived a life that he felt he couldn't share with her. Thank goodness for Graham and John. She imagined they were a great support to him. She would speak to them and try and find out about her uncle's partner. She wanted to meet him. Perhaps he would want something to remember her uncle by.

After this revelation, they had tried in vain to get into the garage, the key to which was still nowhere to be found. Shilpa was now desperate to get in there and was going to call a lock-smith until Tanvi had pointed out that it was past six o'clock and that she would have to pay an extortionate amount of money for an out-of-hours one.

'That's her,' Tanvi said, sidling next to Shilpa as she placed the last cupcake on the stand. Tanvi had been listening in on Harriet's conversations, the first with a work colleague. 'She was very corporate,' Tanvi said. 'Apparently she has something to do with the social media campaign surrounding the company. She was droning on about it. She probably posted one tweet. When Harriet moved on to speaking to her friend though, her tone changed. "It sounds terrible", Harriet said, "But I can't help but think there was a reason for all this happening to me". Those were her exact words.'

Tanvi was surprised that Harriet could find serendipity in Mason's death, but Shilpa wasn't. As she was arranging the cupcakes, two young women who looked to be employees at Drew Accounting came up to her, eager to try them. After telling Shilpa how delicious they were, they carried on with their conversation in hushed tones. They were talking about Harriet and Mason. Shilpa was in earshot, but they didn't seem to mind.

'She knew he had lovers,' one of the women said, explaining that a week before the engagement party Harriet found out that Mason was seeing one of his exes. The woman looked around her. Ignoring Shilpa, she said in a whisper, 'They say that's why she did it.'

'Who said that?' the other friend asked. Her friend didn't answer. Instead she spoke at length about Harriet, who was overheard saying once that she didn't suffer fools. This was reason enough for the young lady to believe that Harriet killed Mason.

'He cheated on her, and she wasn't going to take it lightly,' the woman had said.

Tanvi poured both Shilpa and herself a glass of wine.

'I'm not sure the staff can drink at events like this,' Shilpa said.

Tanvi made a face. 'Stop me,' she said, taking a sip of wine. She looked at the bottle of red. 'This isn't bad.'

Shilpa followed her lead and tried the Merlot. It slipped down easily. 'Have a cupcake too while you're at it,' she said. Tanvi raised an eyebrow.

'Don't tempt me. Tell you what else I overheard. Sounds like the Drew Accountancy firm is in a bit of trouble over not spotting some gaps in the Connolly accounts.'

'What do you mean?'

Tanvi explained that it sounded like someone was embezzling money from the company. 'I heard two of the junior staff talking about it. I wasn't the only one eavesdropping though.

That man over there with the scarf,' Tanvi said, looking towards the man in question. 'He was listening in too, and from what I gather, he works with Drew Accounting. He didn't stop to correct them. I think there's some truth in what the graduates were saying. Perhaps you should go and talk to him?'

'Why? I'm not interested in the Connollys' bank accounts. I want information on Mason Connolly's death.'

'It could be connected, and anyway, I think he's a family friend,' Tanvi said confidently.

Shilpa gave her friend a look. 'You just said he worked with them.'

'You know what it's like with these rich families. Work, play; it all gets intertwined, and look, there he is joking with that lady.'

'June.'

'You know her? She looks very beige. She clearly got the memo that black is for waiting staff only,' Tanvi said, looking down at her own attire and grinning.

'She's Mason's mother. Maybe I'll go over and say hello.' Shilpa left Tanvi by the cupcakes and headed towards the old man with the neckerchief.

'Shilpa,' June said. 'Lovely to see you again. I didn't get to thank you for the cake you made.' June turned towards the old man. 'This talented lady catered for Mason's funeral.'

'Oh, I just made the cake,' Shilpa said, not wanting to take all the credit.

'And what a sumptuous cake it was. Everyone mentioned just how good it was. You really are talented. And you made the cakes here today? The flavour is just exquisite. I've not tasted anything like it.'

Shilpa smiled. She needed someone like June around. She was single-handedly promoting her in Otter's Reach, and with success. 'It's sweet lime. An Indian fruit, a little like an orange, but the flavour is more delicate. You have to be careful cooking with it; if you don't use it soon after cutting the fruit, it can be extremely bitter.'

'Oh, where are my manners,' June said, making introductions. 'Lewis and I go way back. He, Steven and I were friends many moons ago.'

'When we were young,' Lewis said. Shilpa noticed that although Lewis had grey hair and from a distance looked like an older man, up close he looked to be of a similar age to June and Steven.

'If you ever need legal representation, Lewis is your man,' June said. Her eyes darted away from them and towards Steven, who was heading towards the microphone set up in the corner of the room. 'Oh, please excuse me,' June said, colour rising to her cheeks. 'I must go and congratulate Steven on his achievement here today.' And with that, June was off, leaving Shilpa with Lewis.

They watched as June stood in the sidelines while Steven prepared to speak. He shuffled the paper in his hands and then started to talk, thanking his team for their efforts – and of course, his daughter, the social media whizz.

Lewis chuckled at this. 'I'm cruel. Ignore me,' he said. 'I've known the Drews for a long time and love them dearly. Harriet is many things, but a whizz kid is not one of them. At my age, you tend to say things how they are, but I shouldn't. My wife says it's rude, and she's right.'

Shilpa looked towards Harriet, who was now standing close to Evan. She had seen him before at Leoni's, and Tanvi had commented that he looked a little like Gavin Henson with his small eyes, sharp nose and chiselled jaw. Shilpa, who had never been into sport, had to google the rugby player on her phone to get the idea. Looking at Evan now, she could see the resemblance. They could have been brothers.

'I hope it works out better for Evan and Harriet than it did with her last two fiancés,' Shilpa said, trying to keep her tone light.

'Oh, indeed,' Lewis said.

'A terrible thing to happen twice. First Finley and then Mason. It would give anyone else in her position a complex,' Shilpa said, looking at Lewis from the corner of her eye. 'It certainly would me,' she added. 'A murdered partner at your engagement party and a dead fiancé on his stag do. That's what I heard.' Shilpa was impressed by how freely she was talking to Lewis. She was never ordinarily this blatant.

'Finley didn't die on his stag,' Lewis said. 'Harriet was with him. It was their last holiday together before they were to be wed. It's a funny story. The two of them went to a private villa in Crete, paid for by Harriet's father, Steven. Of course, Harriet didn't know that Steven had paid Finley to leave her. Can you believe? But the boy was a smart cookie. He took the cash and went on a luxury holiday with the man's daughter. Steven didn't want Harriet to know, so he didn't tell her. What a fool he had been made to look, but it all came out eventually, and Harriet wasn't happy. Luckily for Steven, the poor chap met with an accident before he returned, or I think Steven would have killed him himself on the lad's return. You have to laugh – not at the poor chap's death, of course, but at Steven's stupidity. What did he think would happen? He won't try that again.'

Shilpa recalled what Graham had told her. 'I thought Finley died on his stag do in Turkey.'

'That's what everyone around here believes, and you can understand why the Drews are happy to let them think that. They wouldn't want any fingers pointed, and Steven is desperate not to let anyone know about his attempted bribe. I only know because he confessed to me one evening after too many whiskys, and of course, I had seen Harriet at the airport.'

'What do you mean?' Shilpa asked. She felt sorry for Steven. Despite his efforts, everyone knew about his attempted bribe.

Lewis explained that Finley had booked the holiday to Crete as a surprise, so he hadn't told many people in Otter's Reach. Most of his friends lived in London, and so when he said he was going away, people assumed it was his stag with his London mates. Lewis happened to be at the airport taking a flight to Zurich at the same time that Finley and Harriet were boarding for their Crete escape. Lewis didn't approach the couple. Harriet had been wearing dark glasses and a scarf tied around her head, which Lewis had thought a little strange as they were inside, but in his line of work he knew when a woman didn't want to be recognised and so he had left her alone.

Shilpa looked back at Harriet and Evan. Why didn't she want anyone to know she was with her fiancé when he died? Had she had something to do with his death, or had her father? Steven Drew didn't want either Finley or Mason in his daughter's life. Had both father and daughter worked together to get rid of Finley and then Mason? It was definitely a possibility.

'What kind of accident did Finley have?' Shilpa heard herself asking.

'He lost control of the moped he was on. Fell off the side of a cliff.'

Shilpa gasped and put her hand to her mouth. 'How awful.'

'Yes. These mopeds abroad can be cruel. I would have thought Finley would have known what he was doing though. Apparently, he had travelled around India on a moped when he was younger, and they are notorious for terrible driving. His poor mother was distraught, and of course, she thinks something untoward happened. She thought her son was a good rider. Like so often when you lose a loved one, you want to assign blame to someone, something, anything but the one you've lost.'

'Did she find anything or anyone to blame?' Shilpa asked.

'Ah, but of course. First there was the shoddy moped – and she took the company that rented it to her son to task. But she couldn't prove anything. The moped was in pieces, and I don't think officials in Crete were too concerned. I expect this thing happens with tourists and mopeds more than we hear about. His mother travelled out there. There was even a piece written in the local rag – you know, the kind that mothers read to their children before they go on their first grown-up holiday without their folks.'

'I see,' Shilpa said.

'His mother dropped it after a while and then went after the Drews. Well, she did and she didn't. By this time, she was a bit of a wreck, and people weren't paying much attention to her. I don't think she knew Harriet was in Crete at the time, because in one of her monologues to me she did mention it, but without much conviction, and I wasn't going to be the one to give her the ammunition she so badly needed. I remember it, because the woman didn't know me from Adam, but everyone at this point certainly knew about her. She thought she would bend my ear, and so she did. Told me that she believed Harriet was in Crete with Finley and that it was strange that Finley would be on a moped without his fiancée unless said fiancée had designed it that way.' Lewis twirled the stem of his glass between his fingers. 'She made the police aware, so they must have looked into it. The woman has been rather quiet for a while, but it wouldn't surprise me if she came out of the woodwork now that Mason has died under such terrible circumstances. I'm sure she'll think this is her opportunity to open the case into her son's death again. She'll be somewhere, pointing fingers, you mark my words. But I suppose an accident is called an accident for a reason. It isn't something you plan.'

'Harriet was lucky she wasn't with him,' Shilpa said, and she genuinely meant it.

'Quite,' said Lewis. 'Quite.'

Chapter Twenty-Four

'So, you've left your friend home alone?' Theo put his glass of gin and tonic on the table and speared a piece of chorizo and a prawn with a cocktail stick. 'These are good,' he said.

They were sitting in a small tapas bar just off the High Street. Tanvi had convinced Shilpa to invite Theo out after she had cancelled on him on Monday night. Thankfully, Theo had called her just before she plucked up the courage to call him, saving her the fear of rejection. She had instantly agreed when he suggested an evening out. Three drinks and several plates of tapas later and they were getting on well. The tapas bar had charm. It was dark and cosy and beautifully decorated with low-level lighting and draped fabrics. Soft Spanish music played in the background, and the barmen were generous with their measures. Theo now knew about her move from London to Otter's Reach, although she was selective with her reasons for moving, and she missed out the bit about being lonely at thirty-five.

He told her about his Greek heritage. He spent his child-hood growing up in Rhodes, which explained his faint accent, and had lived in Sheffield until two years ago, when he moved to Devon. He was Theophilus, not Theodore, as she had incorrectly assumed. His last relationship ended when his long-term girlfriend decided to give up her worldly possessions and live in Costa Rica. Theo, heartbroken, had wanted time out from women, although she was sure he had bedded quite a few since then. That was another trait that would have previously been a turn-off, but she found herself drawn to him. Shilpa was the first woman he had dated in a long time, he confessed. She hoped she wasn't his delayed rebound.

'Tanvi's at the cinema,' she said before turning the conversation to the Connolly case.

'Here we are having a nice, well, I think it's a nice dinner, and you bring up work; death, even,' Theo said.

'You did say death was par for the course in your line of work,' Shilpa said with a coy smile.

'Touché. There was something I wanted to ask you about that day actually. Although you seem rather keen. Maybe I need to do this officially back at the station, without any alcohol present.'

'I'm only keen because I was there, remember? My life isn't that interesting. This is the first exciting thing to happen to me in ages. Otter's Reach is rather quiet compared to London,' Shilpa tried.

'Oh, don't be one of those,' Theo said playfully.

'What do you mean?'

'Someone who moves away from London but never stops talking about just how amazing it is. You chose to move here, didn't you? And Otter's Reach is tiny, but Devon is full of things to do, and it's all on your doorstep. There are beautiful coastal walks, amazing gastropubs dotted around the place, not to mention sailing. I should know; I was the same when I first moved here. It's different up north, but I soon saw sense.'

Shilpa put a finger to her lips. 'No more talk about the

bright lights of London. I know people like that, and I'd hate to be one of those. I hope that isn't the impression you've got of me?'

'Quite the opposite,' he said, staring at her again with those intense brown eyes. Their eyes locked, and Shilpa found it difficult to look away. 'Anyway,' he said, a little flustered now. 'The engagement party. Did you notice a tall woman in a full-length black dress?'

'A black dress?' Shilpa tried to recall the party, the dresses she saw and the hats people were wearing. She shook her head. 'I like fashion and checking out what people are wearing, but I don't think I saw anyone matching that description.'

Theo fiddled with the fork on his plate. 'A few guests at the party said they saw someone matching that description before midday—'

'About the same time Mason went missing.'

'Right,' Theo said, looking up. 'You know your stuff.'

Shilpa smiled and leaned back in her chair with her drink. She knew there was good reason to investigate Mason Connolly's death. Theo was asking her questions, admitting she could have information from the party he wasn't aware of. She was well placed to investigate Mason's death. She had been at the party, and having just moved to Otter's Reach, she didn't have any existing views of its residents. She could be completely objective. Plus, she had been at the Drew house when Mason had been murdered, she was sure of it, so in all likelihood she had seen the murderer at the event. The thought raised the hairs on her arms. It was unnerving but at the same time fascinating.

Theo smiled back. There was definitely something between them. Shilpa caught their reflection in the large mirror opposite. They certainly looked good together. She looked away. This time she wasn't going to let her thoughts run away with her like they had with Danny. Just thinking about him sent a wave of fresh humiliation through her.

'What are you doing to me?' Theo said, leaning back into the sofa next to Shilpa. 'I could get into trouble for this.'

'Only if someone finds out,' Shilpa said. 'And how will Drayton ever know?'

'The DI has eyes and ears everywhere, although at least we are a safe distance away from Glass Bay. News may not travel that fast. Don't mistake his Rottweiler personality for something people avoid around here. He knows how to turn on the charm when he wants something, and the people around here have respect for the man.'

'I don't want to get you into trouble, but if you want to talk about anything to do with the case, I'm here. You know, test ideas, that sort of thing.'

Theo was silent for a moment while he studied Shilpa's face. 'I guess a little information wouldn't hurt,' he said. Shilpa leaned in. 'You didn't hear this from me, but there was a smear of foundation found in the sink of the annex where Mason's body was found.'

'Make-up?'

Theo nodded. 'It doesn't match any shade owned by the Drew women.'

Shilpa was silent for a moment. She thought of Alison's pasty complexion and Izzy's sun-kissed skin tone. 'A dark shade? Maybe a match for the woman in the dark dress?'

Theo was silent.

'Did the dress have long sleeves?'

Theo tilted his head and studied her. 'From what people have said.'

'I've got it,' Shilpa said with triumph.

'Go on then, Miss Marple.'

'Well, not Marple exactly. But I've seen a movie where the killer covers up most of the time because they have changed the colour of their skin with tanning lotion or what have you to commit the dastardly deed.' The thought of Alison frantically applying dark foundation to her skin popped into her mind, but that red hair was hard to hide, and her hair was most definitely red at the funeral, because she saw her straight after at the reception. It could have washed out easily after the party, or she could have been wearing a wig.

'So Devon has inspired you to turn into an armchair detective.'

'You don't think much of my theory,' Shilpa said, a little deflated.

'It has legs, but we need a motive and a suspect, don't you think?'

Shilpa sighed. He was humouring her. She could tell by his smirk. Her idea was far-fetched. And she had overheard Izzy saying that Alison had been wearing a blue-and-yellow dress. Izzy had been wearing her signature green – the Matthew Williamson she had mentioned to her lunch date earlier in the week. Tanvi and she had googled the dress after their boozy lunch. It didn't make sense, but perhaps another ex-girlfriend was at the engagement. Shilpa asked Theo, but he was evasive. They had interviewed all those present at the party. They had the guest list. But did they have everyone on the list? Perhaps it was time Shilpa tried to speak to Alison herself. Mason's mum would know how to get in contact with her. She would message her later.

'Can I ask you one last thing?' Shilpa said.

'Shoot.'

'Was the knife the murder weapon?'

'That's a serious question,' he said.

'I know, but I found it, and my prints will have been on it, so I was wondering…'

'Yes, you did contaminate that piece of evidence. You're

lucky you are not a suspect. I can't really tell you if it was the murder weapon.'

'But I can guess that it was.'

Theo's silence said it all.

It was dark by the time they walked back up Estuary Road to Shilpa's house. Theo insisted he walk her home, which made Shilpa's heart sing.

'I can't let you walk alone,' he said. 'Not when there's a murderer on the loose.'

'You may think it's funny, but it's true. There's someone out there,' Shilpa said. She didn't tell Theo that recently she had the distinct feeling of being watched, of someone following her on quiet roads and at busy marketplaces. She had read about people having that feeling, victims who said they just knew someone had been following them months before they were attacked. She'd always assumed that it must have been psychological. Something victims projected on to themselves following an awful incident – their minds trying to find some reason for an often unprovoked attack. But now she felt it keenly; that day walking home from the funeral, and then in the café with Danny. Since then, the frequency of that feeling had increased. She looked over at Theo and wondered if she was just being paranoid.

'You,' a woman in a mid-length skirt and T-shirt said, pointing at them as they walked towards her house.

Shilpa and Theo both stopped and looked at the woman. Her hair was frizzy and wild, and she looked like she hadn't slept in days.

'Mason Connolly is dead. Found at the Drews',' said the woman. She didn't take her eyes off Theo.

'How can I help you?' Theo said gently, as if this sort of thing happened to him all the time.

'You're a detective on the case, the Connolly case,' the woman said, looking directly at him. He nodded. 'Then you'll know who's to blame for his death.'

Theo didn't say anything. Shilpa just watched as he looked at the woman, poker-faced.

'It's the Drews, of course. Harriet's the one you need to question. You haven't arrested her,' she said. 'I've been watching youse, and you haven't made an arrest yet, have you?'

'I can't disclose anything to do with the case, I'm afraid.'

'No, of course you can't. My son died at Harriet's hands and you lot in Crete wanted nothing to do with it. No one was bothered here either, because she's a rich woman, a daddy's girl who always gets her way, and nothing can touch the rich, can it?'

Both Theo and Shilpa were silent. The woman's ramblings were starting to make sense. This was Finley's mother, the woman Lewis had told her about at Steven Drew's digital launch party.

'He died at her hands or her father's. One of them is to blame, and my money's on Harriet. How many more men are going to die before you stop her?'

'Were you at the Drews' on the evening of the–'

The woman cut Theo off. 'I've not been there in months,' she said with a sneer.

'If you have some information that you think could help our investigations, then you should come down to the station at Glass Bay and make a statement,' Theo said.

'I don't want to make a statement. All I want to know is that you are going to look very closely into the Drews. And when you do, when you find your killer, then you reopen the case into my Finley's death.' She took a step closer to Theo. 'Two dead fiancés, what more do youse need?'

'We have to be somewhere,' Theo said kindly and put his hand on the small of Shilpa's back, steering her past the woman. The woman stared at them as they passed, and when Shilpa turned around, she was still there staring at them as they walked away.

'That was creepy,' she said to Theo.

'She's just looking for answers. She can't accept what happened to her son, and I guess she's looking for someone to blame. She's well known around here. I think the trauma of losing her only son has taken its toll on her. To be fair, I can understand it.'

'You can?'

'I have a suffocating, larger-than-life Greek mother. She would probably be the same if anything were to happen to one of her children.' Theo smiled. 'I had just arrived at the station here when her son died. I didn't really get involved with the case, but I know the DI and the team at the time did their best.'

'Yeah, I guess my mum would be the same too,' Shilpa said, although she wasn't quite sure she believed it. Her mother certainly knew how to fight for what she thought was right, like that time in Poundland when she was overcharged for tooth-paste. She had caused quite a scene, and Shilpa had wanted the ground to open up and swallow her whole. But somehow her mother liked to blame the victim. When Kirran Aunty's baby came three weeks too early, she blamed Kirran for eating too many pickles; and when her uncle died from a heart attack, she blamed his undiscerning appetite for both sweet and savoury pastries. Shilpa knew that some of this was just a front, putting up defences, making light of a dark situation. Her mother loved Dipesh. He was her brother. Shilpa had seen it herself, the way her mum called and fussed over him, sending him food stuffs through the post. Although she still hadn't forgiven her for denying her brother's sexuality – that was, if she knew about it. Now she had more time to consider the whole situation, she wasn't sure if her mother had known the full story. Perhaps Dipesh had kept his private life private.

The shock of Finley's mother approaching them had got her thinking about her date tomorrow night; the one with the stranger she was meeting at the Old Cinema. The Old Cinema was now an art gallery and café. How would she know who she was looking for? She supposed it wasn't her problem. Whoever had invited her knew exactly who she was. They had probably taken up residence in her garage. She momentarily thought about asking Theo to break in, but it was too soon. She didn't want him thinking she was paranoid.

As they approached her house, she fumbled around in her handbag for her keys, unsure whether to invite Theo in. It was late, and the lights were off. Was Tanvi asleep, or had she gone for a late showing at the cinema? Knowing Tanvi, it was probably the latter. It was too soon, she reasoned, to invite him in. It was their first proper date, and she liked him. She didn't want to ruin it. It probably wasn't something millennials were supposed to think about. They were supposed to just go with the flow, weren't they? But she was thinking about it. She didn't want to get a name for herself in Otter's Reach. Although a goodnight kiss wouldn't be a no-no, she thought as Theo leaned in towards her.

'Shilpa? Shilpa Solanki?' She heard an unfamiliar voice behind her, which made her jump. She turned to see a silhouette of a man on her porch. He had been waiting for her, crouching in the corner.

'Wait here,' Theo said, putting out an arm gently to warn her to get behind him. She took a step back as Theo took one forward with a confidence that made her fall for him even harder.

Chapter Twenty-Five

The man who had been crouching by her front door started towards them. 'It's me,' he said.

'Who?' Shilpa asked from a safe distance, behind Theo.

He stepped out of the shadows. 'Brijesh,' he said. Shilpa and Theo stared at the short man with frameless glasses and thick black hair.

'Sorry,' she said. 'I'm not sure—'

'My aunty told me you were expecting me.'

Shilpa looked at him blankly.

'Bippu Aunty,' he tried.

Now it started to make sense. The day of Mason's funeral, when she was running late, her mother had told her some story about a nice boy with a pharmacology degree who wanted to visit England. Her car had been playing up and she was late. She hadn't paid much attention to her mum, but she did recall her saying she had given this man her address. Because it wasn't enough that she may have a stalker, her mother was handing out her address willy-nilly to strangers. She could hear her mum's voice now, reprimanding her. 'He's not a stranger.

He's Bippu Aunty's nephew.' Like that made a difference. Nine out of ten murders were committed by people you knew.

It should have shocked her that in this day and age someone could turn up at your front door unannounced like this, but it didn't. Nothing in her big Indian family shocked her anymore. Just last month the same thing had happened to a cousin of hers, so it was expected. The Solanki family had a lot to answer for. Shilpa noticed that the man had two suitcases with him. One was sealed in a cellophane wrap, suggesting he had important luggage, but it was probably just mangoes. Her relatives loved sending her mangoes and then immediately called to enquire if she had received them, like they were some precious cargo of gold.

'But these are different,' her mother would say, holding one close to her nose and taking in the aroma. 'These are *Manku-rads*. Forget Alphonso varieties. The Mankurad is the true Goan mango.'

'Okay, Mum,' she would say. She had to admit, the taste was unlike anything she had ever eaten before; sweet and delicious. Not like the insipid imports you got at the local store. Maybe she would make a mango cake with Brijesh's haul.

'You know him?' Theo said, looking at her, his hand on her forearm now.

She nodded slowly. Theoretically she didn't, but she supposed she knew of him. 'My mum–' she started, but Theo cut her off.

'You don't need to explain. I have a big family, remember? I've had several potential girls deemed to be wife material sent to my door.'

Shilpa felt a sudden stab of jealousy. 'Oh no,' she said in a whisper, trying to clarify the situation. 'He isn't a suitor.' But she knew this was a lie. How often did her mother send a man her way if he wasn't potential boyfriend material?

'I take it Bippu Aunty isn't a blood relative,' Theo said.

Shilpa looked at Brijesh, his suitcase and his thick jacket on this warm summer's evening. 'Stop it, Theo. He's definitely not husband material,' she said under her breath.

'Phew,' he said. 'I was beginning to feel a little jealous.'

Shilpa looked at him and smiled. She wanted to kiss him there and then, but she refrained. She couldn't do that to Brijesh, not when he had travelled so far. And definitely not if she didn't want to get an early-morning wake-up call from her mother telling her to be ashamed of herself.

'I'll leave you to it?' Theo said, putting his arm around her waist and giving it a squeeze.

Shilpa nodded.

'I wasn't just waiting here,' Brijesh said, as Theo said goodbye and started walking back down Estuary Road. Shilpa watched him as he went. 'Well, actually, I was,' Brijesh continued, oblivious to her yearning for Theo. 'I tried the doorbell, but there was no answer.'

'I was out,' Shilpa said, turning towards him and trying her best smile.

'Obviously,' came Brijesh's reply. 'I tried your number, but there was no answer, so I thought I would wait.'

Shilpa took her phone out of her bag. She had three missed calls from an unknown mobile number. The tapas bar had been noisy, and she hadn't thought to check her phone. She slipped her key in the door. Tanvi must have been at a late showing. Great. She would have to deal with this newbie by herself. She realised as she opened the front door that Tanvi was in the guest room. Brijesh would have to camp in the lounge.

∽

'And then my Mumbai connection was delayed also,' Brijesh said as he took the tenth mango out of his case and laid it on the kitchen island. The smell was so intoxicating, Shilpa asked if she could eat one there and then.

'Sure,' he said. 'They are a little past the season, but still good. The summer came late this year in Goa.'

'So, you're from Goa?' she said as she sliced into the deep orange flesh and cut it into several pieces.

'Originally Cal.' Brijesh saw Shilpa's confusion. 'Not California. Calcutta, or Kolkata, as people say now. You know – Bombay is Mumbai, Bangalore is Bengaluru.'

'I get it,' Shilpa said. She devoured the mango, licking the juice from her fingers.

'Yes, you don't need a history lesson from me,' Brijesh said, looking at his feet.

'No, it's interesting,' she said. 'I've never been to Goa. I know nothing about India or my heritage. I really need to make the trip.'

Brijesh's eyes lit up. Shilpa hoped she hadn't opened the floodgates, allowing him to talk at length about his hometown. She did want to know more about India, about Goa and Delhi. She wanted to go there sometime, but now wasn't the right time. There never seemed to be a right time.

After her mango, she excused herself to retrieve the spare bedding from the trunk in the lounge and started making up the sofa with a duvet, pillow and a sheet.

'And you're just here on holiday?' she asked, trying to sound casual and not just wanting to know how long she would have a house guest for.

Brijesh shook his head. 'I have a work permit. I have a sponsorship from a pharmacology lab in the Midlands.'

'Oh, when do you start?' she asked, but she wasn't really listening. Her mind had drifted to what Theo had said about the woman in black and the foundation in the basin in the annex where Mason's body had been found. She tried to recall anyone wearing black but couldn't. It was an extravagant party. Someone in black was hardly likely to stand out. She was sure it held some relevance or Theo wouldn't have mentioned it, but maybe it was just a red herring. If Mason frequented the annex often, then perhaps he was meeting other women there. Although it was unlikely he would do this right under his fiancée's nose. Perhaps Harriet used a darker shade than necessary. Who knew? Maybe the person Shilpa was meeting tomorrow would shed some light on it. Yes, tomorrow she would know more.

'And the company has gone into administration,' Brijesh said as Shilpa tuned in to what her house guest was saying. 'They didn't tell me before I left Goa, so here I am. I suppose with everything going on they forgot.'

'What are you going to do?' Shilpa asked, wondering if this man would be staying with her indefinitely.

'I can stay for a couple of weeks and have a nice holiday. That's why I thought I'd come down to Devon and see you. Devon is supposed to be lovely.' Brijesh looked out of the window towards the estuary. 'Although I can't see much of its beauty now.'

'No,' Shilpa said, suddenly very tired. 'You'll have to wait till morning.'

'Or,' Brijesh said, 'I could try and find another sponsor. I've always wanted to try a different career. Maybe this is my opportunity.'

'Maybe,' Shilpa said through a stifled yawn. She was too tired to talk anymore, especially to someone making a career decision. 'If you don't mind, I'm completely exhausted. I think I need to get to bed.'

'Of course,' Brijesh said with a slight bow of his head. 'Don't let me keep you. I'm still jet-lagged myself. I only got into London two days ago.'

Shilpa smiled and said goodnight. It was only once she was in bed that she thought she'd better warn both Tanvi and Brijesh of each other's presence, but before she could muster the energy to get out of bed, she had fallen into a deep slumber.

Chapter Twenty-Six

Alison looked through the window. She watched the man scan his surroundings before opening the car bonnet. She focused her camera as the man looked inside and then started his work. Occasionally he looked up, but he wouldn't be able to see her; she was confident of that. When he was done, he calmly closed the hood and slipped into the garage, returning minutes later with a large carrier bag. He let himself into the house.

Alison looked at her watch. She could tell by the fresh flowers on the kitchen work surface and the welcome note that the guests would be arriving soon.

Living in a tourist spot where letting one's home out to complete strangers was commonplace had its perks. By using the rental site app with its 'book-it-now' function, it was easy to find out which properties were vacant and available. Vacating tenants usually left a window or door open or on the latch, with the keys on the table, as instructed by the owner. The owner always left it an hour or two before they inspected the property. People were so trusting, especially in sleepy Otter's Reach. It gave her enough time to pick up the keys and get them cut. She had a drawer full of keys to holiday rentals around Otter's Reach, and having a key fitted her needs perfectly, because she could come and go as she pleased.

Alison had hit gold with this prime location right opposite the house she had her eye on. Plus, she had a key, so she was in whenever she wanted. She just needed to make sure the place was empty, so she used it in between short lets and occasionally when the tenants were at the pub or on the beach. Tourists didn't stay in their accommodation much. They just used it for sleep and breakfast.

She admired the calm nature of the man she had been watching for some time. She had no choice really, because he clearly had a thing for the woman she had taken to following. What sort of thing he had for her she wasn't quite sure. But she would soon find out. She just had to be patient. An unsuspecting man with an unsuspecting woman, she mused.

Alison considered her own predicament. If only she had kept her calm that day, the day Mason died. She was a fool to have flown off the handle at Mason. It wasn't his fault; it was Harriet's, or perhaps it was Izzy's. Both women had wanted him; they had stolen him from her in one way or another. She had flown at Mason in a rage and fled. If she had kept her cool, she wouldn't have made mistakes. Her car had been parked outside the house for all to see, and then there had been the clothes – her stained clothes. They were still heaped on a sheet of plastic on her floor. She couldn't look at that blue-and-yellow dress in the same way again, yet she hadn't disposed of them yet. Tomorrow, she thought.

Still, there was some hope. The police hadn't come knocking yet. They had spoken to most of the attendees at the party. She knew that from her careful watching. She wasn't on the guest list, and it was unlikely that anyone had seen her. Her car was pretty nondescript, and there weren't any cameras outside the Drew house. Of course, Izzy could have seen her that day. If Izzy had been going to say something she would have said it by now.

Alison checked the time and then focused her attention back on the house she had been watching. The man appeared from the house, locked the door behind him and headed towards the slipway. It was time for her to leave.

She left the apartment as she'd found it and made her way back home. Once inside, she had a shower and changed into her pyjamas. Then she selected something comfortable to wear for the following day. It was going to be a long one.

She went to her room and took out a small pocketknife encased in leather. She held it in the palm of her hand and recalled the warm breeze outside the store when she had bought it many summers ago. Now she slipped it into her handbag. She had to be ready. Just in case.

Chapter Twenty-Seven

Shilpa massaged her temples. Today was her meeting at the Old Cinema, and she wanted to be at her best. Miss Marple didn't solve crime with a banging headache. She had had a terrible night. After waking up at midnight to two blood-curdling screams – one being Tanvi's, the other Brijesh's – she had managed to calm them both, introduce them and retreat to her bedroom.

So much for Brijesh's jet lag though. The two of them had seemed to hit it off, and she heard them laughing and talking for the next few hours. Of course they were. Tanvi was a night owl and loved company. Brijesh was a ready audience. She didn't want to be her mother and tell them to keep it down. She refused to be that person. Instead she had silently whinged, in the privacy of her own bedroom, until she fell asleep.

This morning Tanvi was as bright as a button. 'He's a laugh,' she said to Shilpa whilst Brijesh was taking a shower.

'I didn't get that impression last night. He nearly scared me half to death creeping about the flowerpots on my porch.'

Tanvi let out a cackle. Her phone beeped. She took it out of her skirt pocket, looked at it and put it away. 'Listen to you,

Miss Suburbia – flowerpots on the porch! Speaking of being scared, are you ready for seven?'

Shilpa hesitated. 'I guess. Do you think I should tell Danny or Theo?'

'Probably,' Tanvi said. 'But you're not gonna take my advice. At least I'm coming with you. We could take Brij too.'

'It's Brij now, is it? No, keep him out of it. I don't want this getting back to my mum. She'll be on the next train, and that's the last thing I need.'

'In case she meets Theo?' Tanvi said with a laugh. Her phone beeped again. She ignored it.

Shilpa looked at her watch. 'The market this morning shouldn't take long. To be honest, I haven't made much to sell.'

'Tut, tut,' Tanvi said, causing Shilpa to throw a tea towel at her.

'I've been busy, okay?' she said. 'With unexpected visitors.'

Tanvi nodded. 'And a date,' she said with a wry smile.

Shilpa ignored her. 'Let's leave around six. Is that okay?'

Tanvi nodded. Her phone started to ring.

'Someone wants to get hold of you, don't they?'

Tanvi headed for her room.

'We're late,' Shilpa said as they hurried towards the Old Cinema. The market this morning had gone well. She had sold out in two hours and returned home for a much-needed nap. She had overslept, and it had taken an age to get Tanvi out of the house.

'Why were you so keen to let Brijesh tell you that story about Shah Jahan and the guavas?'

'It's our heritage,' Tanvi said. 'I find it fascinating.'

'I don't want to miss this. It could be the key to who killed Mason Connolly.'

Tanvi ignored Shilpa and read a message on her phone.

'So, are you going to tell me what's going on?' Shilpa asked.

Tanvi looked at her friend. 'It's Jason. He's coming here. He's on the train. Taking a cab from Exeter. I guess he'll be here in the next couple of hours. But don't worry, I'm not leaving you with some nutter. I've got your back. As agreed, I'll mill about in the shop, which has a clear view of the café, from what I could see online. Jason can come meet us there afterwards.'

'Listen,' Shilpa said. 'I'll be fine. I'm in a crowded place. You carry on and meet Jason. You've a lot to sort out.' But to Shilpa's relief, Tanvi was adamant that she was staying, because Shilpa's safety came first.

As they pushed through the glass doors into the Old Cinema art gallery, they each went their separate ways. Tanvi, glued to her phone, headed towards the shop, while Shilpa walked casually towards the café. She eyed the drab selection of cakes and left one of her cards by the till as she ordered a piece of insipid-looking madeira cake and a hot chocolate, even though she felt like neither. She took her purchases to a vacant table closest to the gallery shop where Tanvi was pretending to look at a series of postcards. She sat down and waited.

'It's been an hour. Whoever left me that note was having a laugh,' Shilpa said, a little dejected now.

'Oh dear.' Tanvi was looking at Shilpa, talking to her on her phone as she sat on the stairs leading to the gallery.

'You go,' Shilpa said, looking at her watch. 'Jason'll be here any minute now.'

'You sure?' Tanvi said.

Shilpa nodded. 'I'll head back.' The feeling of being

watched had disappeared. She disconnected the call and headed to the ladies to use the facilities.

Once inside, she bent over the sink and splashed her face with cold water. When she looked up, there was another woman with pale skin and red hair standing beside her, staring at her in the mirror.

'It was you,' Shilpa said. She looked towards the bathroom door.

'The facilities are closed for cleaning,' Alison said. She turned to Shilpa. 'Did you need the loo?'

Shilpa shook her head. She wasn't going to walk into an even more confined space with this unstable woman. She swallowed. 'You left me the note.'

Alison nodded. 'You brought a friend. I'm not stupid.'

Shilpa thought about denying it then thought again. 'Can you blame me? You have something you want me to see?'

'Why're you so interested in Mason?'

'I was at the engagement party,' she said. There was no harm in telling Alison the truth. 'So I feel some kind of connection. What was it you wanted to show me?'

'Do you know why I chose to show this to you?' Alison asked, playing with a wisp of hair. She didn't give Shilpa a chance to answer. 'You're different from the others.'

'Others?'

'Just, you know, people.'

'In what way?'

'You too have enemies, like me,' Alison said with a small smile.

'Enemies?' Shilpa asked. Alison had the demeanour of a schoolgirl. The way she raised her shoulders to her ears, the way she giggled. It was unnerving. 'Are you going to show me what it is you wanted me to see?'

'Of course, silly,' Alison said. She reached into her bag, and Shilpa watched her carefully.

'I'm only getting my phone. Don't be such a drama queen,' Alison said. She retrieved her mobile from her bag and fiddled with it. 'I want to show you something, as you've taken quite an interest in the case, and I like you. Not to mention you seem to be getting on quite well with Otter's Reach's police force, so you may be able to pull some strings.'

'What do you mean?' Shilpa asked, although she knew very well what Alison meant. She wondered now if it had been Alison who had been following her. Had she been lurking in her garage? Did she have the missing key? With the warm weather, Shilpa often opened the bi-fold doors that led to the garden. The garden was accessible from the front of the house too. If she were in her bedroom or down on the slipway with her balcony doors open, Alison easily could have accessed her house.

'I wanted you to see this,' Alison said, ignoring her question. 'This clearly shows you who killed Mason.' Alison thrust her mobile phone at Shilpa so that the screen was visible.

Shilpa noticed Alison's chipped nail polish, her nails bitten to the quick. She focused her attention to the picture on the phone. She looked back at Alison. 'This doesn't prove anything.'

Alison scowled.

'It's a picture of you and Mason with Izzy hovering in the background.'

Alison pursed her lips. 'So, you know her then?'

'I know of her,' Shilpa said. 'The same way I know of you.' She relaxed. This woman was clearly delusional, but harmless.

'Look at the venom in her eyes. She couldn't stand that Mason was with me, so she took him away from me. Then when he was with Harriet she thought if she couldn't have him, no one else could.'

'Did she take him away from you?'

'As good as. She provokes people to do things they

wouldn't ordinarily do.' Alison crossed her arms over her chest. She wore a maroon-and-white summer dress with a denim jacket, a cross-body bag and clips in her hair. She looked so fragile, Shilpa wanted to put her arm around her. She didn't.

'Can we go for a walk?' Alison said meekly.

Shilpa nodded. They left the bathroom, and Shilpa noticed that Alison had placed a yellow cleaning sign in front of the door they had just come out of. Alison deftly moved it out of the way. *She is unbalanced*, thought Shilpa, *but at least she is considerate.* They left the Old Cinema, and Alison started walking two steps ahead of her. Shilpa followed her as she headed down an alleyway. It was getting dark, and there was a chill in the air. Shilpa put her hands in her pockets as she caught up with Alison.

'You don't believe me, do you?' Alison asked.

'The picture just doesn't prove much. You were at the engagement party, weren't you?'

Alison nodded.

'The police don't know though, do they?'

Alison stopped and turned to look at her. It was a narrow alley, and the way Alison was looking at Shilpa sent a chill down her spine. 'You're not going to tell them, are you?'

Shilpa shook her head as Alison inched closer to her. Shilpa took a step back.

Alison turned and walked on ahead. 'Why were you at the party?' Shilpa asked. She couldn't help herself.

'Who told you I was there?' Alison asked, walking on ahead.

'I saw you,' Shilpa lied, not wanting to bring Izzy into this. The two clearly didn't like each other, but it felt like they were protecting one another. Alison hadn't gone to the police with her photo, and likewise Izzy hadn't told the police that Alison was at the party. It didn't make sense.

Alison turned and sneered at Shilpa. 'What's it to you if I was there?'

'Did you speak to Mason?' Shilpa asked. She was provoking Alison, but she couldn't help herself.

'Mason wanted to speak to me,' Alison said. She stopped towards the end of the dark alley. They were near the rough end of town. The streets were poorly lit, and there were few people around.

'So you told him to meet you at the annex?'

'He didn't want to go there.' Alison started to cry, her mascara running down her cheeks. She wiped her face with the sleeve of her denim jacket, smearing black make-up across her face.

'You shouted at him outside until he agreed?'

Alison looked up, and something in her demeanour changed. 'Shut up,' she screamed. 'Shut up, shut up, shut up. You don't know anything.' She was yelling now; a different person to the meek girl in the summer dress. 'I loved him,' she said. 'I was the only one who truly loved him. Harriet is with Evan now. She never loved Mason.'

'Is that why you hurt him?' Shilpa asked. Alison started to sob. She lifted her eyes up to Shilpa's and tilted her head to one side. It was then that Shilpa saw it – the familiarity of the woman wearing the green scarf in that Audrey Hepburn sort of way that day at Magdalena's when she was having tea with Danny. She'd had the feeling of being watched, and now she knew why. The woman in the coffee shop had dark hair and a slight tan, unlike Alison, but that bone structure was unmistakable. She was surprised she hadn't noticed it sooner, but her red hair had distracted her. That's how Alison knew she had some police friends. She must have been wearing a wig. If she would go to that length to follow someone she hardly knew, what would she do for murder?

It was starting to make sense. At the engagement party

Alison changed into a black dress shortly after Izzy had seen her. Black wasn't a colour Alison would wear with her complexion, so it was the perfect disguise. The foundation smear the police had found in the sink must have been hers too. Alison must have used it to change the colour of her complexion like Shilpa had explained to Theo. She would have worn a wig to cover her red hair. Shilpa could see it now. Alison, dressed in blue and yellow, approached Mason at the party. She screamed to make a scene. Izzy had witnessed the fuss she made. That was her plan, because it was exactly what Mason didn't want. He must have ushered her inside the apartment. Once inside, she asked him to call off his engagement to Harriet. He laughed at her, and that's when she lost it.

Alison attacked him. She had taken the knife from the kitchen earlier. She changed out of her bloody clothes into black and used the foundation to disguise herself and return to the party. But why put the murder weapon back in the knife block?

The woman in the black dress would give people an illusion to focus on when they eventually started looking for the murderer. She must have taken her bloody clothes with her somehow and later disposed of them.

Shilpa took a step back. 'It was you in the black dress.'

Alison stared at her, her expression not giving anything away. 'You aren't any different from the rest of them. You don't know anything,' she screamed. 'Look at you. Do you even know what your neighbours are doing? What they're capable of?'

Alison didn't give Shilpa any time to think. She reached into her bag and pulled out a small knife, deftly lifting it up to Shilpa's neck. 'You've got no evidence I was there that day, and you're definitely not going to tell the police.'

Shilpa took a breath, and Alison leaned in closer. Then she pointed the knife towards her own arm and jabbed it. She barely flinched even as the blood seeped through her denim jacket.

'I could hurt you,' she said, 'and say it was self-defence.'

There was a noise behind them, a clattering to Shilpa's left. It was dark. She couldn't see if someone was there or if it was just a cat knocking over a bin. Whatever it was, it startled Alison, and she momentarily looked in the direction of the noise. Shilpa saw her chance. She pushed the knife away from Alison and ducked narrowly, avoiding the blade as Alison reached towards her. Shilpa ran in the other direction. Alison let out a blood-curdling scream as she chased Shilpa down the empty street. Two youths on bikes and in hoodies looked on, but Shilpa didn't stop. She ran towards the centre, past the Old Cinema, towards Estuary Road. It was dark, and the road was deserted. She couldn't see Alison behind her. Her heart was thumping in her chest. She walked quickly, too scared to stop to take out her phone from her bag, afraid Alison would jump out at her, wielding her knife. For once she was glad to be going back to a full house.

She reached her front door, let herself in and bolted it behind her.

'Hello,' she shouted, but she was met with an eerie silence. She immediately took out her phone, dialling Tanvi and then Brijesh when she didn't get an answer. No response from either of them. She checked the bedrooms. No one was home.

Alison had killed Mason Connolly and now she wanted Shilpa dead too.

She unlocked the screen on her phone and dialled Theo.

Chapter Twenty-Eight

'You should have told me,' Theo said.

'I didn't even think she was on your radar,' Shilpa said.

'This isn't a game. Someone killed Mason Connolly. You can't go around playing detective.'

'I thought if I told you or the police I would scare them off. I also thought you'd think I was getting too involved.'

'You're correct on both counts,' Theo said. He stood up from the sofa and walked towards the bi-fold doors that led to the balcony. It was pitch black outside, and Shilpa couldn't help but wonder if Alison was out there, waiting, watching. She walked over to Theo as he made a call and pulled the curtains shut.

Theo disconnected the call and turned to Shilpa, putting his arms around her. 'I've let Drayton know. There's a patrol car looking out for her now. We're locating an address for her, and then another car will go there.'

'You don't know where she lives?' Shilpa pulled away from Theo and sat back down on the sofa. It had been foolish to investigate Mason's death and meet Alison on her own, but given the police knew less than her, maybe it wasn't so ridiculous after all. She told Theo her theory again but this time named her suspect.

Theo looked at her as if deciding whether or not she could be trusted. 'Sod it,' he said. 'Why would Alison change after she killed Mason? Why not just leave the knife in the apartment and go? She wasn't invited, so she would have stood out. She had more of a chance of being seen doing what you say she did.'

'It's obvious,' Shilpa said. 'She got a kick out of it. Or maybe she was planning to hide the knife somewhere else, but something disturbed her, so she ended up slotting it back in the knife block.'

Theo nodded. His phone rang. He answered it. A few moments later he disconnected and turned to Shilpa. 'I have to go. I'm sorry,' he said. 'I don't want to leave you alone.'

'O-of course,' she stuttered. 'You go. I'll be fine. I'll keep the doors locked.'

'Have you heard from Tanvi yet?'

She shook her head. 'It's late. But maybe she and Jason made up and got a hotel. Although it's unlike her not to check in.'

'And Brijesh is out too?'

'Maybe they're together,' she said, although she thought it unlikely.

Theo kissed her on her cheek and headed for the door. 'Don't worry. I don't think Alison is coming for you.'

Shilpa stood up and walked behind Theo. 'What do you mean? She could be out there.'

Theo opened the door. 'I don't think she is,' he said. He kissed her cheek again and closed the door behind him.

'I can't believe it,' Tanvi said. 'We were in this awful bar in a basement and there was a lock-in, and I had absolutely no reception. I even tried a text message.' Tanvi put an arm around her friend. 'I feel just awful. I'm a bad friend.'

Shilpa looked up at Brijesh. 'Not a word to your mum or aunty or anyone back home. I don't want my mum on the phone.' Brijesh, who had sat in silence while Shilpa regaled them with the details of her traumatic meeting with Alison, looked at her in horror. He was hungover. There was nothing worse than a Tanvi hangover. She would have made him drink tequila shots and vodka. At least she had made him a bacon sandwich. Tanvi was surprisingly alert, but then she and Jason seemed to have resolved their issues.

'I can't believe that all this happened, and here of all places. You would think the city is a much more dangerous place,' Brijesh said.

Shilpa stood up, taking her coffee to the kitchen. The morning sunlight streamed in through the windows. Brijesh was right. Just how dangerous was Otter's Reach? Yesterday, Alison had said something about her neighbours. She padded over to the window and looked to the house on the right. Mrs Alden lived there, an elderly woman who rarely left the house and looked harmless enough. She had a nurse that visited twice a day. Occasionally, Shilpa would see Mrs Alden on her balcony and she would wave. She was hardly capable of standing, let alone something more sinister. If anything, she was the one who was a terrible neighbour. Wasn't England suffering from a loneliness epidemic? Didn't people die of loneliness? She made cakes; she could easily take one around to her and pop in for a chat.

The house to the left, like most of the houses here, was rented out on short lets. She could hardly count the never-ending changes of tenants. She finished her cup of coffee. Why was she listening to someone as delusional as Alison anyway?

She returned her cup to the sink and picked up the photo album of her uncle and his lover and flicked through it. Instinctively her eyes went to the boiler cupboard. She opened it and looked at the hook where the garage key lived. She expected it to be empty, as it had been for days, but the garage key was hanging there as if it had never disappeared.

'Tanvi,' she said. 'Did you put this key here?'

Tanvi's look said it all. If Tanvi hadn't replaced it, who had? She picked up the key and Dipesh's photo album, grabbed her cardigan and marched to the garage.

The garage only contained a couple of boxes, but she was sure there had been more the last time she looked. Searching, she could definitely tell from the dust marks on the floor that boxes had been moved around, and possibly some were missing. Why would someone want Dipesh's stuff? As far as she knew, he didn't have anything valuable. Her relatives would have taken anything worth something. She shook her head. Maybe she had remembered wrong. With what had happened last night, she was just on edge. She had a missed call from Theo in the early hours, but she had been asleep and hadn't heard her phone ring – knocked out by the brandy, no doubt. He had left her a voicemail saying it had been a long night and that he wouldn't surface till midday. He would call her then. He wanted to see her. She looked at her watch. She still had a few hours to kill.

Shilpa looked in the boxes. There wasn't much there. Perhaps her aunts had taken away anything that implied a relationship between her uncle and another man. She eventually found another album – pictures of Dipesh and locals in and around Otter's Reach. There were quite a few of Dipesh with John and Graham on their boat. It was a shame Dipesh hadn't spent the day with them like they had wanted. Instead he died alone. She looked towards Mrs Alden's house. It would be awful to die alone. She would definitely make her a sponge cake and take it around. Still holding the album Tanvi had found amidst the pile of books in the house, Shilpa left the garage and headed down the slipway.

Chapter Twenty-Nine

Shilpa wrapped her long cardigan around her. She was wearing shorts and a simple T-shirt, perfect for a day of mooching around the house and garden, but now on the water's edge, in the cool morning air, before the sun had broken through, she felt a slight chill.

'Graham? John?' she called from the slipway.

Graham emerged on deck. He motioned to her to stay where she was. He was heading over to collect her on their tender. The tide was in, so she couldn't just walk along the muddy floor of the estuary in wellington boots to their boat, like she sometimes did. It was an odd way to live. But only odd to her because she was so used to living on land, in a house. So many people lived in narrowboats and out on the water. When Dipesh was alive, he had told her about the couple that lived on a boat attached to his mooring, but she had never stopped to consider it.

'Jump in,' Graham said as he approached her.

'Look, I don't want to take up much of your time,' she said. 'But I've been meaning to show you something – to ask you something, really.'

'You'd do me a favour by coming on board. We are in the middle of packing.'

'Packing?' Shilpa asked.

'Well, stowing things away for France,' Graham said, like she should have known. 'Our annual summer trip.'

'I like your thinking,' Shilpa said. She couldn't remember the last time she'd had a holiday. She hopped into the tender, looking back at her house as she made the short trip to Graham and John's boat. Brijesh and Tanvi were standing at the window, waving. She waved back. She hadn't caught up with Tanvi about Jason. It sounded like they had kissed and made up and that Tanvi would be staying with Jason in Hope Cove before heading back to London. She hadn't asked her friend for any details like she ordinarily would have. She had been so shaken up by her ordeal last night.

Shilpa looked back at Graham, who was tying the tender to the boat, and considered telling him about Alison, but then decided against it. She didn't want to answer more questions about what had happened, and she didn't want him to worry like she knew he would. She slipped her hand into her pocket and checked her phone. Nothing from Theo. It was nice to be out on the water with Graham, and her uncle's lover was a good distraction from what had happened yesterday.

Graham climbed up onto the deck and held out a hand. Shilpa took it. In her other hand she held tightly to Dipesh's photo album. She saw Graham looking at it curiously.

'This is what I wanted to ask you about,' Shilpa said, handing the album over as she followed him into the lower cabin. She looked around. There were several brown boxes labelled with various provisions. She felt a stab of jealousy. How carefree it would be to sail to France with your loved one. She looked back at Graham, who was studying a photo in the album.

'Where did you find this?' Graham asked.

'In amongst some of Dipesh's possessions.'

'Just one album?'

Shilpa nodded.

Graham made a face. 'He probably took the rest.'

'Who? Do you know who that is? The whole album is full of pictures of Dipesh and this guy. And later on, there are a couple of the four of you on your boat.'

Graham swallowed. 'That's Craig.'

'Craig. A name, that's great. I knew you'd know. Looks like they were in a serious relationship and travelled together quite a bit. We always thought Dipesh went alone to all these places. It's lovely to know he had someone. Sad that he felt he couldn't tell us about him, but still.'

Graham was silent. He put the album down and started packing a box. 'Need to wrap some of these ornaments up. Sailing can cause a bit of havoc in here,' he said.

'But who was he?' Shilpa asked. She stepped over to where Graham was and handed him a paperweight.

He took it from her and sighed. 'Dipesh loved Craig for a time, but then he left without so much as a goodbye. It broke your uncle's heart. I'm afraid I can't tell you much more than that.'

'How long were they together?'

'A year, perhaps.'

'Didn't my uncle try to find him?' Shilpa asked.

Graham stopped what he was doing and looked up. 'I don't think Craig wanted to be found.'

'But he left a note?'

'I don't know the ins and outs of their relationship. Your uncle was a reserved man. Kept his private matters to himself. That's probably why you didn't know about it.'

Shilpa could see that Graham wanted the conversation to end, but there was so much more she wanted to know. There was a part of her uncle's life that he had kept hidden. But she was living in his house. She wanted and needed to know more about him. He wasn't just an old bachelor who led a lonely life, as her mother had made her believe. He had a life filled with love and laughter. Before Craig there may have been someone else.

'Craig must have left for a reason,' she continued. 'It would be good to hear why. I mean, he must have had his reasons. They seemed so well suited in those photos.'

'It was one album,' Graham said as he wrapped a porcelain vase in tissue and put it in the cardboard box. 'You didn't even know…' he mumbled under his breath.

Shilpa looked away. The boat rocked gently, telling her another vessel must have passed them. She steadied herself and watched Graham wrap another ornament to put in the box. He was right. Dipesh had kept Craig a secret for a reason. He didn't want her snooping around his private matters in life, so he wouldn't want it in death either. It was time to drop it, but she couldn't help herself. She pursed her lips. She was her mother's daughter, after all.

'I can't help thinking that–' she started.

'If your uncle didn't tell you about him, he either didn't want you to know or he didn't want to be reminded of that weasel.'

Shilpa picked up the photo album that Graham had discarded on the table and nodded. 'I guess you're right. There wasn't a mention of him in his will, although he had written it some time before his death, and it probably needed updating. You don't expect your life to end in your late fifties.'

Graham walked over to Shilpa and put a hand on her shoulder. 'If I were you, I'd put that album up in the loft or something and forget about that man. Remember your uncle how he wanted to be remembered. Now, let me take you back.'

Shilpa looked around her as Graham busied himself with a

box. 'Yes, you need to get on with things here. When do you leave?'

'In a few days.'

'And when'll you be back?' Shilpa asked, feeling a sense of loss. She had grown used to having Graham and John around. They would be the first people she would call if she ever needed help, and with people like Alison around, she needed people she could trust close to her. Her phone vibrated in her pocket. She immediately retrieved it, expecting it to be Theo. It wasn't. She walked up and out onto the deck and looked up at her house. Tanvi was on her balcony, waving frantically, pointing to her phone. Shilpa looked at the message her friend had just sent, then she felt a hand on her shoulder, which made her jump.

'Sorry,' Graham said, immediately removing his hand. 'Didn't mean to startle you.'

'Oh, don't worry,' Shilpa said. 'I'm a little jumpy after last night.'

'Last night?'

Shilpa shook her head. She couldn't get into that now.

'I'll take you back,' Graham said.

'Sorry,' Shilpa said. 'I've interrupted your day.'

'Nonsense. Don't be sorry,' Graham said with such warmth that Shilpa had to refrain from giving the man a hug.

'Will I see you before you go?' she asked.

'We'll certainly wave,' Graham said as he climbed down into the tender. He held out his hand and she took it.

Five minutes later she was climbing up the steps to her balcony. She walked through the bi-fold doors to see Tanvi on her sofa, staring intently at her phone. Tanvi looked up when she heard Shilpa say hello.

'You've got to see this,' she said, passing over her device.

Her friend was looking at a local news site. 'Body found at

Fish Cove,' she said, looking over Tanvi's shoulder at the screen.

'Not that,' Tanvi said. 'I didn't know it was so dangerous here. Apparently, the body of a man was found washed up weeks ago. The body is so decomposed they can't identify who it is. Creepy. Sounds like he was pushed overboard.'

'He could have fallen in. You're being overdramatic.'

'Overdramatic!' Tanvi said. 'That's rich coming from you, who found a bloodstained knife. I don't think you can be over the top around here.'

'When I found the knife, I didn't just assume someone was murdered.'

'You kind of did… eventually, like within twenty-four hours,' Tanvi said with a smile.

Shilpa couldn't help but smile too. She thought back to last night, to Alison holding a knife against her neck. She could have been a decomposing corpse right about now. The smile quickly faded from her face.

'It's the story below that you need to see,' Tanvi said.

Shilpa scrolled past the story of the body found at Fish Cove. She saw now why Tanvi was so excited. It showed a block of apartments in an area of Otter's Reach she was unfamiliar with. Police tape surrounded the entrance, and there was a picture of two men carrying a stretcher. There was clearly someone on it, but it was partially blocked by the paramedics, so you couldn't quite see. Theo too was pictured, looking towards the ambulance. No wonder he hadn't been in touch. Shilpa slumped down on the couch, barely registering that Brijesh had appeared from somewhere and was making a sandwich in the kitchen. Her hands started to shake as she found her phone and dialled Theo.

Chapter Thirty

Shilpa listened as Theo spoke, guilty for having phoned him. He had called her over, and she had driven to his house. He had managed four hours of sleep. Despite his exhaustion, he was going back to the station, because after what had happened last night, sleep wasn't a priority.

Theo sat next to her and started lacing his shoes. They hadn't been seeing each other for long, but it felt like they had known each other forever. Shilpa was beginning to think that her humiliation with Danny had been worth it. She looked around the lounge, which was open-plan with the kitchen. The two-bedroom house was similar to hers, but the wallpaper wasn't outdated. The walls were a simple off-white, with stainless steel and anthracite-grey kitchen units. There were few ornaments or pictures in his space. It was minimalist, to say the least. She supposed it suited his lifestyle: a single man with a demanding job. He didn't have time for curios. She hoped he had time for her. She noticed a half-empty bottle of vodka on the kitchen work surface standing next to a glass.

'So, by the time you found her she had already been stabbed?' Shilpa asked, shifting her eyes from the vodka to

Theo. She still couldn't understand how Alison, the woman who had threatened her yesterday, the woman she was certain had murdered Mason, was now dead.

'You're connected to two murders. I shouldn't be telling you this.'

'I didn't kill Alison,' she said. 'Or Mason for that matter. You know exactly where I was last night. You were with me until you had to go.'

'She was a voyeur,' Theo said. 'There were loads of pictures of Mason, Izzy and Harriet plastered over her walls.'

'A stalker.' But was that all she was?

Theo sighed. 'She died in the ambulance on the way to the hospital.'

Shilpa asked if Alison had said anything about her attacker. Theo rubbed his temples. He looked at her as if weighing up whether or not he could trust her. He hadn't known her for long, and he was taking a big risk by dating her. She knew that. A thought occurred to her. Had Theo done this before? Dated a suspect? Not that she was a suspect, but he was right – she was connected to two murders.

Theo's momentary doubt disappeared. She could see it in his eyes; in his manner as he picked up his keys from the leather-and-glass coffee table and straightened his shoulders. 'She couldn't say anything really,' he said. 'Just two words again and again, and they didn't make sense.'

'What were they?'

He looked at her. 'Never mind. I can't tell you that. This is just so…'

'I'm not going to tell anyone,' she said, although she was pretty certain she would tell Tanvi. But Tanvi didn't count. She didn't live in Otter's Reach and was hardly likely to go blabbing.

Theo leaned over and kissed her on her cheek. 'You need

to go to the station and make a statement about last night. It's better you go before they send a patrol car to get you.'

Shilpa nodded. 'Fine,' she said, conceding. 'If you don't want to tell me what Alison said, that's okay too. You know, when I mentioned the woman in the black dress, she looked at me curiously. I'm not sure it was her.'

'You mentioned that to her?' Theo stared at her.

'It was hardly a secret,' she said in defence. 'You said loads of people had seen someone in a black dress at the engagement party.'

Theo was silent.

'Do you think Alison killed Mason even though she's been murdered too?'

Theo grabbed his coat from the back of a chair. 'What else did she say when you asked her about the black dress?'

'Nothing,' Shilpa said.

'You've no idea what you're doing,' he said. There was an awkward silence between them. Then Theo sighed. His tone softened. 'Look, I didn't tell you this, but we have a witness that places Alison away from the Drew house at the approximate time that Mason died. We need to verify the claim, so don't go talking about it. But it seems improbable that she killed Mason now. Her car broke down on the way back from the Drews to her home. Her clothes were covered in grease. We found them on a sheet of plastic in the corner of her kitchen. I guess she hadn't got around to washing them. It stands up to what the witness said he saw.'

Shilpa understood his frustration. Theo wanted to close the case, put a murderer behind bars and get some decent sleep again. It suddenly made any work stress she'd ever had seem insignificant. It was one thing making a mistake on a client's account, another to mess up on a murder investigation. She was probably complicating matters, and that didn't help Theo.

Shilpa stood up. 'Thanks for telling me,' she said. 'I'll leave you to it.'

Theo shot her a smile that made Shilpa relax a little. They walked together to his front door and she noticed a solitary family picture by the console table next to the entrance. In the photo, Theo was standing in the middle of a group of about a dozen people. They were gathered next to a boat. A fishing trip somewhere in the Mediterranean, she assumed. Theo was holding up a big fish. She bent down to look at it.

'Is this your family?' she asked.

'Most of them.'

'So, you do have a big family. Who's missing?' Shilpa studied the picture and made assumptions on who his dad and his brothers were.

'My mama left my father when I was a kid. She had a whole other family. I have a half-sister who isn't in that picture, and Mama's missing too.'

'Do you get on, you and your half-sister?' She couldn't imagine one of her parents having another family and them all getting on.

'Sort of. She can be a bit difficult. Used to getting her way. That sort of thing. But you can't pick your family,' Theo said, stepping in front of the photo.

Shilpa kissed him. It was understandable that he didn't want to go into detail about his relationship with his mother's other family. Theo moved towards the front door and opened it. They stepped outside, and he locked up.

'The bag,' Theo said as they parted.

'What?' Shilpa said.

'That's what Alison kept saying before she died. '"The bag" – over and over. We didn't find any bag of any interest at her apartment. Anyway, I'll see you later.' Theo walked towards his car. Shilpa stood alone on the pavement, wondering what Alison had meant.

It was clear to Shilpa now. If Alison hadn't killed Mason, she had a good idea of who had. Theo had said that Alison's front door had been open but that there had been no sign of a forced entry. Alison knew her attacker; she must have let them in. Her body had been found in a pool of blood on the kitchen floor, stabbed several times and once fatally in the lung. Not too dissimilar from how Mason had been found, she imagined. Was that final jab of the knife luck or judgement? Alison wasn't all there, from what Shilpa could tell, but even she knew that so many stab wounds wasn't an act of self-defence. Alison's attacker intended to kill. He or she was angry about something and wanted Alison to suffer.

The attack wasn't random; that much was clear from what Theo said. The way Alison's apartment had been left didn't look like a burglary gone wrong, because as far as the police could tell, nothing had been disturbed, and it wasn't obvious that anything was missing, just her mobile telephone. Alison must have called the killer. She must have invited them into her home, ready to expose them, tell them what she knew.

What did she know? The photo she had been so keen to show Shilpa had proved nothing. She must have known who was wearing the black dress. Maybe she had a photo of the killer wearing it. It was likely, given the number of photos Theo said they had found. Theo said only her mobile was missing, but maybe an incriminating photo had been taken too. Surely the police could see that. Shilpa reassured herself that they would. Theo couldn't tell her everything.

Theo had told her that forensics had been all over Alison's apartment, dusting for prints and searching for clues in her well-ordered home. Blood-soaked felt leopards lay next to her body. According to Theo, there were heaps of these little felted creatures all over her flat.

Shilpa parked on her drive and got out of her car. Could she have inadvertently got Alison killed by mentioning the black dress? Could Alison have suspected Harriet and called her over to confront her? Had the black widow aptly dressed in black to murder her fiancé; a colour so dark it would disguise the blood? She had been notably absent from her own engagement party to start with. Her own mother had commented that Harriet was taking an age to get ready. Harriet conveniently appeared at the last moment after Mason had already been missing for some time.

The timing was certainly convenient, and she easily could have met her fiancé at the annex prior to midday in order to murder him. Had the spoiled Harriet been bored with her beau? If she had killed before – and here Shilpa was thinking of poor Finley – then perhaps she just had an evil streak. The engagement party was at Harriet's home. She easily could have changed into black, arranged to meet him at the apartment, telling him there was something she wanted to share with him away from everyone else, something private, something that couldn't wait. After the deed was done and the bloodstained knife put back in the knife block – why it had been put back like that was still a mystery to Shilpa – she could have slipped back to her room and changed. It was definitely a possibility.

But supposing the black dress was just a red herring. What did Alison mean by repeating the words 'the bag' over and over again? And what about Harriet's dad, Steven Drew?

Where had Steven been the day Mason had been murdered? He was definitely returning from somewhere as she had been leaving that evening. Why would you leave your daughter's engagement party? Had Steven killed Mason and then, covered in blood, realised he couldn't return to the party? He was sure to have a change of clothes at one of his offices in town. It would explain why he'd left in the first place. And didn't Graham say that it was Steven who had found the body?

That was very convenient indeed. He could have been in on it with his daughter and his wife, for all Shilpa knew, because Harriet's mother was hiding something too. She had blatantly lied to the police about being in her husband's study. What was in the old bureau that she had wanted? And hadn't a guest commented on Margery's outfit as she stood talking to her in the kitchen? Margery too had changed her clothes under the pretence of her previous choice being unsuitable for the hot weather. The Drews were a peculiar family.

Shilpa let herself in. She thought about Dipesh and the part of his life he had kept hidden. The Solankis had their fair share of secrets too. But then most families were not connected to two suspicious deaths. Finley's death was officially recorded as an accident, but was it? And now there was Mason. Shilpa walked down the steps to the lounge. Her eyes were drawn to the sofa. When she saw what was there, she froze.

Chapter Thirty-One

Tanvi and Brijesh looked sheepishly at Shilpa. They were both sitting on the sofa in their dressing gowns. Tanvi had her legs draped over Brijesh and was playing with his glasses. Even more shocking was that Tanvi was wearing Shilpa's new White Company grey towelling robe that she hadn't yet worn.

'What happened?' Shilpa asked. She put her hand out to stop Tanvi from answering. She couldn't do that to Brijesh. He looked mortified. 'I know what happened,' she said. The tightening in her chest took her by surprise. She had no feelings for Brijesh, yet it seemed like another rejection.

'You won't tell my mum, will you?' he asked.

She shook her head. 'What about Jason?' she asked, turning towards Tanvi. 'I thought you'd kissed and made up.'

'I don't think I love Jason,' Tanvi said, removing her legs from Brijesh's lap and straightening. She adjusted the gown around her and tightened the belt.

'You don't think,' Brijesh said, meekly looking down at his bare feet. Never in a million years would Shilpa have put Tanvi with Brijesh. 'I think I'll take a shower,' he said. He stood up and crept out of the room. Tanvi suppressed a giggle. They heard the bathroom door close.

'What were you thinking?' Shilpa asked. She headed to the kitchen with the idea of baking a rose-and-pistachio cake. She was tired of thinking about death and murder. At least she could relax a little now that Alison was not going to come after her with a knife. She would try and forget about Alison and Mason for a couple of hours and bake her neighbour a cake. It was time she paid Mrs Alden a visit.

She looked at Tanvi. The feeling of rejection had been fleeting. And at least Tanvi and Brijesh were providing some light-hearted distraction. She selected the ingredients she needed – the butter, eggs, sugar, flour, rose syrup and the chopped pistachios. Tanvi was quiet. She looked back at her friend, her ingredients now neatly assembled on the counter-top. 'You like him,' she said.

'I don't know.' Tanvi padded over to the coffee machine, slipped a capsule in and pressed the flashing button. Taking her mug of coffee, she perched on a bar stool at the island while Shilpa started to sift flour.

'Don't mess Brijesh around. He's so innocent. And what about Jason?'

'He's going back to London today,' Tanvi said, her hands around her coffee cup.

'Does he know that you two are over, or is he going back filled with hope?'

'Probably the latter,' Tanvi mumbled.

'Oh Tan, you're going to have to tell him.'

'I'm not sure I can trust him. I was excited to see him when he came here, but when we met, the spark seemed to have just disappeared. I don't know. Our make-up seemed forced, and I was glad Brij was there to lighten the mood. We really hit it off.' Tanvi stared into her coffee. 'Which is surprising. He's not my type at all.'

~

'I've told you where I was,' he said. 'What more do you want?' Steven Drew looked at his wife. She hadn't been herself since Mason died. At first, she had been strong – the stoic woman she had always prided herself on being – but slowly the façade had fallen. Had she known what Mason was doing? She couldn't have. But in the last week she had turned on Harriet for carrying on with Evan so soon after her fiancé's death. She couldn't understand how Harriet could move on so quickly.

Didn't she know their daughter at all? He had no doubt that Margery would have done the same herself had she been in the same position thirty years ago. So why the change of heart now? Was it because it looked bad? His wife was sniffling into her handkerchief. She was a constant blubbering mess these days, and he couldn't stand the sight of it.

'Just pull yourself together,' he snapped.

Margery looked towards the photo of Mason and Harriet hanging on the wall. 'I suppose that should come down,' she said, her hands shaking. 'I can't bear to look at it anymore. Plus, Harriet has some other plan, which I'm sure you know about.'

Evan was a breath of fresh air as far as Steven was concerned. He walked over to his study and was about to slam the door behind him when he saw Margery following him. He went over to his Chesterfield and sat down.

'It just sounds a little odd, you leaving the engagement party like that and where you said you went. It doesn't make sense,' Margery said, facing away from Steven and looking intently at the bureau.

'Are you calling me a liar?'

'Why would you leave your daughter's party, where there is plenty of expensive food, to go to a fast-food place for something to eat?'

Steven looked away. 'There were so many people here enjoying our hospitality, and most of them are just leeches and social climbers. I wanted to get some space, and I like fried chicken.'

'And you managed to get grease stains on your shirt, which is why you needed to change. You lied to the police. You said you were here the whole time.'

'Because Margery, dear, it was irrelevant.'

'I didn't mention to the police that you had changed, but someone else may have.'

'Nobody saw me,' Steven said. 'You changed too. I remember you wearing something completely different when I left compared to when I returned. You don't see me questioning you about it.'

Margery seemed to have not heard his last remark. 'And you're sure that no one saw you because you were looking around to make sure that no one was following you? So you were deliberately being careful?'

Steven ignored her. He wasn't going to get into this again.

His wife wrung her shaking hands. 'You shouldn't have bothered changing… All that blood. It wasn't worth it,' Margery said.

Steven stared at her, but she didn't turn to look at him. 'What?' he asked.

'You were the one to find Mason. You were covered in blood after changing. So really there was no need to change.' Margery turned and stared at her hand which, Steven noticed, was firmly placed on the bureau.

'If there's something you want to say, dear, just say it.'

His wife's moment of determination suddenly faded, and a tear rolled down her cheek. Steven didn't know which was worse – her playing the emotionally unstable wife or the scheming one. He had seen both sides in their long history together. She had exhibited this same behaviour with the whole Finley debacle too. Perhaps she should have been an actress. He didn't dare mention it. It was possibly another dream she had harboured until she married him and found herself a kept woman. She would have some resentment towards him, holding him responsible in some way or another. Looking at her hand pressed firmly on his bureau, he wondered just how much she knew. Perhaps she was keeping the information to use at a later date, or maybe she was just scared of what would happen if the truth was exposed. The latter suited him better.

Steven stood up and walked towards her, his arms outstretched.

'We should have a dinner,' Margery said, holding back the tears. 'With Harriet too. There is much to discuss, and I'm fed up with all the lies. There are so many.'

Steven put his arms around his wife, and she buried her head in his chest. 'Is that what you want?' he asked. 'For everything to be laid on the table, expose everything?' His tone had softened, and he stroked her hair. He felt Margery sigh in between sobs. 'Do you really think that would be wise?'

'No,' he heard his wife whisper. 'No.'

'What's going on?' Steven heard his daughter's voice from the doorway.

'Oh, Harriet,' he said, pulling away from his wife and standing in front of her. 'I didn't hear you come in.'

'Is everything okay?' Harriet asked.

'Fine,' Margery said, stepping out from behind him. 'Everything's fine.' Her eyes were red and filled with tears. There was no getting away from the fact that she had been crying, but Harriet wouldn't ask why. 'I was just saying to your father that it would be nice to have dinner together tomorrow tonight. Can you join us?'

Harriet nodded. 'I was going to see Evan, but I can meet him after. Anyway, there are things that we need to discuss,' she said.

'That's settled then,' Margery said, walking past her husband and daughter towards the kitchen.

Chapter Thirty-Two

Shilpa had lunch with Theo in Glass Bay after giving her statement about what happened with Alison. Something was going on in the Connolly case that Theo couldn't tell her about. He hinted that they were going to make an arrest soon but didn't give anything else away.

'A man or a woman?' she had tried, but he remained tight-lipped. He wouldn't say, not after she had screwed up so royally last time. Theo promised to fill her in as soon as he could, but for now he had to keep his intelligence to himself.

Shilpa returned home to find her rose-and-pistachio cake where she had left it. She had warned Tanvi to leave it alone as she left for the police station, but she could never tell with her best friend. Tanvi was going to walk Brijesh into town to prep for his interview with a telecommunications company. Somewhat different to his pharmaceutical background, but he seemed to know what he was doing. Working in the back office of a phone store was certainly something different. But Shilpa could hardly judge. She had gone from a healthy city salary to a meagre wage so that she could fulfil her dreams of making cakes for a living.

Sometimes you just needed a change. A change of job could mean a change in another part of your life, like love, for instance, which was what Shilpa now realised this whole change in lifestyle came down to. She had wanted something different. She was tired of the same old dates with self-centred bankers. A change of job and location had certainly come up trumps with Theo.

She quickly iced the cake, garnishing it with freeze-dried rose petals and chopped pistachios and placed it in a newly branded Sweet Treats cake box; over a thousand boxes in various sizes had been delivered that morning. She looked at her market stall to-do list. She needed to get baking to have a decent spread for the next stall. She wondered how long her house guests would be staying. Tanvi would be heading back to London in a week's time, because she had only taken two weeks off, but Brijesh was an unknown quantity.

Her mother had called her as she made her way back from the police station.

'How's the boy?' her mother had enquired. For a moment Shilpa thought her mother was referring to Theo, but then she realised it was impossible. It was Brijesh she wanted to know about.

Shilpa filled her in on the issues with his job.

'What a shame,' her mother said. 'Who would have ever imagined something like that happening. I hope you've been a comfort to him. You don't know anyone working in pharmaceuticals who can give him a job?'

'No, Mother,' she heard herself say.

'You are getting on well?'

Shilpa didn't destroy her mother's hope by telling her about Tanvi or give her a reason to point out her numerous failings as a grown woman, so she agreed they were getting on well. She did not mention Theo, because she definitely did not want to go down that road. Instead she had asked her about Dipesh's love life.

'I didn't know,' her mother protested. Shilpa was silent, and eventually her mother confessed that she had her suspicions. 'But I didn't like to ask, and he didn't tell, so there was nothing more to it. I couldn't just tell everyone something he hadn't yet admitted to me.'

Shilpa was silent, unsure whether or not to be angry at her mother. She decided against it. Her parents were old and stuck in their ways, but they were not bigots. Maybe they had, for once in their lives, chosen to respect someone else's privacy.

Mrs Alden looked frailer in person than she did standing on her balcony. Shilpa greeted the old woman with a smile as she explained she was just being neighbourly.

'Oh, how lovely,' Mrs Alden said. 'Please come in, and do call me Elaine.' She stepped to one side, allowing Shilpa into the large lounge that had the same view as she did over the estuary. The sitting room was painted a pale blue and was filled with trinkets and exotic ornaments that told of a well-travelled life. Shilpa could see by the neat order of the house that Elaine was once a house-proud woman, but now her ornaments collected dust on the countless shelves. Shilpa felt her heart give a little.

'I've been here in this house for over three decades,' Elaine said. 'And you're the first neighbour I've had come and introduce herself.' Elaine touched her grey hair that was combed back neatly and held in place with a coral Alice band. 'I used to know everyone in this town, and they all knew me. My husband was quite a prominent member of the town council, but he passed away seven years ago.' Elaine put the kettle on and took two cups out of the cupboard.

'Let me,' Shilpa said, and Elaine smiled. She pointed out where the teabags were kept and then, turning the volume down on the television, seated herself in a well-used chair that faced the estuary. She looked lost in thought for a moment, but then she looked up at Shilpa as the kettle came to the boil and said, 'Now people probably think I'm some eerie old lady that lives in the house at the top of the hill on Estuary Road, who sits by her window to watch the tide turn.'

Shilpa smiled. 'I haven't heard that. I don't think people talk as much as they used to. People are so busy with their lives and their phones.'

Elaine laughed. 'They are. I can guarantee that people talk in Otter's Reach though. My nurse keeps me up to date with the goings-on in the town. I know all about the poor Connolly boy and your cake venture. I think you'll do very well in this place from what I've heard.'

Shilpa brought over two cups of tea and gave one to Elaine, then she went back to the open-plan kitchen to cut two generous slices of cake. She brought them over and sat next to Elaine, looking out over the estuary.

'The Connolly case,' Shilpa said, taking a sip of her warm drink. 'I know all about that.' She doubted the old woman could tell her something she didn't already know, and in all honesty, she wasn't in the mood to talk about it. She wanted some normality for an afternoon.

'I gather you did a delightful cake for the engagement party. Your first commission here at Otter's Reach?'

'You do know everything!' Shilpa said. She put a forkful of cake in her mouth. It passed her standard. She would make a few of these for the market.

'And what I don't hear, I see,' Elaine said, giving Shilpa a knowing smile which made Shilpa feel a little self-conscious.

'Did you know my uncle?' Shilpa asked, trying to move the conversation along.

'Dipesh?' Elaine asked. 'He was your uncle?'

'He left me the house.'

'Oh, how generous of him. He had a big heart though. I met him when I was more mobile, and he often left a jar of his lovely jam for me outside my door,' Elaine said, taking another bite of cake. 'This, my dear, is one of the best cakes I have eaten in a long while, and that is saying something. All I do these days is take pills, drink tea, eat cake and watch the news.' She motioned to the muted television screen. 'But then I do have this beautiful view to compensate as well as the telly. At least I'm not in an old people's home… yet.'

Elaine dabbed at her mouth with a handkerchief before continuing. She liked to talk, and Shilpa wondered how often she had visitors. 'I was glad that your uncle was with people the day he died. To see him that day, you wouldn't have thought that anything was the matter. He was so full of energy, helping Graham with the tender and whatnot.'

He wasn't with Graham and John the day he died. Graham had told her as much. Elaine must have been mistaken. She didn't correct her. It was also plausible that he had helped them with their boat before they set sail.

'You never know with problems of the heart, do you?' Elaine said. 'He had problems with his heart for some time, didn't he, dear? That's about the only organ I have that is functioning well, so I can't say I'm an expert, but they say, well we all know, that you can get a heart attack at any time, and if he was close before…'

'Before?'

'Oh, he had an episode last year at the annual summer fair. Although it's unlikely to be annual for much longer. Numbers are dwindling these days and it isn't well attended. The youth now prefer to go to Salcombe or be out on the water. They're always trying to get a better attendance by mentioning it at every opportunity on the Otter's Reach blog.'

'What happened to Dipesh?'

'I only know second-hand, dear, but I read it online.'

'My uncle's near heart attack at the fair was in the blog? That seems a little odd.'

'Not for around here, dear. You'll see. News is news.'

Shilpa nodded. The authors (she'd heard from Leoni there were several) of the Otter's Reach blog had written a piece on Mason's gruesome end only days after he died. It was informative to a point but wasn't in good taste and didn't take his family into consideration, or the Drews. Although she doubted either family followed that sort of publication. And she was sure they would know to avoid it around a tragedy that involved their families.

'I'm not sure if it was a near heart attack. I think it was more like angina or something. The whole town was talking about it. It was definitely heart-related.' Elaine smiled at Shilpa, who was looking out at the estuary. John and Graham, by the looks of it, were still getting supplies for their trip. John was approaching the boat in their tender, laden with shopping bags.

'You can certainly see all the comings and goings here, can't you?' Shilpa said.

'As can you, dear. But I'm sure you have better things to do with your time, like running a successful business.'

Shilpa smiled. 'Did you ever see my uncle with a man, slimmer build than him, taller, dark hair?' The question was out before Shilpa had time to consider what she was saying.

Elaine tilted her head to one side. 'There was a man fitting that description who was always with your uncle. Those four used to be out all the time, as thick as thieves. But I didn't know much about him. He was here for a time, possibly a year or more – you know how time just flies – and then he wasn't.'

'I was trying to track him down, but John and Graham were not much help. They say he just disappeared one day.'

'Oh, that's a shame if he didn't even tell those two where he went. He was always doing odd jobs for them…' Elaine trailed off, her eyes fixed on the television screen to the right of Shilpa. 'Well I never,' she said, reaching out for the remote control, which sat next to a pillbox on a small nesting table.

Shilpa turned to look at the screen.

Chapter Thirty-Three

Shilpa stared at the picture of Craig on the television, dumbstruck over the coincidence.

'Oh dear,' Elaine said as she turned up the volume. 'And we were just wondering what had happened to the poor chap.'

'Craig Worthing,' the news presenter announced, 'was found dead at Fish Cove. His body was too decomposed to identify immediately. Authorities were uncertain how long the body had been underwater but finally managed to identify the body through cross-referencing the persons reported missing in the last six months with dental records.'

Elaine and Shilpa looked at each other as the news presenter rattled on. Poor Craig had met his end out at sea. After much investigation, forensics had concluded that the victim hit his head and fell into the water, subsequently drowning. They didn't say whether they thought it was foul play or not. Sailing accidents did happen. But it was obvious that something was amiss. There was no unmanned boat found in the days following his death, and no one had reported a man overboard. The news presenter as well as both she and Elaine could read between the lines.

'I read about the body found at Fish Cove,' Shilpa said. 'I didn't know it was Craig.'

'They've only just released a name. That's two mysterious deaths in and around Otter's Reach,' Elaine said. Shilpa didn't tell her it was in fact three, if they counted Alison as well, but perhaps the news hadn't reached her yet.

'Where is Fish Cove?' Shilpa asked.

'Not far from here. It's a small cove just past East Portlemouth. A stunning little bay, really. If you catch it at the right time of day, with the sun high in the sky on a summer's afternoon, you would think it was somewhere in the South of France. Personally, I think this part of the world is better, but there are many that would disagree. Coastal England has a certain charm though, don't you think?'

Shilpa took a breath and nodded. She was avoiding the Connolly case but instead felt like she was in the middle of uncovering a murder closer to home. She tried to move the conversation along with Elaine, enquiring into her past, her career and what life in Otter's Reach used to be like. But she couldn't evade her thoughts. Did her uncle have anything to do with Craig's death? Had the man died before her uncle had? Or was it just an unfortunate coincidence? Craig was an enigma. He could have been a vagrant taking advantage of her uncle. No, she was being paranoid. The pictures of Craig and Dipesh told a different story. They clearly loved each other. Dipesh had a heart attack, and an autopsy had proved it.

Shilpa managed half an hour of conversation with Elaine before she realised she needed some fresh air.

Evan pulled up outside the Drews' and turned off the engine. He checked his watch. Harriet was late. The Drews were making this a habit. It wasn't enough that Harriet had cancelled their dinner at the last moment, but now she was going to keep him waiting. After all he had done, after all he had been through. He wondered if this was what it would be like living with Harriet – would it just be take, take, take? By now she should have told her parents of their plans – the destination wedding by the Italian lake. It was too soon after Mason's death to make anything official, but at least they had a plan. They would get engaged over the Christmas break, when work in Otter's Reach was pretty much non-existent. Tourists were never interested in the bleak winter coast that was often ravaged by storms and driving winds. But that was when Evan liked it best. It was real. The weather exposed a certain side of Devon that he loved, something raw and authentic. Sure, he couldn't venture out on his paddleboard on days like that, but he loved nothing better than standing in his living room, staring out at the lashing rain, the harbour on the other side of the bay barely visible and the estuary a barren landscape.

They would marry the following summer in Italy, near Lake Maggiore. Harriet was reluctant to tell her parents with Mason barely cold in the ground, but those were his terms.

'Aren't you scared?' Jasper, one of his friends, had asked him when he confided his plans.

'Scared?' he had asked, taken aback.

'Two of Harriet's fiancés have died. I don't want it to be you next, mate.'

Evan looked at his bruised knuckles as he remembered the moment. Jasper wouldn't be making any statements like that anytime soon. When he and Harriet had discussed their wedding plans and he had mentioned Italy, she had been like an excited child who had just been told they were going to Disneyland.

He had friends over in Italy that lived close to the lake. It wouldn't be that difficult to organise a wedding there, and Harriet had the time. She could travel up and down, if needed.

He could go with her too. That would be romantic. Give them time to catch up with each other after years of wanting to be together but never quite managing it. Harriet liked the idea of Italy because it would be different to what she had imagined her wedding to be like in England. Twice she had been so close to getting married in Devon. Twice it wasn't meant to be. Evan smiled. Harriet felt indebted to him, and that was something he could certainly live with. The wait, the deaths, it had all been worth it.

Evan checked the time again. This just would not do. He reached for the door handle on his new Porsche Macan but then retracted his hand. He saw the flashing lights follow a black saloon car into the gravel drive of the Drews'. Once again he remembered the weight of the knife he had picked up that day, the same day that Mason's body had been discovered – killed by that very knife. He let out a breath and watched. Detective Inspector Drayton, who had only recently inter-viewed him, the same man he had been forced to lie to, stepped out of his car.

Another man, in plain clothes, also got out of the car. Another detective inspector, perhaps, a detective sergeant? What were they doing to require further backup? A police car had parked right behind them, blocking the drive, and two police officers got out. There was no way Evan would be leaving anytime soon. He contemplated getting out of the car and running as the four of them stood in front of the black saloon, chatting.

Five minutes later, it was too late.

All four men were looking straight at him. Had they come here for him? Perhaps it was better that he had refrained from knocking on the Drews' front door. He wouldn't want his future in-laws to witness this.

DI Drayton walked towards his vehicle, the other three men walking closely behind. They looked determined. They meant business. He didn't know Drayton. He had been a recent recruit, not like the older detectives working on the force; home grown and partial to a backhander.

Evan took a breath and opened his car door. He stepped onto the gravel and held out his hand to the approaching detective. He stood with his legs apart, his broad shoulders pulled back, and gave them a confident smile.

'Detective,' he said. 'How can I help?'

Chapter Thirty-Four

Steven sliced into a purple heritage carrot and pierced a piece with his fork. He heard the distinct sound of a car pulling up on the gravel outside but refrained from walking to the window and peering through the curtain to take a look. His family always accused him of being too nosy. 'It's probably someone just turning around,' Margery would say if she saw him twitch, a statement which enraged him almost as much as the act itself. In this instance, the car definitely came to a stop on the drive. He could hear the low hum of the engine outside. Harriet had no doubt left the gates open when she arrived. She always left them open and paid no heed to his constant nagging about it. He was tempted to close the gates with the remote. Lock whoever it was within his property so they would have to ring the doorbell to ask to be released. He would enjoy giving them a menacing stare as he pointed the remote to the gates.

'So you see,' Harriet was saying, 'it really is the best time.'

'I wouldn't say the best time, dear,' Margery said. Steven noticed that the food on his wife's plate had barely been touched. But he had to hand it to her, she was doing a good impression of acting cool when she was probably seething with rage. 'I mean, Mason is barely cold in the ground, and I'm just worried about you rushing into this,' Margery carried on.

Harriet turned to her mother. 'What you mean is that you are worried about what people will say. You're always worried about what people will say. You probably wouldn't mind Mason being dead if he had died someplace else, somewhere more convenient. I'm the one that has been left with two dead fiancés.' Harriet paused. 'I bet that bothers you more than it does me. What are people saying about that, Mother?'

'I wouldn't know, dear,' Margery said, pushing a potato around her plate. 'I don't socialise much these days.'

'No,' Harriet said, looking between her mother and father. 'I don't suppose you do.'

Margery cleared her throat, and Steven braced himself. After her outburst earlier, he wasn't sure what the woman would say. She wanted an end to the lies, but she didn't want exposure, he was sure of that. He noticed how his wife gripped the sides of the table as she spoke.

'How are you feeling about Mason's death? We haven't really talked about it.'

Harriet shot her father a look, then she turned back to Margery. 'We don't though, do we? We don't talk about things like that in this family. Why are you bringing it up? You know just how I feel.'

'If you want to get something off your mind, here is the best place to do it. At home, within these walls, where you are safe.'

'Is that what we're doing now?' Harriet asked, cutting into her lamb. 'Talking about our feelings, opening up?'

'It might be a way forward for us,' Margery said curtly. Steven noticed that she managed to eat a new potato as her hands moved away from the edge of the table and towards her knife and fork once again.

Harriet laughed.

'What's so funny?' Margery said. Steven avoided his daughter's piercing stare.

Harriet stood up abruptly, throwing her napkin beside her plate. 'You know how I feel,' she said, looking from her mother to her father. 'You know exactly how I feel, both of you. I heard what you were saying yesterday, Mum. You're tired of the lies? Well, so am I. God knows there are enough secrets buried in this family's history.'

'Harriet,' Steven said. 'That's enough.' His daughter studied her uneaten food – he looked down at her plate, the blood seeping out of the rack of lamb, the carrots tainted by the red liquid. He looked up at his wife, but her gaze was steely.

His daughter sat down and replaced her napkin on her lap. 'I've known Evan a long time, and he's right for me,' she said. 'Now I've had time to reflect, I realise Mason wasn't the one for me. It would have been a huge mistake. I was lucky really.'

Margery was silent.

'What else am I supposed to do?' Harriet said, tears filling her eyes. 'My luck when it comes to men isn't very good, is it? Hopefully, this one will last.' She turned to her mother, her tone calm. 'Mum,' she said, her eyes pleading. 'I'm going to be thirty. Everyone has someone. All my friends are settling down.'

Steven sighed, watching as Margery softened too. Thirty was a big thing. He remembered his own thirtieth and the slight dread that accompanied it. It was nothing but a number once you were past it though. And besides, he hadn't the luxury of time to think about that milestone. He was too busy setting up his business, making plans, and Harriet was on her way. After years of struggling to conceive, they had finally done it. Looking back now, he must have been fairly fulfilled at thirty. Margery too. He allowed himself a small smile. They were happier back then, with the world at their feet.

'I know, love,' Margery said. 'Evan is right for you. I can see that. He has always been fond of you.'

'Yes,' Steven said, putting his knife and fork down. He looked towards the window. He was sure he heard another couple of cars pull up on the drive, but with Harriet's noisy outburst, he couldn't be sure. It could have been a car turning, or worse, one of those electric cars. They were unnervingly silent. 'He's a lucky man to have you, and ambitious. Although he could do with dressing a bit better.'

'You always have something to say, Daddy,' Harriet said in her best little-girl voice. She wanted this marriage more than the others, and she was going to make this work. Steven could tell. It wouldn't end like the last two had done.

'So, the engagement would be at Christmas, with a wedding next summer?' Margery asked.

Harriet nodded and found her appetite. She speared a piece of bloody meat on her fork and put it in her mouth, taking another large gulp of wine. Steven noticed her eyes drift to the large grandfather clock that stood in the dining room. So Evan was outside. He saw why she had accepted their dinner invitation this evening. She wanted to set the tone for what was to come, to make sure everyone knew that she was coping fine with Mason's death and that she would move on swiftly, like she did after Finley. Harriet was going to win. Margery could see it now as well. He looked up to his wife, expecting a smile, one they shared when they were both confident of what their little girl was thinking, but her gaze was hard. Since Harriet had mentioned the secrets within the family, Margery had given him a cold stare every time he looked in her direction; like this was all his fault and she was just trying to keep the family together.

Steven locked eyes with Margery until she looked away like a faithful dog. She turned to her daughter. 'A destination wedding sounds right for this. I think Tuscany or even Limoges would be beautiful and suit you both.'

Steven finished the remnants on his plate and studied his wife as she and his daughter started talking animatedly about the wedding. He wondered how much Margery knew. How much did Harriet know? Did they know about the blackmail? Did they know what Mason was threatening? If they had known, would they have done anything about it? Margery was too weak to do anything substantial, although she was cunning. He had seen her scheming with Finley. She had taken Finley to task, warning him that if he loved her daughter, he would stay with her despite the money Steven had offered him to leave. But later Margery had come around to his way of thinking. Finley thought he could outsmart the Drews and get away with it, and look how that turned out.

The young boy had been deluded, and he got exactly what was coming to him. Even Harriet saw that in the end. His daughter was the most precious thing in his life, but she would soon fly the nest, and he doubted they would see much of her, perhaps until babies came along. Women tended to want their mothers around for that. The thought of grandchildren filled him with a moment of happiness. It was time that Harriet settled, and Evan was a good candidate, worthy of his daughter. He looked towards the annex, the place where Mason had met his fateful end, and then he looked back to his daughter.

Margery and Harriet cleared away the plates and returned from the kitchen with dessert.

'Lemon syllabub with blackberry compote,' Margery announced, like it was the last supper. She had gone to a lot of trouble to make sure the meal had been just right. She had even used the good wine glasses that needed hand washing.

Steven put his spoon into the dessert. He looked up towards the window. He was sure he could hear voices outside. Margery glared at him from across the room. Evan would be outside waiting for his daughter, probably on his phone like all youngsters were these days. They could never just sit in silence for a moment. Apart from occasionally glancing at the clock, Harriet didn't seem worried. *Good girl,* he thought to himself. *Let him wait for you.*

Harriet was smart, much smarter than she often let on. She must have known about the bevy of foolish women that had pursued Mason. She had forbidden that redhead from attending the party. She hated her with a passion, once confiding in her father that Alison had it in for her; that she was determined to split them up. When he asked his daughter how she knew, she said she just did.

Steven's phone buzzed. He looked at the screen and let a small smile hover on his lips before returning it to his pocket. He looked over at Harriet and Margery; neither had noticed him looking at his phone. Harriet didn't have to worry about the crazy redhead anymore, or Mason. They were both dead.

The doorbell chimed, and Harriet immediately got to her feet, leaving her half-eaten pudding. 'I told Evan I would be out when I was ready,' she said.

'Invite him in, dear,' Margery said. 'There's another syllabub in the fridge. I can fetch it.'

'He won't want it, Mother. We're going out for drinks,' she said as she walked towards the front door. Steven and Margery looked at one another. They could hear voices. Not just Evan's and Harriet's but another voice, someone vaguely familiar. Margery must have realised whose voice it was a moment before Steven did, because he saw her face fall. He saw the fear in her eyes, and in that split second, he knew exactly who had come for them.

Chapter Thirty-Five

Shilpa pulled out another banana loaf from the oven and wiped her brow with the back of her hand. She placed it on the wire rack to cool and checked her list. She had just about finished Leoni's order, but she still had a mountain of cakes to make for the stall. She wasn't sure where to start. Tanvi and Brijesh were out, and she found she missed them. Thoughts of Craig and his bloated body found in Fish Cove came back to her. Elaine seemed to think John and Graham had been close with Craig and her uncle. She was also under the impression that they had spent the day with her uncle the day he died. But Graham had told her otherwise. It was easy to mix up your days when you were stuck at home all day, but somehow Elaine didn't seem the sort of woman to muddle days.

'Professional baker?' Tanvi asked, walking through the front door and down the steps into the lounge. 'You're covered in flour!'

'Ha, ha, ha,' Shilpa said. 'Take your jokes elsewhere. You two can help. Hi Brij,' she said as he followed Tanvi into the sitting room. 'Tanvi, you can ice the mango-and-lime cupcakes. I've made up the frosting in the glass bowl over there.'

'Yes, sir,' Tanvi said, saluting her friend. She walked over to the sink, washed her hands and then took the tray of cooled cakes and the icing to the dining table. 'Are you not going to ask Brij how the job interview went?'

'Oh, I'm sorry. Of course,' Shilpa said. 'Did it go okay?'

'Better than okay,' he said. 'I got it.'

'Amazing,' Shilpa said, pouring her cake mix from the mixer into a round tin.

'The interview was sooo long,' Tanvi said. Shilpa watched her friend ice the first cupcake and, pleased with the result, she looked away.

'But it was worth it,' Brijesh said.

'What will you be doing?'

'Back-office stuff for the phone company on the High Street.'

Shilpa looked at Brijesh. 'Great,' she said, although she wondered how that place stayed open. It always looked so empty. 'So, from pharmaceuticals to phone repairs?'

'Something like that,' he said. 'And the good news is that I also found a rental in town. I'll be out of your way soon.'

'It's nice having you and Tanvi here,' Shilpa said, although it would be nice having her space back too. 'What do you know about cars?' she asked.

'A little,' Brijesh said. 'My friend back home was a mechanic. I picked up a few bits from him.'

'My car won't start again. I've used it since Graham got it going and brought it back from the Connollys' for me, but I tried it earlier, and it just won't start. I need to take these cakes down to Leoni's before she closes at five. I don't suppose you could take a look at it? I don't fancy walking in this heat.' A day's baking in the summer was tiresome and often left her irritable, with no energy to make small talk with her customers. It was on days like this that she missed the cool air conditioning of her London office. She complained at the time that it was far too cold in the office and joked that her work wardrobe was the same in summer as it was in winter because of the temperatures. But she appreciated it on those hot, sticky days, when taking the Tube was like walking into a sauna with a million other people. Just the thought of having to do that again made her shudder.

She'd take baking cakes on a warm summer day in Devon any day over having to take the Tube again, and as a bonus, she had the beautiful view of the estuary too. The water was in, and the boats tied to their moorings bobbed up and down, the sun glimmered on the water, and the view instantly calmed her.

'The car's open, Brijesh, but take the keys. They're there.' She pointed to the steps where her keys were, and Brijesh disappeared with them.

He reappeared half an hour later. 'All done,' he said.

'What?' Shilpa asked incredulously.

'The ignition fuse was missing. Did you take it out when trying to get it to start?'

'I have no idea what an ignition fuse even looks like. I didn't even know cars had fuses,' Shilpa said.

'Anyway, I've fixed it. I walked down to the garage and bought one. It was a pretty easy fix. I'm going to take a shower now,' Brijesh said. 'It's pretty muggy out there. It needs to rain or something.'

'Thanks,' Shilpa called after him. She turned to Tanvi. 'Don't you think that's odd? A fuse that isn't working is one thing, but one that's missing is something else.'

'Unless Graham took it and forgot to replace it,' Tanvi said, concentrating on icing the last of the cupcakes.

'But I've used it since Graham dropped it back. I usually

leave my car open though. It's easier when I have to put boxes of cakes in the boot so often.' Shilpa put her finger to her lips. 'When I met Alison at the Old Cinema, she said that I didn't know much, that I didn't even know what my neighbours were doing.'

'Who does?' asked Tanvi. 'I don't know the names of my neighbours.'

'But that's London,' Shilpa reasoned. 'Anyway, I know this side is just rentals' – she pointed behind her – 'so she couldn't have been referring to them, and I went to see the old lady who lives over there yesterday.' As she rolled out some pastry Shilpa motioned with her eyes to the house visible through the long gable window in her lounge.

'So, after nearly being killed by some crazy loon, you decide to go into your neighbour's house? I'm beginning to wonder about your sanity.'

'Elaine's an old woman. She could barely make a cup of tea, let alone stab me.'

'Those are the ones you need to watch; the quiet sorts. I'm just saying, if Alison warned you–' Tanvi started, but Shilpa cut her off.

'What if she was referring to another neighbour?'

'Like? The ones opposite?'

'Exactly,' Shilpa said.

Tanvi looked up through the little window towards the road. 'Honestly, all the properties around here look like they're rented over the summer. I'm sure I saw a family with two little girls in summer dresses clutching buckets and spades getting into their car this morning as I waited outside for Brij.'

'Brij, yes. I see you two are still friendly. You still planning to go back at the end of the week?'

'I have a job that I can't just walk out of. Not all of us are as lucky as you.'

'So, you'd move down to this backwater if you had inherited a house here?'

'I didn't say backwater,' Tanvi said, making a face.

'You'd rent the place out like the rest of the second home brigade and make a killing, spending your summer in Paris instead, more likely.'

'Perhaps,' Tanvi said with a smile. 'Although I'm glad I came to see you.'

'Because you found another poor soul to dig your teeth into.'

'It's not like that. I told you. I don't think this is going to be a summer fling. I think there might be more to it. Anyway, look at what I've done.'

Shilpa put the circular cookie cutter down and walked over to the dining table. 'Well done,' she said, admiring the perfectly iced cupcakes. 'If I had one, I'd give you a gold star.' She looked through the picture window towards Graham and John's boat. They were going to set sail today or tomorrow, from what Graham had said.

'Ah, I see,' said Tanvi. 'Those are the neighbours you're referring to. The ones that fix your car and provide a shoulder for you to lean on.'

'They may live on water, but that's where they live. What if Alison was referring to them?' She quickly filled Tanvi in about Craig and her uncle, about what Graham had said to her about not spending time with Dipesh the day he died and Elaine Alden contradicting his story. Brijesh had walked in halfway through their conversation and had busied himself with a magazine on the sofa.

'So, those two,' Tanvi said, looking at their boat, 'could have had something to do with Craig's death.'

'Or maybe your uncle's,' Brijesh said, looking up from his magazine.

Shilpa and Tanvi looked away from the catamaran towards

him.

'You mentioned a heart condition, right?' he said.

Shilpa nodded.

'Anything inconsistent in the autopsy report or the coroner's findings?'

'No idea,' Shilpa said. 'I didn't look at it, and even if I had done, I wouldn't have any idea what to compare it with. Is looking at autopsy results a regular hobby of yours?'

Brijesh shook his head. 'No,' he said. 'I was just wondering if there were any elevated levels of sodium chloride—'

Tanvi interrupted him. 'That's salt,' she said, smugly. 'Sodium chloride is salt.'

'Wait a minute,' Shilpa said. 'My mother did mention something about raised salt levels and assumed it was his diet.'

'A young bachelor not having a nice young wife to take care of him, na?' Tanvi said in an Indian accent. Brijesh laughed, but Shilpa wasn't smiling.

'Elevated salt levels in his bloodstream could suggest something sinister. If someone knew your uncle had a heart condition and wanted him dead, they could induce a heart attack.'

'What?' Shilpa said.

'Say he was injected with potassium chloride; it would pretty much be untraceable apart from some elevated levels of salt in his bloodstream. In the body, potassium chloride breaks down into potassium and chlorine. The chlorine binds with naturally occurring sodium in the body to create sodium chloride, which is salt, as Tanvi pointed out. If your uncle had a heart condition and a bad diet and the coroner found no other evidence to suggest foul play…'

'Foul play such as a puncture wound from an injection or something?'

'Possibly, unless he didn't look properly because it was pretty much an open-and-shut case—'

'What do you mean open-and-shut?'

'Say a report came back from your uncle's doctor saying that Dipesh was told that if he didn't change his diet soon, a heart attack was likely, and say his arteries were clogged, then a lax coroner may not go hunting for a puncture wound from an injection. I mean, why would he? And the body is a big mass, with freckles and age spots, nooks and crannies. Perfect hiding places for a wound as small as an injection needle to go unnoticed, especially if it isn't being looked for.'

'Wow,' Tanvi said. 'You know a lot for a phone technician.'

'I am a pharmacist, just not practising. And there was a time in my life when I had a morbid fascination with death.' He looked at Tanvi. 'Don't worry, I think I've outgrown it now.'

Tanvi walked up to Shilpa and put her arm around her. Her friend looked visibly shaken. 'He's just talking in what-ifs, Shilpa. Don't worry. I mean, where would you even get the right amount of potassium chloride to kill someone? How would you know what to use if you weren't a doctor or a pharmacist?'

'The dark web,' Brijesh said.

'The what?' Shilpa asked.

'A part of the internet that you don't stumble upon. It's easy to get information and whatnot if you know where to look,' Brijesh said.

Tanvi turned to Brijesh and gave him a hard stare. Then she turned back to her friend. 'Why would anyone want your uncle dead? This whole case with Mason Connolly, Alison and now Craig whatshisname, it's making you see murderers everywhere. You need some time out. Dating a detective sergeant doesn't help either. Come back to London with me for a few days.'

Shilpa shrugged off Tanvi's arm and headed back to the kitchen. 'I've got a stall to prepare for,' she said. 'Anyway, you're right, it's all what-ifs, and there's no reason why anyone would have wanted my uncle dead. Graham didn't even know about Dipesh's heart condition. He was quite genuine when he told me, and this was before the thought of murder had even crossed my mind.'

Tanvi threw a cushion from the armchair at Brijesh. 'Perhaps you should stick to phone repairs.'

Chapter Thirty-Six

'Have you seen the news?' Tanvi said as she settled in front of the television with a tumbler of gin and tonic.

'No,' Shilpa said, stacking Sweet Treat boxes in jute bags. 'I need to get these to Leoni before her shop shuts, but when I return I'm expecting one of those, chilled to perfection, with lots of ice and a large measure of gin. I'll need it for tonight's baking.'

'More baking? How much do people buy around here?'

'I've run out of stuff at the last couple of markets, and I don't want people to think I'm lazy or unprofessional.'

'You sell out because your cakes are so good.' Tanvi turned up the volume on the television.

Shilpa's phone vibrated in her pocket. It was Theo apologising for having his phone switched off. He had been unreachable. She had tried his phone several times to find out if they had any more leads on Alison. He had sent her a message saying that they didn't. In his opinion, Alison's phone, which was missing, held a key piece of the puzzle.

Unofficially, they thought the two crimes, the death of Alison and of Mason, were linked. Another message followed in quick succession saying he had something to show her – photos that one of the officers had found in Alison's apartment that he thought she should see.

That last message piqued her curiosity. She was late for Leoni, but Theo couldn't keep her hanging like that. She called him quickly. He answered and spoke to her in hushed tones, telling her that he was just entering a briefing. He mumbled something about them having made an arrest before hastily saying goodbye and disconnecting. It was better than nothing.

She focused on the television screen. A journalist was talking in front of the Drew house; she wore a pink scarf, and her eyes were full of excitement. The reporter seemed to think a man had been arrested and quite unprofessionally implied it was Steven Drew, but they couldn't confirm it. The large white-washed house on Honeywell Drive looked devoid of life. There were no lights on, and none of the curtains were twitching.

Shilpa looked at her watch. 'I'm so late,' she said. Brijesh had now joined her friend on the sofa with a gin and tonic. She could do with one of those. Even at ten to five in the evening it was warm. The tide would be turning soon though, and when-ever it did, the weather changed. As the tide went out, the clouds gathered, and the estuary was often overcast. It was a strange phenomenon, but something she was slowly getting used to; like the sound of the black-and-white barnacle geese that often woke her up in the early hours of the morning and the pungent aroma of the mudflats which drifted into her bedroom.

Shilpa gathered her boxes of banana loaf and lemon polenta cake and headed to her car. She sat inside and put her key in the ignition, hoping that her little red Fiat would start. It wasn't every day that you found out someone had tampered with your vehicle, and it unnerved her.

Steven took a sip of his water and stared back at the detective. 'You've got the wrong person,' he said.

'I'll ask you again,' DI Drayton said. 'Why did you lie to me when I asked if you'd been at the engagement party all day?' The detective had a piece of paper in front of him which he was now jabbing with his finger. 'We have your statement here, Mr Drew.'

'I was confused. And when I did remember, I didn't think it was relevant,' Steven said.

'So you left your daughter's and Mason Connolly's engagement party and went to a fried chicken restaurant, where you ate a chicken burger and chips, got tomato sauce on your shirt and went to your office on the High Street to change. It strikes me as odd that you'd do that.'

Steven could see why. His wife didn't like his explanation either.

'And is there anyone who can vouch for where you were during those two hours?'

'Someone in the chicken shop,' he tried. 'The office was closed. I don't normally close the office, but this was a special occasion.'

'And you don't have any CCTV on the premises?'

'It's wiped clean every day. I don't know why you're trying to pin this on me,' Steven started.

'We've been looking into Mason's affairs, and we have reason to believe that you gave him a large sum of money the month before he was found brutally murdered.'

Steven stiffened in his chair.

'You've done this before, haven't you, Mr Drew? Paid off one of your daughter's boyfriends so they'd leave her. What kind of father would you say that makes you?'

'A good one,' Steven said. 'Do you have children?'

Drayton nodded.

'Then you wouldn't want them to end up with someone unsuitable.'

'I'm not sure it's ethical to pay them off, is it?'

'It's not really breaking the law,' Steven said. It was unbearably warm in the interview room. He looked around for some kind of ventilation system. There was nothing; just a small window behind Drayton which was slightly ajar.

'Does your daughter know about the payments?'

'With Finley, yes…'

'Although that didn't really work. From what I hear, he took the money and carried on with Harriet until his unfortunate but convenient demise.'

'Just what are you trying to imply?'

'For the record,' Drayton said, 'can you confirm why you transferred money to Mason Connolly on July the 22nd?'

Steven was silent. A police officer knocked on the beige door and then stepped inside, calling Drayton out. Drayton switched off the video recorder, leaving Steven alone for several minutes before returning. He then started the recorder again.

'Where were we, Mr Drew? Oh yes, the money.' Drayton cleared his throat. No apology for leaving the room, Steven noted. They thought he was their man, that he had killed Mason. What did they have on him? A one-off payment a month before his death was not evidence. Maybe they would get to a motive, but they couldn't pin this on him. He wondered if his wife and daughter were being questioned again. If they would say anything different the second time around. Whether they were ready to expose the lies and secrets of the Drews.

'How well do you know Bernard Connolly?'

Steven made a face. 'June's husband?'

'Yes,' Drayton said. 'Mason's father.'

'Sure, I know Bernie.'

'And how well do you know his wife?'

'A little,' Steven said, shifting in his seat.

'You might want to expand on that. We've got reason to believe that you and Mrs Connolly were having an affair.'

Steven put his hands on the table in front of him and withdrew them again. 'Who told you that?'

Drayton ignored his question. 'How long has it been going on for?'

Steven was silent.

'Did you think that no one knew about your lover? That we wouldn't find out? It's a small town, Mr Drew. Surely even you know that nothing here stays a secret for long. Is that why you made that large payment to Mason in July this year? I'm sure you'd like us to believe that you paid Mason to stay away from your daughter as you've done before. But, in fact, you were paying Mason to keep quiet about your affair with his mother. He must have been quite a heartless son to not even consider his own mother's feelings. Or maybe he thought by threatening you, you would back off and leave his mother alone.'

Steven didn't respond. He should have waited for his lawyer. The man was on his way, or so he said an hour ago. He had instructed him not to speak to the police, but Steven was impatient. The longer they kept him at the station, the more it incriminated him, and he couldn't just sit about. They had kept him for long enough already. He decided to speak to the police. He knew how to handle them. He was a successful businessman, after all. He'd negotiated deals; he dealt with the wealthy on a daily basis, catering to their whims and demands in his accountancy practice. A DI would be no different.

'It wasn't just a young boy trying to make a quick buck, was it? It was a substantial payment that you made,' Drayton continued.

'What evidence do you have to prove this utter nonsense?' Steven asked.

Drayton sat back in his chair. He smirked. 'I think you're forgetting that this is a murder investigation. A serious crime has been committed, and we have access to the victim's social media, email, bank accounts and his personal devices. We know what he was threatening you with.'

The colour drained from Steven's face. He cleared his throat. 'And what was that exactly?'

'Exposure.'

Chapter Thirty-Seven

It had started with a feeble attempt at a threat, but it had soon escalated into something much bigger. Harriet was helping Margery clear away the dishes after dinner one evening, and Steven and Mason had retired to the drawing room. The photo of Mason and his daughter had been hung, just that morning, in place of Finley's. Mason walked over to it and ran his finger around the frame. Steven could still remember the smug look on his face, like the cat who had got the cream. It made his stomach turn. He poured them each a large measure of brandy and walked over to where Mason was standing.

His daughter's boyfriend turned towards him and took the glass Steven was holding out. 'You don't like me, do you?' Mason asked, looking Steven straight in the eye.

Mason's directness had taken him by surprise. He had always been fairly quiet. Steven had taken it as a mark of respect, but he was pleasantly surprised by the boy's directness. This was a side to the boy's character he hadn't seen before. A side, he had to admit, he found more favourable than what he had seen so far. Perhaps the lad had some personality after all.

'I think you're punching, to use a phrase the young use today,' Steven said, without so much as a blink.

Mason laughed, but Steven noticed he was the first to look away. A small victory, but nevertheless a victory.

'I think you're right. Harriet's definitely special to me and someone I'll always take care of.'

'On your father's coin,' Steven said. The words had left his mouth before he could stop himself. He hoped Harriet wasn't listening at the door. 'Although,' he added, 'there's no harm in that when you pull your weight.'

'Precisely,' Mason said. Either he had completely missed the point or he was rising above it. *Touché*, thought Steven.

'Your opinion matters to Harriet,' Mason said. 'It's why I wanted to speak to you.'

Steven felt the dread rising from the pit of his stomach. He wanted time to stop. He definitely didn't want Mason to ask what he was about to. He wasn't ready to go through all that again like he had done with Finley. Not so soon.

'I want to marry your daughter,' Mason said.

There it was: the gut-wrenching statement.

'I'm doing the right thing,' Mason continued. 'I'm asking for your permission.'

Steven eyed Mason. He knew about the boy's past – the girls that fawned over him, his reputation as a ladies' man. The boy had limited ambition, a leech on his father's business. Was he worthy of his daughter? He couldn't offer him cash to get out. No, he had made that mistake before and had paid the price. A smile formed on Mason's lips with joyous expectation, and Steven's grip on his brandy glass tightened. Just who the hell did Mason think he was? What kind of future could he give his daughter? Harriet certainly knew how to pick them. What was Evan White doing? It was about time he made his move.

'No,' Steven said, swallowing the dark liquid in his glass.

Mason's eyes widened, and Steven momentarily enjoyed the satisfaction of the boy's disappointment.

Mason took a step closer. 'I think I misheard you,' he said, pulling something out of his jacket pocket.

'I don't think—' Steven started, but Mason cut him off.

Mason had his phone in his hand. He was scrolling through his photos. He stopped at one and showed it to Steven. Steven did his best not to grab the phone from the boy's hand and fling it across the room.

'I thought so,' Mason said, a smile spreading across his face.

'What are you boys chatting about?' Margery said, walking into the room with a pot of tea. Mason, Steven noticed, had pocketed his phone. Harriet followed his wife closely with a tray of cups and a plate of petits fours.

'Man stuff,' Mason said, without so much as a stutter.

'That sounds interesting,' Harriet said.

'Oh, it is,' Mason said, looking at Steven, who avoided his gaze. Mason walked over to Harriet and put his arm around her waist, kissing her on her cheek.

'Young love,' said Margery.

'Stop it, Mum,' Harriet said.

'Tea?' Margery offered.

'God, no, woman,' Steven said, reaching for the decanter.

'I'll have one, Mrs D,' Mason said, his voice like nails on a blackboard. Steven took a breath before pouring himself another large measure and falling into his Chesterfield.

Days later, Harriet announced their engagement. With no engagement ring, Steven should have seen what was coming next, but he didn't. He didn't think the boy was that hard up. Mason's father was strict with his allowance, everyone knew that, but for something such as this, especially given Bernard's enormous wealth, he thought his father would turn a blind eye to the boy's spending. Margery opened a bottle of champagne and Harriet gushed over plans for the engagement party. Steven had foolishly thought it was over. He was going to make contact with Evan. He was going to let Evan take matters into his own hands. But then Mason had complicated matters.

A week later, Mason sent him an email asking for money. Not just a couple of hundred, but thousands.

Steven had invited Mason over the same evening. If the boy was going to extort him, let him ask him to his face. It turned out that Mason had no qualms about this. He was only too happy to oblige. It was a thunderous night with rain lashing down, and they would find out the next day that Slapton Ley had flooded and that the road to Torcross was impassable.

They had sat in the kitchen that night. Both Harriet and Margery were away on a spa weekend in Somerset. Steven didn't offer Mason a drink. Instead he sipped his whisky, his rage intensifying with each mouthful.

Mason had reiterated what he had asked Steven for in his email.

'And what if I don't pay you?' Steven asked. He noticed the new knife block on the kitchen counter. Only yesterday Margery had commented that the knives were so sharp that they sliced through the joint of beef she was preparing like butter.

'What do you think would happen?' Mason asked. 'My father would find out what you've been up to, and my mother would be mortified. She wouldn't be able to show her face at parties, at those charity gala dinners she attends. And Margery would be upset too, I presume. Not to mention Harriet.'

'Why are you doing this?'

'Your daughter has expensive tastes.'

'I'm paying for the wedding,' Steven said.

'I'm paying for the engagement ring.' Mason had the audacity to wink at him.

'If you can't ask Bernard, ask your mother,' Steven said

flatly, wondering if Mason actually needed the money or if this was just some show of power.

Mason looked away. Everyone knew the story of Mason's older brother marrying a waitress in Vegas and losing half his wealth in the divorce that soon followed, which had made Bernard think twice about the allowance he gave his younger son. No doubt Mason had spent his allowance and more, so he was coming after his wealth. Was that why he was marrying his daughter? For the money? Steven's anger soared.

'Don't you care about your mother?' he asked.

'She doesn't need to know unless you want her to… publicly.' Mason hesitated. 'Her behaviour has been shocking. It's not something I'd expect from June, but Dad's away a lot, and when he's around, he isn't really there. So, I guess I can see why she strayed. It was a momentary lapse of judgement.'

Bernard Connolly lived to work, and that made him a very dull man. Steven had known Bernie and June since school. He could see why June had wanted something more.

Growing up, June was beautiful, but Margery had the looks, the wealth and a certain edge that put her a league above. He'd considered dating June back then, but he was already with Margery. You would never go behind Margery's back, not then, when they were in college. He had witnessed her harsh and a little unfair treatment of a girl, her arch-rival, Vicki Cross. When Vicki had attempted to flirt with him, Margery hadn't thought twice about slapping her adversary in front of their year. Margery soon earned a reputation. He certainly hadn't dared go behind her back in all their years of marriage – well, not until now.

He had been smitten with Margery back in college; her bold and determined nature had impressed him. Other women were so feeble. Although he had been slightly unnerved one evening when they were dining at an exclusive restaurant with her parents. They had taken a stroll in the grounds and had seen one of the waitresses fumbling about with a diner they had previously seen in the restaurant. They had both laughed about it at the time because it was a sackable offence. One of their mutual friends had lost his job there after a similar incident. But no sooner than they were back in the restaurant Margery complained to the management and Steven had been gobsmacked at how Margery could so coldly snitch on the poor young lady when she knew exactly what her fate would be. It seemed so spiteful and for no good reason.

Margery had changed over the years. After Harriet was born, she had softened, and when she stopped working to become a full-time mum, she definitely lost her confidence and volatility. Occasionally he saw a glimmer of the old Margery, the woman he had fallen in love with, but more often than not she was just a fretful woman. The anxiety and constant worry had started when Finley died. Margery had put her life into her daughter, but her daughter was making her sick with worry because she wasn't living the life she had planned for her.

It wasn't long after Finley's death that he had seen June in his office dropping off some accounts for Bernard. Things just progressed from there. A chance encounter turned into a drink, then dinner, and then spending the night at June's house. It was amazing how a shared youth and nostalgia could draw people together. He loved June. Not so much that he would leave his wife for her, not just yet at least, but he loved her in his own way. June felt the same; she had said it in not so many words. It wasn't Bernard she was worried about but their only son. Mason was her everything, and she wouldn't hurt him, even though he was a grown man. Steven understood. He felt the same way about Harriet. You would do anything for your kids. He knew that better than anyone.

Steven looked over at the knife block again. He imagined walking over to it, picking up the butcher's knife, feeling the weight of it in his hands and plunging it into Mason's chest.

The boy deserved it. He looked at him with pure hatred. This would be the first and last time the boy extorted money from him. He promised himself that.

'Okay,' Steven said through gritted teeth. 'I'll give you what you want. This is a one-off. You threaten me again and I'll let you talk. Share your photos with the world for all I care.'

'Oh, you care, Mr D,' Mason said, standing up.

Chapter Thirty-Eight

'I didn't do it,' Steven said, his eyes focusing back on Drayton. 'I found him.'

'It's strange that no one could access the property before you turned up.'

'They could. They chose not to.'

'The key code had changed.'

'But they all had the code.'

'Who are *they*, Mr Drew?' Drayton noted something down on the pad of paper in front of him. 'The victim was found in your property with multiple stab wounds. You had motive to kill Mason, and opportunity. You slipped out of the party. You may have gone for a chicken burger and a quick change at the office after you killed Mason, because you certainly had time to do that. And a change of clothes would have been needed after what you did. Given the lies you've told before today and your circumstances, it is all pretty incriminating, wouldn't you say?'

Steven didn't respond. He stared at Drayton. The detective's patience was wearing thin. 'Did your wife know about the affair?'

Steven clasped his hands on the table. 'It's stuffy in here,' he said, looking towards the small window, wedged open. He closed his eyes and recalled the night Mason had visited him, threatening to expose his secret. Before he left that night, the boy had handed him an envelope. Steven had opened it, and explicit photos of him and June fell out. Mason must have been at home one night when he and June were at her house. He must have taken the photos then. The sick boy. Mason's business card was inside the envelope too, his bank details scribbled on the back. He should have disposed of the photos there and then. He could have put them on the fire. Instead he hid them away in the drawer of his old bureau, certain no one would look there.

'Margery had no idea about the affair,' Steven said. Margery never went into his office, not since finding the cheque he had written to Finley.

'You're sure? She never confronted you about it?'

Was that what Margery was referring to when she mentioned that she was sick of all his lies? He brought his hand to his face and bit his fist. If Margery knew, she would want to protect what they had and push what Mason was threatening to expose under the carpet, pretend it wasn't happening, because if it was then she would have to do something about it. He shook his head. Margery was now weak and afraid. She wouldn't confront anyone like she had done with Vicki Cross all those years ago, would she?

Steven hesitated. 'I'm sure,' he said.

Shilpa parked outside Leoni's. The car started fine after Brijesh had replaced the ignition fuse. She had tested the brakes too, just to be sure. She hoped the whole tampering episode was behind her. She got out of her car and took the bags of cakes from the boot.

'Ah, you're here,' Leoni said, poking her head around the front door. 'Come on in. I've just brewed a cuppa.'

'Sorry I'm running late. I wanted to get here earlier.'

'No matter,' Leoni said. 'Brian's out tonight, and this way we can have a catch-up without any customers listening in.' She winked at Shilpa, who followed her inside and put the bags on the countertop.

'Now that you've mentioned the cardamom in the banana bread, I can smell it. I'll put these out back for tomorrow,' Leoni said. 'Make yourself comfortable.'

Shilpa sat down at the table closest to the counter, where there were two cups of tea. She took one and held it in her hands. It had been such a rush leaving the house that she hadn't had time to think, but now she recalled that the television reporter had implied that Steven Drew had killed Mason. Had Steven also had something to do with Finley's death? His poor grieving mother certainly thought so. Maybe she wasn't barmy after all and there was some truth in her accusations.

'The things people do for their children, eh?' Leoni said as she returned from the back room, pulled off her apron and slumped down into the seat opposite Shilpa. 'It feels good to sit down. I've been on my feet all day. That assistant of mine didn't show today. Bet it was because of the weather.' Leoni paused. 'Didn't I tell you that Harriet's dad was a bit of a control freak? He's only gone and butchered the poor Connolly boy.'

'You know for sure?' Shilpa asked.

'It's obvious, isn't it? They made a big arrest at the Drew house. Who else could it be?'

'Well, Harriet,' Shilpa suggested. 'Her mother.'

'Margery's a goody two-shoes. It isn't going to be her. The daughter, now she's a character, like I said, a black widow. She could have done away with both Finley and Mason.' Leoni looked wide-eyed at Shilpa. 'Ay, you don't think she did do it and her dad's taking the fall for her?'

'I did hear that Harriet was in Crete when Finley met with that terrible accident,' Shilpa said. She regretted saying the words as soon as they left her lips. She knew better than to gossip with Mrs Blabbermouth.

Leoni smiled. 'That doesn't surprise me in the least. It could well be her then.' She took a gulp of her tea. 'I wouldn't go sharing that knowledge with Finley's ma though. She's already a penny short of a pound, if you know what I mean. She'll become your best friend overnight and hound you no end. She made herself a regular here after Finley's passing. It were all right to start with, but then she stopped washing her hair, and that put some of the customers off after a while. I'm glad you popped by.'

Shilpa began to feel uneasy. Just moments ago, she had believed that the police had caught the right person. Now she wondered if there was any truth in Leoni's deduction. She shook her head. That was all this was – another armchair detective having a guess. For years she had watched cosy crimes on television; from *Murder She Wrote* to *Midsomer Murders*. It was easy Sunday night viewing. She wondered at the time, in a life that was a million miles away from the one she was currently living, how little villages were the setting for such calculated events. But now she knew. Little towns like Otter's Reach had a limited number of people who were often in each other's pockets. Everyone knew everyone else's business. They often made it their business to be in the know, and that frustrated people – to the point of murder? Maybe not often, but she could certainly see why it happened.

'You all right, love?' Leoni asked.

Shilpa looked at Leoni. It wasn't the Connolly case she was interested in talking about today. Since her chat with her neighbour, she couldn't stop thinking about her uncle's death. What

Elaine had said about Dipesh's heart condition and then what Brijesh had told her about the potassium chloride was playing on her mind. 'Tell me about my uncle and Craig,' she said.

'Ah,' Leoni said. 'So that's what it is. Thought you looked a little bit absent-minded. They've found his body, haven't they?'

'Fish Cove,' Shilpa said. 'I didn't even know about his relationship with my uncle until recently.'

'You didn't? They were very much in love. They spent all their time together. Practically lived together. I'm surprised Craig's stuff wasn't all around the house.'

'My aunts cleared most of the house before I got there. They're of a generation and can be quite closeted in their thinking. So maybe they got rid of a load of stuff. There was just one album I found buried under a pile of romance novels.'

'Or maybe your uncle got rid of the stuff when Craig took off like he did,' Leoni suggested.

'How did he take off?'

'Didn't Graham and John fill you in? They were all very close.'

'They didn't mention it,' Shilpa said. Leoni explained how Dipesh and Craig were planning for their future together and that Dipesh was the happiest he'd been in a long time. It had taken the locals some time to warm to Craig, given he was from out of town, but they soon got his measure as they got to know him when he helped out at the stall selling jams and in Dipesh's shop.

'But Craig decided he wanted out?' Shilpa asked.

'I don't know the ins and outs of it all. But from what your uncle said, he just took off one day, no note, nothing. Left all his stuff at Dipesh's house.'

Shilpa asked if they had been arguing, but Leoni couldn't confirm it. Dipesh had filed a missing persons report. Leoni explained that it wasn't taken too seriously, as Craig had a house in Dartmouth and his passport was missing.

'It didn't surprise me when your uncle died not long after,' Leoni said.

'Why?' Shilpa asked.

'You can die of a broken heart. I know it usually happens with older people who have been together decades, but there's no telling when it comes to matters of the heart.'

Shilpa nodded, but she didn't quite believe a broken heart caused her uncle's heart attack. Another idea was forming in her mind, an idea that she'd had earlier when Brijesh had told her about the elevated salt levels and the effect of potassium chloride. It had been a random thought, but now it was starting to make sense.

'Leoni,' she said. 'Did you know about my uncle's heart problem?'

Chapter Thirty-Nine

L eoni leaned forward, moved her cup of tea to one side and rested her arms on the table. 'Sure. He had a problem with his heart at the local charity summer fair last year. Angina, maybe. It wasn't a big deal, but it was being talked about, and it was written about on the blog that a local community group has set up. They write about anything and everything, and you should read the comments on some of their articles. People around here don't hold back when they can hide behind a different username. Like we don't all know who *123Cuttlefish* is!'

Shilpa gave Leoni a curious glance. She had no idea who Leoni was talking about.

Leoni stared at her for a moment. 'It's that barking mad professor who owns the bungalow with the bright-pink windows.'

Shilpa nodded as if she knew who Leoni was talking about, but in reality, she had no idea. 'The Otter's Reach blog?' she asked.

Leoni nodded.

Shilpa already knew this. Elaine had told her. If she wanted to know anything more, then she would have to come straight out and ask her.

'Do you think Graham and John knew about it?' she asked. They could have missed it. They had probably been in France at the time. 'I could ask them but they are so busy right now. I spoke to Graham a few days ago, and they were diligently stowing things away for their annual France trip.' She was talking at speed, something she did when she was nervous.

John and Graham had done so much for her since her arrival, and just thinking that they could have been responsible for her uncle's death felt like a betrayal. They had made her feel so welcome in Otter's Reach, inviting her over for dinner in those early days. They told her all she needed to know about the locals, warning her that Leoni's nickname was Mrs Blabbermouth. They had been spot on with that, and now here she was asking Leoni about them. She tried to suppress the guilt in the pit of her stomach.

'I think you're mistaken about their *annual* trip to France. Them two never go anywhere.'

'Oh,' Shilpa said. She couldn't have been wrong; she had seen Graham packing things to stow away. Maybe Leoni was mistaken.

'Those two are always in Otter's Reach,' Leoni confirmed. 'I can't recall that they've ever gone to France for the summer, but they are going this year. Bri told me, as John needs him to moderate the blog, what with all those comments. Bri hasn't been asked to step in for ages, so it's unlikely they went anywhere last year. And that answers your question; them two knew about your uncle's heart. John moderates the thing. Nothing goes on that blog without his approval.'

Shilpa felt her stomach turn.

Leoni put her hand on Shilpa's. 'You okay? You don't look right.'

Shilpa stood up. 'I need to see John and Graham before

they leave.' Her phone beeped. She took it out of her bag and held it in her trembling hand. It was a message from Theo. She opened it.

About what I mentioned earlier, was all the message said. She could see by the three dots that he was typing another message. She felt nauseated. She had messaged him asking to see what had been found in Alison's apartment.

Two picture messages followed. The pictures were crystal clear. Her jaw dropped. A longer message from Theo followed. He wanted to show her the pictures in person, he said, but it was going to be another late night, and he wanted her to see them sooner rather than later.

'You okay, love?' Leoni asked again.

Shilpa couldn't speak. She could only nod.

'It's pointless you rushing off, love,' she said. 'According to my Bri's blog debriefs, they'll be well on their way to France by now. They were setting sail this morning.'

Shilpa stared at Leoni. She had seen their boat earlier. They wouldn't leave so late in the day, would they?

'I've got to go,' she said. She ran through the door and jumped into her car, plunging the key into the ignition of her red Fiat.

Shilpa parked her car next to the slipway on Estuary Road, took her phone from her bag, tucking it into the back pocket of her chinos, and exited, leaving her handbag on the passenger seat. Running down the slipway, she could see John and Graham's boat still tied to the mooring. She breathed a sigh of relief. A couple of RIBs full of tourists sped past, waving and cheering as they made their way back from town to Salcombe and beyond. A small boat was tethered to the slipway, and a young father and his son were crabbing off the pier. Despite the light evening, there was a distinct chill in the air, and the clouds looked heavy. It would rain later. She assumed the boat belonged to the father and son. She jumped in, hoping they were too engrossed in their activity to notice, and started rowing towards the boat moored in front of her house.

John and Graham had been using her uncle's mooring for years. Dipesh had been so good to them. They had said it themselves. So, what had gone wrong? Graham and John had treated her like an old friend too, but they were not who she thought they were. She tied the small rowing boat to the catamaran and climbed on board.

Graham was instantly on deck. 'What's up? Where did you get that delightful craft from?' he asked, putting his arm on hers. Shilpa instinctively flinched and pulled away. John opened the door to the rear deck and stepped outside.

'What's happened?' he asked. But he didn't seem concerned. Shilpa could tell by looking from John to Graham and back again that they knew something was wrong. 'We're about to set sail for France,' John said.

Shilpa took a breath. What was she doing? It hadn't been long since her ordeal with Alison. She would have been lying to herself if she said she wasn't scared approaching John and Graham in this way, without any kind of backup, without telling anyone what she was doing. But her mind had been reeling when she left Leoni's, and she didn't have time to explain it all to her friend. Likewise, there was no time to stop at home to tell one of her house guests what she was about to do. She realised she should have taken her time, and now, standing in front of the two men, she could hardly whip out her phone and text Theo or Danny.

Every cell in her body was telling her that what she was about to do was crazy; but she owed her uncle this.

'You're leaving so late in the day?' Shilpa asked. 'You should wait for morning.'

'What is it?' Graham said, stepping towards her.

Shilpa took a step back, and Graham stopped. He put his hands up, his palms facing her. 'Okay,' he said. 'I can tell you're bothered by something. I'm not sure what's happened here.'

'I know what you did,' Shilpa said.

'And what's that?' John asked, resuming his usual casual demeanour.

'With my uncle, with Craig.'

'You're not making any sense,' John said. 'Look, why don't you come inside. We can talk about whatever it is that is bothering you.'

Shilpa ignored him. 'Graham,' she began, 'you said you didn't know about my uncle's heart condition.'

'Because I didn't.' Graham made a face at John as if to say *I'm not sure where this is going*, but Shilpa wasn't going to be taken in by him again.

'The whole of Otter's Reach knows. It was in the blog you moderate,' she said, looking at John.

'I don't recall that. I wouldn't lie to you on purpose. It must be difficult coming to terms with your uncle's death. Perhaps you think we could have done more to help. John and I wonder that same thing often. The truth is, we didn't know, or we would've kept a better eye on him,' Graham said.

'You knew,' Shilpa said, 'and you used it to your advantage.'

'You're not making any sense.'

'You killed my uncle,' Shilpa said. As the words left her mouth, the reality of what she was accusing them of hit her. Now she had said it out loud, she felt the conviction of her words. In the split second that followed, she saw a look pass over Graham's face. It was a look of fear which he shared with John just momentarily before they resumed their usual composure. It told her everything she needed to know.

'Why'd we do that?' Graham asked. That was the question,

the question she had turned over in her mind during her short journey from Leoni's Café to Estuary Road.

'You said you were away the day my uncle died, but that was another lie, wasn't it?' The dark clouds were gathering; the tide was turning. In under an hour, the water would drain from the estuary and they would be on the mudflats again. She heard shouting in the distance. The young boy and his father must have realised their boat was missing. But she couldn't think about that now. They would soon be stranded, and so would John and Graham.

'We weren't here,' Graham said. John was silent.

'You were seen with my uncle that day.'

John looked up at Elaine Alden's house. He sneered. Her eyes followed his, but there was no one sitting at the window. She hoped Elaine was making her way over to the Glass. She had told Shilpa how she liked watching the tide go out.

'Look, Shilpa,' Graham said, taking a step towards her. 'I don't know who's said what, but we would never have harmed your uncle.'

'And Craig? Did you harm him?' she asked.

This time Graham didn't look to John for support. Instead, he took another step closer and grabbed her wrist. He held it tightly. 'What is it you're trying to say?'

'I think you took Craig out on your boat. Just a trip somewhere around here, and something happened. There was a fight, or maybe it was an accident. Craig hit his head, from all the accounts online.' Her eyes wandered to the low coffee table with the sharp edges, the one they had warned her about when she visited. It was an odd fixture for a boat like this. Treacherous. After what Brijesh had implied about her uncle's death, she wanted to find out as much as she could about her uncle's lover. She had spent the best part of two hours reading some wild theories online about how he could have died. All the sources were certain that Craig had died from a blow to the head.

'You dumped his body in the sea, weighted down, hoping it wouldn't surface, but it did, at Fish Cove. Hence your trip to France, something I know you don't do annually.'

'This is ludicrous,' John said, stepping forward.

Graham released his grip on Shilpa. 'It is,' he said. 'Anyway, what's it to do with you or your uncle?'

'My uncle found out,' Shilpa said confidently, although it was all assumption. She knew in her gut she was right as she pieced together what Elaine and Leoni had told her. 'He went out with you the day he died. He confronted you about what he knew, and you killed him.'

Chapter Forty

'I'm sorry,' John said, his tone changing. 'You come into our home and accuse us with these lies. Just get out. Go back home with your stupid accusations, which are no doubt based on local gossip.'

'I have two pictures of you, Graham,' she said, gesturing to her phone. 'One taking things out of my garage and the other tampering with my car.'

'If you've forgotten, we sorted your car out and drove it home for you,' John said.

'You knew how to fix the damn thing because you've been tampering with it. I have a picture of you outside my home fiddling with it. The photo is dated after you returned the car to my house.'

'I-I was checking it was running okay,' Graham said.

'Funny, because someone had removed the ignition fuse when I tried it,' Shilpa retorted. 'And the other picture. I have it right here, and I can tell you exactly what you were doing. You see, I thought I was losing my mind when the keys to the garage went missing, when I could hear noises in there. Then when the keys did reappear, when you decided to return them to me, I went in there and saw some of the dust marks on the floor. Some of the boxes had been moved. You had been removing evidence of Craig's existence.'

Graham and John didn't respond.

'I thought that my bigoted aunts had removed any trace of a gay lover from Dipesh's house, but I realise now that you must have had a key. My trusting uncle had given you a house key, which you returned to me, but not before you had a copy made. You used it to access my house and take my spare car key to tamper with the fuses. You took the garage key and searched my property for anything incriminating. That evening on your boat, at dinner, you asked me if I had been through my uncle's things. Now I know why. I mistakenly accused my aunts of destroying Dipesh's old photo albums, but it was you. I had told you that all my uncle's boxes were in the garage. It's why you concentrated your efforts there. You might have looked for Dipesh's belongings in the house as well, but you missed that one album because it was buried under some books.

'You've done nothing but lie to me,' Shilpa said. 'Why did you tamper with my car? Did you want me to die as well?'

'I didn't take your spare car key. You always leave it open. Anyone could have tampered with it.'

'But it wasn't just anyone. It was you. You were angry that I had discovered my uncle's photo album. You wanted to cause me distress because I had asked you about my uncle's lover.'

'It was just the ignition fuse on a car that was playing up,' Graham snapped. 'It was hardly going to cause a fatality.'

'Shut up,' John said, giving Graham a stern look.

'She has the pictures,' Graham said. 'She knows it was me.'

'We haven't seen anything yet,' John said, lunging for her. He grabbed the phone out of her hand, and as he did so, Graham held her back. Shilpa was so weak compared to him.

She tried in vain to wriggle out of his grasp, but she couldn't. John scrolled through her pictures.

'Was it an accident?' she asked Graham, her tone softening.

'Craig?' Graham said. 'He knew too much. He came onto our boat much like you have now and confronted us. I pushed him. It was an accident, but once it happened, it happened, and we thought it was best he was out of the picture.'

'Shut up,' John growled. 'Photos don't prove anything.' He waved the phone around in his hand.

'Confronted you about what?' Shilpa asked.

'He knew what we were doing at the Drews',' Graham said. He turned to John. 'She knows. She already knows what we've done.' Graham let go of her hands and sat down. He looked defeated. John disappeared inside the boat with her phone. She wanted to stop him, but Graham was ready to talk. She didn't want to give him any time to change his mind.

'The Drews?' Shilpa asked, sitting next to him. Graham explained how John's niece worked for the Drews, doing the accounts for some of their oldest customers. The Connollys were one of her clients. It seemed like the Drews and the Connollys were intrinsically linked. John's niece had been covering up his fraudulent activities while working for the Connollys. Graham explained how John would create fictitious suppliers and pay them through the books. For such a large shipbuilder, their purchase order and supplier set-up was anti-quated, so it wasn't difficult to do. Graham's reasoning for why they were embezzling from the Connollys was that they needed the money for her uncle's mooring, which they paid for along with the fuel. 'Living on a boat is more expensive than you'd think,' Graham said. Craig had found out what they were doing from someone he knew who worked in the Connolly finance team.

'He confronted you that day on the boat,' Shilpa said. She remembered Tanvi overhearing two graduates at Drew

Accounting talking about gaps in the Connolly accounts at their digital launch party. She hadn't paid attention at the time, but somehow this was connected to her uncle's death. Shilpa swayed and realised that the boat's engine had started. Graham was looking out towards the other side of the estuary. She looked back to the father and son on the somewhat exposed slipway. The tide was going out. John wouldn't want to be stranded on the estuary with no means of escape, and she didn't want to be stuck in the middle of the ocean with two murderers. She looked up towards Elaine Alden's house. The old lady was sitting by the window. She waved, but Shilpa didn't dare wave back and risk Graham seeing her. Instead she turned back to Graham as he started to speak again.

'We got into a scuffle. I'm not sure how. I think John pushed him and he pushed back. John retaliated. There was a bit of a scrap. Craig said he was going to tell the Drews and the Connollys what we were doing. I pushed him, and he fell backwards onto that table,' he said, his eyes focused on the lethal object. 'That stupid thing. I told John we had to sort it out, but it was always tomorrow, tomorrow.' The table was fixed to the deck. It looked old, but the edges were sharp, and the height was definitely a trip hazard – an addition by the previous owners, probably. It wasn't something a boat builder would install. 'He fell badly. He was knocked out. He was dead.'

'You could have called the coastguard. You could have taken him in the tender to the shore.'

'We panicked. We waited till nightfall when we had the tide on our side, then we went out towards Fish Cove, where we wrapped, weighted and dumped the body,' Graham said.

'And Dipesh?' Shilpa asked. The boat had started to move. John lived by the tide. They would soon be out of Elaine's line of vision. If they were going to do anything terrible to her, let them do it with a witness present.

Graham was silent.

'He knew? Is that why he had to die too?'

'He didn't know. Craig hadn't told anyone. In that respect, the man was decent.' Graham put his head in his hands. 'He was a pretty sound guy.'

'So then why did you kill my uncle?' Shilpa was standing up now. She held her clenched fists by her side and steadied herself as the boat made its way down the estuary.

Graham started to weep. 'He was worried about Craig. He didn't believe that his partner would just go off like that.'

John appeared on the deck. 'I told you to write a letter from Craig to Dipesh,' he said to Graham. 'But you didn't listen.'

'Your uncle was insistent,' Graham said, wiping his tears. 'The day he died, he had come aboard. He wanted answers. We agreed to go back to his and talk it through.' Graham looked up at Shilpa. 'We're not what you think we are. We wanted to explain. The whole thing with Craig was an accident.'

Shilpa shook her head. 'You're telling me you just happened to have a fatal injection of potassium chloride on your person when you went to see my uncle?'

Graham looked to John. John looked at Shilpa. 'Your uncle wouldn't let it drop. He was insistent that we had done something to Craig. Clearly that kind of stubbornness must run in your family.' John dropped Shilpa's phone into the estuary. 'You won't be needing this,' he said.

Shilpa watched as the phone disappeared under the water. 'What the hell,' she said.

'Your uncle had a heart attack. Get over it,' John said.

'She knows about Craig. Just tell her,' Graham said. He looked relieved to have confessed.

John grunted but didn't say anything. The boat was moving away from Elaine's house. She dared not look up to see if the old woman was still watching. She had to make a decision.

Either wait till Graham confessed or jump. She looked at Graham. His head was back in his hands. She was confident she could make him talk. Then she looked at John. She noticed now that he was holding some old rope and duct tape in his hands.

She couldn't risk staying if she wanted to get out of this situation alive. Graham and John had killed both Craig and her uncle. They had even tampered with her car hoping that it would unsettle her. It was the start of a campaign to discourage her from settling in Devon and learning about Dipesh's life. She had seen the photos Alison had taken whilst she had been stalking her proving that Graham had previously been meddling with her car and her house. Graham could easily have tampered with her car again. It was likely that he took the ignition fuse out of her car after she started asking questions about Craig.

John stepped towards her. 'You'll be reunited with your phone,' he said. Shilpa took one look at John and then at Graham, who hadn't moved, his head still in his hands. In one move, she manoeuvred herself to the boat's edge and jumped over the side into the icy depths of the estuary.

The water was cold and winded Shilpa as she sank into its murky depths. She used all her strength to push her way back to the surface to try and breathe, but the icy water had her in its grip. She couldn't catch her breath. It felt as if someone was squeezing her chest. The eelgrass and bladderwrack clung to her legs as she thrashed around in the water, trying to find solid ground. The tide was going out. She had that on her side, but she had underestimated just how deep the water was. It would take at least an hour before the water was shallow enough for her to find a footing and steady herself. It made her panic; her breath was already shallow and reaching, her clothes heavy. She couldn't keep herself afloat for much longer.

She closed her eyes. Her face was just above the water. 'Take a deep centring breath,' she remembered a yoga teacher in London once saying to her group when they were talking about panic attacks, which she had never suffered from. Now she took a breath and tried to clear her mind of negative thoughts. Surprisingly, even though her arms and legs were still flailing about, she felt calmer. She could do this, she told herself. She looked around for the catamaran, which was some distance away now. A figure standing on the deck was watching her. She had been foolish to jump, but how foolish? John would have had no issue binding and gagging her and throwing her out to sea halfway to France. They had pretty much done it to Craig, and they had set out and succeeded in killing her uncle. They were evil. They just masqueraded behind normality. Shilpa started to tread water, just like she had been taught in swimming school when she was young. She was still kicking though, searching in vain to feel something solid under her feet.

Fat raindrops fell from the sky. She looked up towards her house, but the rain spatter made it impossible to see. She couldn't identify anything behind the glass of her bi-fold doors. Her eyes moved from her house to Elaine's. Elaine was standing at the window, leaning on the large pane of glass. She was just a blurry silhouette, but Shilpa tried to focus, wiping the rain off her face. She saw then that Elaine was frantically waving at her. Relief flooded her. Elaine would have called someone. She just had to hang in there or try to swim to safety. For the next five minutes, she tried to swim towards the shore, but the tide was stronger than she had ever imagined, and she soon saw that she was being dragged out with it. She was beginning to lose hope again when she heard what sounded like a speedboat heading in her direction. She looked towards the noise and saw a flash of orange and white. She recognised the colours of the Mermaid Point rescue station. She had only seen them in action once before, when a young family got caught with the tides and found themselves stuck in the thick sludge of the estuary on a cold and wet day. Thank goodness for Elaine. She hoped Mrs Alden could see her relief, her gratitude, but when she looked up again, she realised she had drifted quite a way from her house.

Chapter Forty-One

'Your week isn't getting any better, is it?' Tanvi said, handing Shilpa a hot chocolate. Shilpa was still shivering despite a hot shower and a change of clothes. She took a sip of her warm drink.

'That feels good,' she said. The coastguard had rescued her. Ordinarily she would have felt embarrassed, but she was grateful that she was alive and that they had turned up so quickly. She didn't think she could have stuck it out in the icy water that much longer. She could still taste the fetid, brackish water she had swallowed when she had jumped into the estuary and the cold had seeped into her bones. She wondered if she would ever feel normal again. She took another sip of the sugary drink and swallowed down the taste of the estuary. Her hands trembled as she warmed them around her mug.

She felt quite lost without her phone. She had no idea what Theo's telephone number was, and she needed him to know what had happened. The coastguard had wrapped a foil blanket around her after they pulled her from the water and had called a police officer to the rescue station as they made their way back to Mermaid Point. The officer had been waiting for her when she got there, as well as a paramedic, who had checked her over after she changed into dry clothes. Finally, an hour or so later, she had been given the all-clear.

'What happened to the boy and his father?' Shilpa had asked the officer, concerned that she had left the two stranded in her quest to speak to John and Graham.

'Who?'

'I borrowed a boat from a young man and his son,' she said.

The officer looked at her blankly and then walked away and spoke to a colleague. He returned minutes later and told her the man and his son were safe and well. 'They managed to walk along the pier and the foreshore back to Estuary Road before the tide came in,' he said, giving her a look.

Shilpa breathed a sigh of relief.

The officer had taken her statement and assured her that they would find the catamaran and its owners for questioning. The young man taking her statement looked at her sideways, wondering whether to believe her story about Craig and her uncle. In that moment, it didn't matter. They would have to investigate, and Theo would see to that. The officer seemed even less interested in her personal reasons for wanting to get a message to Theo.

'I can give you his station number,' he said. Shilpa had taken the number down the old-fashioned way on a scrap of paper, which she had pocketed in the joggers they had given her to wear. She later passed the number to Tanvi when she reached home. Shilpa looked at the clock on the wall. Her watch wasn't waterproof and had stopped. Tanvi had called Theo over an hour ago and left a message for him to call back on her mobile urgently. He still hadn't called. Is this what it would be like dating a detective sergeant? Never knowing when he would call back; prioritising other people's lives over hers? His job was important. She couldn't expect him to have the same freedom as someone who ran their own business selling cakes, but she wanted him to prioritise her just a little. By the way Tanvi was looking at her, she could tell that her friend was thinking the same.

'He'll call,' Tanvi said, her face belying her optimism.

'We've not been dating long.'

'Whoever said that expectations are preconceived disappointments was right.'

'That's the Tanvi I know and love.' Shilpa looked over to her friend and smiled. She heard the front door open and looked up.

It was Brijesh. He held up a paper bag with fine rope handles. 'It's the least I could do,' he said. 'Allowing me to stay here indefinitely. And you introduced me to Tanvi,' he added, looking at her friend with warmth in his eyes.

Tanvi walked over to Brijesh and took the bag from him. She put her hand inside and retrieved a white box. 'A phone. How clever of you,' she said, kissing him on his cheek.

Tanvi and Brijesh looked so content with each other, and although she was happy for her friend, it made her feel a little envious. She wanted a little comfort right now.

'That's so generous,' she said.

Tanvi put the box back into the bag and handed it to Shilpa, who had a distinct feeling of déjà vu telling her she was tired. She looked at the bag that was so much bigger than needed, and it triggered something, a memory, just out of reach. She spent a moment trying to figure out what it was, but it evaded her.

'You okay?' Tanvi said.

Shilpa nodded. 'Yeah.'

'That officer who dropped you off told me to keep an eye on you. You've had a traumatic experience.'

'I know, but I'm fine.' Shilpa reached into the bag and pulled out the phone.

'I can set it up for you. You laughed at me working at a phone shop, but it comes in handy.'

'We didn't laugh,' Tanvi said, trying to keep a straight face. 'Anyway' – Tanvi looked at her watch – 'how did you get this? It's like the middle of the night. Surely the phone shop isn't open.'

'Don't worry about it,' Brijesh said.

Tanvi stared at him.

'I didn't steal it!' Brijesh said, looking wounded. 'The manager was working there tonight.'

'At a phone store?'

'You Londoners are not the only ones who work late.'

'Okay,' Tanvi said. 'Don't get defensive. You've just started there, so it's a bit curious.'

Brijesh pulled a paper from his pocket. 'Here's the receipt if you want to check it. Look, in India, if you need a favour, you ask. People don't ask here, so they don't get.'

Tanvi nodded, looking slightly impressed.

'I didn't need a phone urgently,' Shilpa said. 'Tomorrow would've been fine. I hope you don't owe them on account of me.'

'If I thought I was going to be grilled like this, I would have left it till tomorrow. I needed to pop into the store. The manager was there. I asked him if I could pick up a phone. I paid for it and everything.'

Shilpa stood up and walked over to Brijesh. She hugged him. 'Sorry. I guess we're all a little paranoid at the moment. Thank you. I really do appreciate it. Although I'm terrible with phones. It'll probably take me a week to set up.'

'You were on Apple before, right? I can pretty much restore your phone for you. You won't even know the difference,' Brijesh said. 'You just need to call your phone provider and get them to send you a new SIM.'

Shilpa made a face. 'I think my iCloud storage was full. I

kept getting reminders. I'm sure I'll have lost some photos. I should have made up actual albums,' she said. She wanted to say like her uncle had done but refrained.

'Don't you use a photo web portal to save all your photos, like Google Photos or something? I think the popular one here is Herring Photos. It doesn't have the most sophisticated security and malware programmes, but it does the job. Depends how precious you are about your photos. And you have to consider who can get hold of them. You'll have heard about ransomware. People can hack your photos and blackmail you before they give them–'

'We get it,' Tanvi interrupted. She looked at Shilpa. 'Are you sure you're all right? You look a little spaced out. Maybe you should lie down or something.'

'I'm fine,' Shilpa said. 'I have a cake stall, remember?'

'It's almost eleven o'clock. Surely you don't need to do that now.'

Shilpa turned to Brijesh. 'What did you say about photos?'

'I was talking about using a photo-sharing site,' he said, not looking up from her phone as he switched it on.

Shilpa's eyes lit up. 'If I needed to have a look at someone's photos from their phone but I didn't have it, would you be able to get into their photos?'

'If they used a site like Herring then yes, I'm sure I could.'

'What are you thinking?' Tanvi asked.

'Alison was a serial stalker,' Shilpa said.

'Some may just call that amateur photography,' Brijesh said, logging onto Shilpa's laptop, which was on the kitchen island. Tanvi walked over to Brijesh and stood behind him, peering over his shoulder while he navigated the Herring Photo website.

'But she was murdered,' Shilpa said. 'And her phone was taken. Whoever killed her took her phone and any photos she had printed because they were incriminating. If we could see what other photos she had, then maybe we could find out who killed her.'

'She showed you her incriminating photo. It didn't prove anything. You said it yourself,' Tanvi said.

'But what if there was another one, one that was more damning and she just didn't realise.'

'What's her handle?' Brijesh said.

'Her what?' Shilpa asked.

'You know, her name online, her username. It usually has an @ symbol before it.'

'No idea,' Shilpa said, 'but her full name was Alison Bishop. That's what it said online after her body was discovered.'

'Is this her?' he asked. Shilpa walked over and nodded, looking at the picture of Alison on-screen. 'Alison ran a small business,' Brijesh said. 'Felting, mostly woodland animals.' She looked at the little creatures and felt a pang of sympathy for the redhead who had been so brutally murdered.

'Has Steven Drew been charged?' Shilpa asked, recalling what the news reporter had implied before she had to go to Leoni's.

Tanvi picked up her phone. 'I'll check on the news app.' She shook her head. 'They haven't released a name yet. Although all the comments suggest it most definitely was Steven who was arrested.'

'Anyway,' Shilpa said, 'I've been thinking about it, and I don't buy it.'

'What?' Tanvi asked.

'If Steven killed Mason, why do it at his own house, at his daughter's engagement?'

'There were several stab wounds, from what I've read. It was a heat-of-the-moment kind of thing. He didn't plan it. It just happened.' Tanvi looked up from her phone.

'So why kill Alison?'

'Because like you said, she knew or she realised she had evidence, and he found out.'

'No luck,' Brijesh said. 'I've got her email from her website and I've tried to get into several photo-storing websites using her address. I can't get in.'

'Because you don't have her password,' Tanvi said, giving Brijesh a look. 'I can't believe we haven't looked her up on social media till now. We'd make rubbish detectives.'

'I don't think this is the email address she used for storing photos. She must have set up something else. Either that or she isn't using a photo-storing website.' Brijesh turned to Tanvi. 'If I had the right handle, I could definitely get in.'

Shilpa and Tanvi shared a look. 'So, what is it you really do at the phone place you're working at?' Tanvi asked.

Brijesh tapped the side of his nose. 'That would be telling.'

Shilpa patted Brijesh on his shoulder. 'Thanks for trying,' she said. She walked towards the bi-fold doors and looked out towards the estuary. 'Alison may have been crazy, but she warned me about my neighbours. She must have known something bad was going to happen, because she printed those photos. She must have wanted me to see them so I'd know.'

'Okay,' Tanvi said, standing up. 'I think you need to rest.'

Shilpa ignored her friend, suddenly remembering what it was about Brijesh coming into her house and carrying a bag that resonated with her. 'I think Alison realised something the day we met. Theo said that her dying words referenced a bag. And when I asked her about the woman in the black dress at Harriet and Mason's engagement party, she had this look on her face. Alison knew who the killer was or at least had a good idea. I strongly doubt it was Steven, so who was it?'

Tanvi shrugged.

'Exactly.'

Chapter Forty-Two

How much longer were they going to make him wait? Evan looked around the barren interview room. His knee was shaking. He placed his hand on it and then glanced at his watch. It had been over twenty minutes. He stood up and walked over to the door. He had voluntarily agreed to come to the station to answer some questions. He hadn't called in his lawyer because he had thought it would make him look cooperative, but in hindsight it had been foolish. They hadn't arrested him though, so he could just leave. Although it wouldn't look great.

Evan had seen them take Steven Drew away in a police car as he comforted Harriet. Margery had been fretting, not knowing whether to follow her husband to the station or to let him just get on with it. A strange look had come over her as they arrested Steven, somewhat akin to relief. But he knew from speaking to Harriet since that Steven hadn't been charged.

Drayton had been pretty smug escorting Steven Drew out of his home before he had a chance to finish his dessert. Evan felt quite relieved as he watched the detective open the car door for his future father-in-law. But it wasn't long before they were knocking on his door. To be honest, he was surprised it had taken them until now. They must have had their reasons. They always did. Had they been watching him, waiting for him to trip himself up? Harriet didn't know he had been asked to come to the station, and he hadn't told her. He would be late for their date, and she would be annoyed, but there didn't seem to be any phone signal in this concrete room. He could only imagine what a cell would be like. He shuddered.

They had wanted a set of elimination prints. 'Do you mind?' a policeman had asked.

Of course he minded, but he could hardly say that. Instead he had stupidly agreed. He entered a room where a portly policewoman instructed him on how to use the optical screen. He knew these would be run against the prints they had taken from the murder weapon. He had left the Drew house before Mason's body had been found, and he hadn't been on the original guest list for the party, which was how he had managed to evade having his prints taken before now.

Forty minutes after his last print had been taken, Drayton was interviewing him. He should have called his lawyer, because without a doubt his prints were on that knife.

'If I'd been the one to kill Mason, I'd have wiped my prints off the knife, don't you think?' he had challenged Drayton when asked.

Drayton just stared at him.

Evan could hear his mother's voice. 'You never know when enough is enough,' she'd say.

'You were not thinking rationally,' the detective said. 'Most opportunist criminals don't think logically because they are just that – opportunists. The perpetrator makes obvious mistakes.'

'Bloody hell,' Evan said. 'It wasn't me.'

'So, explain why your prints were on the knife. Were you a regular at the Drew household when Harriet was engaged to Mason?'

He explained that he occasionally visited the house. That he had been friends with Mason, sort of. The detective had accused him of moving in on Mason's fiancée a little too quickly. His love for Harriet was the perfect motive to want Mason out of the picture, and in all honesty, he couldn't deny that. Drayton had looked at him intently and asked him if he had left the party for any length of time. He swore that he hadn't.

Drayton looked down at a sheet of paper in front of him. '"In the thick of it" is how you described your presence. But you lied to us, Mr White. We've asked witnesses about your presence at Mason and Harriet's party,' Drayton said. 'You were there all right, but there are some gaps in your where-abouts. You weren't there the whole time, were you?'

Evan sat back in his chair. 'I was.'

'But not when the guests were being seated; you were noticeably absent from your table.'

'I probably went to take a leak,' Evan said. 'Not everyone was seated when we were told Mason had gone walkabouts.'

'From what I gather, it was quite a long absence.'

Evan laughed. 'It was probably a long loo break.'

Drayton's expression didn't change. 'So why were your prints on the knife?'

Evan folded his arms across his chest. 'That day at the party, I happened to be walking through the kitchen. I saw one of the caterers attending to some canapés, watched her for a moment, and then I just picked up the knife…' Evan trailed off, and Drayton looked at him expectantly.

'Do you make a habit of going into other people's kitchens and picking up their knives?'

Evan shook his head.

Drayton looked at the yellow A4 pad in front of him and then looked up. 'Can you see how this looks? There's absolutely no reason why your prints should be on that knife. You were having a relationship with the victim's fiancée. There's a credible motive, and your notable absence right before Mason was noticed as missing says you had the opportunity as well.'

Evan leaned forward, putting his clasped hands on the table. 'I picked the knife up to feel its weight. And my relationship with Harriet only started after Mason's death.'

'You had an on-off relationship with Harriet Drew for years.' Drayton looked at him and then at the video recorder.

'I respected her decision to marry Mason.'

'You like getting your way, don't you?' Drayton said.

'Doesn't everyone?'

'And you just like the feel of a knife in your hand? Can you expand on that a little?' Drayton said.

'It's just a thing I do,' Evan said, wondering if Drayton was buying any of it. How would it look if he called his lawyer now? Not good. Only the guilty called their lawyers. He explained that he was going into the knife-sharpening business with a friend. Sharpened knives delivered weekly or monthly right to their customers' doors. Butchers were already being provided with this service. His idea was to extend this deal to the general public. Then the detective had taken down his partner's details.

Evan looked at his watch. Forty minutes had passed. Had Drayton believed him? He pulled out his phone from his pocket again. Still no signal. He was supposed to be meeting Harriet in ten minutes. If Drayton came back and let him go then he could get away without telling her he had been called in for questioning. He peered through the small window in the door and then walked back to his seat and sat back down.

Perhaps the detective had been given a better lead and they

had forgotten him. It certainly wouldn't be a bad thing. On the other hand, Drayton could walk back in here and arrest him. Worse than that, he could charge him. Would he only get one call?

His knee jigged up and down. He checked his watch. Then he stood up and walked out.

Chapter Forty-Three

'I can't believe you're making me do this,' Tanvi said as they walked under the police tape. 'What if we get caught?'

Shilpa laughed. 'I can't believe you're the nervous one and I'm egging you on to do something illegal.' Her ordeal with Alison and then with Graham and John should have put the fear in her, and to an extent it had, but she found it had given her a new confidence. Twice now she had confronted the people she believed to have done wrong. She may not have been right in the case of Alison Bishop, but she definitely had something on her neighbours. Ordinarily she would never have had the nerve to do something like this, but she had realised over the last few days that you had to step out of your comfort zone to get to the truth.

'We could compromise their whole investigation. What if we tamper with some evidence without realising?'

'That's why I have these,' Shilpa said, handing Tanvi some blue overshoes and latex gloves.

Tanvi shot Shilpa a questioning look.

'Catering,' Shilpa said. 'You never know when you have to

handle something that requires gloves. They're Spontex. Did I tell you what Theo said?'

'That they haven't charged Steven and that they're working on another suspect.'

'Who could be Harriet,' Shilpa said.

'Black widow? If it's her, what are we doing here in the middle of the night?' Tanvi asked while Shilpa picked the lock. 'How do you know how to do that?' Tanvi was looking on incredulously. 'Who are you?'

Shilpa turned to her friend with wide eyes as the door opened. 'I didn't know I could until now. Result!' Shilpa crept into the apartment, and Tanvi slowly followed.

'I think Alison knew more than she was letting on,' Shilpa said, once they were inside.

'Do we turn on the lights or use torches?' Tanvi asked.

'Torches,' Shilpa said as she carefully looked around the apartment. There was still a bloody stain in the kitchen where Alison had been stabbed. A chill ran down her spine. 'Okay, let's be quick.'

'And what is it that we're looking for?' Tanvi asked.

'Anything suspicious. Anything to do with a black dress; a picture of anyone in black from the engagement party; bags.'

'Bags?'

'She mentioned a bag before she died. It has to be connected to either her death or Mason's.'

'You think she was keeping Mason's murderer in a bag in her apartment? Tanvi asked. 'I think the police would've found that.'

'Listen, Tanvi,' Shilpa said. 'Less backchat and more work.' Shilpa started opening and closing drawers and kitchen cupboards while Tanvi gently peered around the sofa. Shilpa shook her head and continued carefully opening and closing drawers.

'If there was anything of interest, the police would have found it, don't you think?' Tanvi said. 'Does Theo know what you're doing? I'm not sure he'd approve.'

Shilpa ignored her friend, although Tanvi was right. She had asked Theo this afternoon if they had found any evidence at Alison's, but he was reluctant to share any details, suddenly conscious about losing his job, especially after messaging her the two photos found at Alison's apartment.

'Alison gave me those pictures,' Shilpa had said, remembering the lie she told in her statement when she had reported what John and Graham had done. She had surprised herself at how quickly and easily the untruth had tripped off her tongue.

Theo had swiftly moved the conversation along, and instead she found herself talking about John and Graham. Their boat had malfunctioned and had been found grounded at a small harbour in Normandy. They had ditched the vessel and were officially on the run. It must have pained them to have to leave their home like that. She knew how much it meant to them, but she felt no pity. They deserved everything that was coming to them. She just hoped the police caught up with them.

Her idea to break into Alison's house had come to her after her conversation with Theo, but she didn't think it wise to share it with him. Plus, she didn't want to get him into any trouble. If he knew what she was doing, it could compromise his job and his position on the case.

Mason and Alison were both dead. Their deaths were most certainly connected. Her gut told her that while Steven may have had a hand in Mason's death, he wasn't the killer, and Theo said they hadn't charged him, which proved they had insufficient evidence. Alison had evidence to put the killer away. Shilpa's comment about the woman in the black dress had triggered something, and her words may have been what got Alison killed. It was therefore her responsibility to find out what she could to help catch her killer.

Whoever had killed Alison had killed Mason too. Theo had as good as confirmed it. Yet it seemed like the police had given up on Alison's flat. Even her comment about the bag as she was dying seemed to have been brushed aside.

'It's a dead end,' Theo had said.

'Did any of the guests have a bag with them?' Shilpa had asked.

'All the women,' Theo had answered sarcastically.

'You know what I mean. A bag of note.'

Theo had cut her short. 'If we could find her phone, that would be something.'

Maybe Alison's apartment was a dead end, but Shilpa wanted to take a look. She had been at the engagement party. Theo and the rest of the Otter's Reach police had not. There could be some clue that she might pick up on that they hadn't.

'Leave Theo out of this,' Shilpa said to Tanvi. 'Just keep looking. Anyway, you have your own criminal to deal with.'

'I know, right?' Tanvi said, sounding a little bit more cheerful. 'Who'd have thought Brij would be into hacking. Do you think he's doing something more than fixing phones at his new job?'

'Definitely. I did think it was odd that someone would give up a lucrative career in pharmacology just to repair old phones.'

'Do people even fix their phones these days? Surely they just buy a new one,' Tanvi said. 'I've gotta say though, a hacker makes a better boyfriend than a phone repair guy.'

'Snob.'

'It's just more exciting, that's all,' Tanvi said. 'I don't think he's hacking into anything major, that's if he's hacking at all. He's got too many morals.'

'He didn't seem too shy when it came to looking into Alison's photos. He was raring to go,' Shilpa said.

'That's different. Firstly, she's dead, and secondly, we're trying to catch her killer, not fleece her bank account. There's a difference. Hmm, my boyfriend, the hacker. I quite like the sound of that.'

Shilpa laughed. 'Did you just use the term "boyfriend"? This week is getting weirder and weirder.'

'Oh, shut up,' Tanvi said. 'I'll have a look in the bedroom.'

Shilpa ran her hand under the desk she was looking in. A tiny fox and rabbit looked up at her as she did it. The felt animals were putting her on edge with their tiny beady eyes, watching her illegal activity.

'I'm trying to find your killer, Alison,' Shilpa whispered. 'Just help me out here. Her hand felt something, like a piece of paper taped to the underside of Alison's desk. Shilpa bent down to take a look.

'Are you talking to yourself now?' Tanvi asked. Shilpa bumped her head as she tried to manoeuvre out from under the desk. 'Nothing in her bedroom or bathroom. A few bags, ugly ones I would never wear. Maybe she was referring to her poor taste in bags when she died. It could have just been a possible regret.'

'Look at this,' Shilpa said. Tanvi squatted and craned her neck to see where Shilpa was pointing.

'I don't get it,' Tanvi said.

Shilpa grinned. 'I think we have what we're looking for.'

'Don't you think it's strange that the police didn't find this?' Tanvi asked, and Shilpa couldn't help but agree. She felt uneasy as she took a photo of the email addresses and passwords. How had the police missed this?

'Come on, let's go,' Shilpa whispered.

Tanvi stood up. 'You're the boss, and quite frankly I'm

glad,' she said, eyeing a felted leopard. 'This place gives me the creeps.'

Shilpa rubbed her eyes and looked at her pitiful offering. She had done well to bake in the time she had, but it was still a paltry selection, and she wasn't confident in the taste of her baked goods either. She had let herself down. She was trying to make a name for herself in Otter's Reach – the go-to baker, the maker of fabulous cakes. She couldn't let her standards drop, and yet she had. But at least she hadn't pulled out at the last moment, leaving Kelly with one less stallholder. She had a good enough reason though, with what had happened to her over the last week. She looked at her watch. It was early, but already the market was busy with locals and tourists, and the two strong black coffees she had swallowed first thing didn't seem to be working.

'Two of those,' an old lady said, pointing to the cupcakes Tanvi had helped decorate. Shilpa boxed them and placed them in the lady's shopper before undercharging her. She sighed as she put the incorrect money into the tin. Perhaps she should have cancelled today after all. One day wouldn't have hurt, but she could hear her father's voice. 'You cancel once, *beta*, you make it a habit. You have a new business. Turning up is what you have to do to make it work.' Her father was right. Murder and espionage aside, this was her livelihood. She had to give it her all. But Tanvi was right too. She was delusional. Just what did she think she would accomplish by breaking and entering at Alison Bishop's apartment so late last night?

'You're distracting yourself because of what happened to Dipesh,' Tanvi had said on their way home in the early hours. 'Have you spoken to your parents about what happened?' Shilpa shook her head as she flicked the indicator and turned left. 'You need time to digest what happened. It has only been a couple of days since you jumped into the estuary, and here you are running about trying to be a detective. Maybe you're running on adrenaline, but… you learned something shocking about what happened to your uncle. This isn't something you can brush over with that gung-ho attitude of yours. Pick up the phone and speak to your mum. Dipesh was her brother.'

'I can't deal with their grief right now,' Shilpa said.

'Why not? What's holding you here? You could hop on a train with me in a couple of days. Just have some time out. Your business won't suffer as a result, I promise you. And you'll feel better for it. Trust me. You'll thank me.'

'What's happened to us?' was all Shilpa could think of saying. 'You're dishing out the advice with a boyfriend at home and I'm committing a crime.' Tanvi had taken the hint and had dropped the topic, but her friend was right. Her parents, especially her mum, deserved to hear the real reason for her brother's death, and they needed to hear it from her before the authorities called them. Theo was certain they would reopen the investigation now there was some question over the cause of death.

She picked up a mini muffin and popped it into her mouth. She was surprised that the taste was as good as if she had baked them without all the drama going on. No one would know that after breaking into Alison's apartment she had returned home and, unable to sleep, wondering if she had left anything out of place during their search, started baking. Perhaps her bakes were better when she was dog-tired and jittery.

In the light of day, the whole escapade to Alison's home had been foolish. She had realised that as the sun came up over the estuary giving the sky a pink luminosity. She felt foolish giving Brijesh her findings to hack into Alison's personal photo accounts. So, she hadn't given him what she had found despite having a photo of half a dozen email addresses and some cryptic letters and symbols which she guessed were passwords. Breaking into Alison's apartment had been pointless. Tanvi was right. She had been looking for a distraction.

As a woman approached her stall, she put on her brightest smile. She needed to pour all her energy into Sweet Treats and make a success of it. More than anything, she needed to forget about Alison and Mason. It was none of her business.

Chapter Forty-Four

Steven watched his wife water the basil and mint plants on the windowsill. The water caught the sunlight as she poured, reminding him of the simple things in life: warm summer days when Harriet was a toddler, playing in the garden and jumping over sprinklers in the heat of the sun. Life was more carefree then.

Margery had known about his affair with June. She had been into his study and into his bureau. He realised soon after Detective Drayton had asked him. How irrational he had been to think that she hadn't. To think that she was too timid to look through his things was reckless. He knew her better than that. He had just believed what he had wanted to preserve his own ego, so he could continue with his philandering. Margery was a kind and caring mother. He had seen her nurturing Harriet from a seven-pound baby into a young woman. She had nursed her when she was sick and had comforted her when she had a falling-out at school. Family was everything to Margery, and she wasn't ready to let that go. Margery would do what she needed to keep her family safe. It was one of the reasons he loved her, but he had lost sight of that, perhaps because Margery herself had lost her identity along the way.

Now, as he watched his wife trim the stalks of basil, he realised how serene she appeared. The anxiety she'd suffered before he had been arrested seemed to have dissipated. She wasn't fussing, and in the short time that he had been back, he'd noticed her manner with Harriet had improved. They were both making a concerted effort.

With his return from Glass Bay, things at home were definitely more settled, perhaps because the police didn't have enough evidence to charge him. The sense of foreboding had dispersed – certainly for Margery, it seemed – but as he watched his wife and thought about her extreme moods of late, he realised that the threat of something terrible was hanging over them.

'You went into my bureau,' Steven said.

Margery turned to look at him, her eyes devoid of any emotion. 'You thought I didn't know.'

When Margery had spoken of secrets a day before his arrest, he assumed she was referring to this; that she had an inkling about an affair but that she didn't know for sure. Now he was confident that she had seen the photos. He looked away from his wife's cold stare. *What have you done, Margery?*

'You saw the pictures?' he asked.

'You kept them.'

'I was going to dispose of them.'

'Then you allowed that woman in my house the day of the engagement for me to see you two together. Was that the plan?' She took a step closer to the knife block, but her eyes were fixed on him.

He watched her carefully, waiting for her hand to reach for

the thick black-and-steel handle. The knife used to kill Mason was still at the station, along with the knife block, but it had been immediately replaced with an identical set, which was typical of Margery's efficiency. He couldn't look at it without picturing Mason, eyes glazed over and bloody in their annex.

'That wasn't the plan. She is—' he started and then corrected himself. 'She *was* Mason's mother. It was his engagement party.'

'She was fawning all over you that day,' Margery snapped.

'She didn't come near me,' Steven said.

'So, you remember what she was doing? That's why you left to get something to eat, wasn't it? You lied to me. You could have waited for a burger or whatever, but you couldn't bear to be so close to her but not with her.'

'Margery—' he started, but his wife cut him off.

'I tried,' she said. 'I tried, like you tried with Finley.'

Steven stood up and walked towards her. Her face had fallen, her chin buried in her chest. He lifted her chin up with the tips of his fingers. 'Tell me,' he said softly. 'We've got through worse before. We'll get through this.'

'You tried to pay off Finley before, so when you made that payment to Mason, I assumed you'd done it again.' She looked up at Steven. 'I'm not stupid. I know what money goes in and out of our accounts.'

'I didn't say—'

'Just leave it. You made a large payment to Mason. I was curious as to why Harriet's fiancé was still here after you had paid him a large sum of money. I thought I'd take a look through your bureau that morning. It was logical. Your confidential items are only ever in that drawer that sticks. You think it's too much of an effort for me to open, but it's the place I first look when I'm suspicious. I expected to find something, but not that. Those pictures,' Margery said, her face pale and wretched. 'I still can't get them out of my mind.' She explained that with the party about to start and being unable to locate Harriet, she had decided to take a look in the envelope. Once she had seen what was inside, she knew it was true. She couldn't bear to hear Steven's excuses. She understood what the payment to Mason was for, and she hated him not just for the affair but for turning a blind eye to what kind of man Mason really was and still letting him marry their daughter.

'You should have come to me,' Steven said, slumping back into his chair. He put his head in his hands.

'You'd have only made it worse,' Margery hissed.

'Mason was Machiavellian,' Steven said.

'It takes one to know one,' Margery said. 'I saw red that day. I haven't felt like that in a long, long time. I thought that part of me had died years ago. That part of me that wanted revenge, wanted justice.'

'Would you rather not have known?'

Margery walked over to her husband and sat in the chair next to him. Tears stained her cheeks. 'Had I not known, I wouldn't have had to do anything about it.'

Steven reached out to her and took her hands in his as she folded forward.

'Mason was going to ruin us,' she said. 'What we'd built together. You were a fool to pay him and not tell me. He'd have kept taking money, and then what? He would have exposed you and your disgusting secret.'

'He was marrying our daughter. He wouldn't do that to her.'

Margery looked up at Steven. 'Ha!' she said with a mock laugh. 'He didn't care for his mother's feelings; why do you think he would care for our daughter's? You fool. You utter fool. You just don't see things clearly, do you? You didn't with Finley and not with Mason either.'

Steven closed his eyes.

'I wasn't going to sit back and let him ruin our lives and our daughter's. I have more guts than you do.'

'What have you done?' Steven asked.

Margery pulled her hands out of his and sat straight in her chair. She leaned back. 'I did what you should have done.'

Steven shook his head. 'No,' he said. 'It can't be.' He tried to see it from his wife's point of view. He tried to see what she was trying to save by committing this heinous crime, but he couldn't. He loved June. He knew that when he had hung on to those pictures, but Margery didn't see it.

'I saw him go to the annex. It was a strange thing to do in the middle of his engagement party, right before we were going to sit down for the meal. It was a little chaotic getting everyone to their table.'

'You followed him?' Steven asked, afraid to look at his wife, remembering that when he had returned to the party Margery was wearing something completely different to what she had dressed in when they had both got ready that morning. He hadn't been the only one to change that day. Steven held his breath, waiting for his wife's response.

Margery nodded.

Chapter Forty-Five

'You're that policeman's girlfriend,' the woman said as she approached Shilpa's stall. She picked up a small mango loaf cake from the display and handed it to Shilpa.

'That's £5.99,' Shilpa said.

The woman handed her a note. 'I see they've got Steven Drew at long last.' It was then that Shilpa placed her. She was Finley's mother; the same woman who had accosted Theo when they had been walking on Estuary Road. With everything that had happened since, she had completely forgotten her. 'I see that woman was killed by his hand as well,' she said. Shilpa gave the woman her change.

'I like mango,' the woman said. Putting the loaf in her bag, she retrieved a printout from the blog. She showed Shilpa the page. 'Another Murder', the post was titled, a picture of Alison, her hair as vibrant as ever, accompanying the story. 'I always knew the Drews were no good.' She leaned in towards Shilpa. 'That Harriet shouldn't get away scot-free though, should she?'

Shilpa realised why she hadn't initially recognised the woman standing in front of her. She looked completely different. Her hair had been combed back neatly and put into a bun. She wore fitted black trousers and a cerise top. Was it just the thought of Steven Drew behind bars that had lifted her spirits? She clearly didn't know that Steven had been released without charge. No one would know as yet, she supposed. That was definitely one perk of going out with a detective sergeant.

'I don't know what you mean,' Shilpa said when she realised Finley's mother was waiting for a response. She looked expectantly at a middle-aged couple standing about five metres away, willing them over. They turned away when she caught their eye and headed towards Olivia's Savoury Bakes.

'I saw her with this young woman,' Finley's mother said, jabbing her finger at the picture of Alison on the paper she held. 'I saw her with this woman the day she was killed.'

Shilpa looked at Finley's mother. The woman, although known for jumping to conclusions, or so she had been told, looked quite serious. Then she recalled the look of pure hatred Harriet had given Alison at Mason's funeral.

'You saw Harriet Drew with Alison Bishop the day she died?' she asked. 'What time?'

'It was late,' she said. 'But I live across the way from Alison, so I know what goes on. Alison keeps herself to herself usually. I can't say I normally take much notice of her. I only ever met her once, and she was quite polite. She was an orphan, you know. Both her parents died years ago.'

Shilpa realised she had been holding her breath. She let it out and inhaled deeply.

'I was checking on my neighbour's hanging baskets. She was away, you see. That's when I saw Harriet. She was pointing her finger at the poor girl, intimidating as the Drews are by nature. But that Alison looked rather pleased with herself, like the cat that had got the cream. Harriet certainly wiped the smile off her face though, because the next thing I know she's dead.'

Harriet must have been waiting for Alison outside her

apartment building. Alison must have called Harriet after chasing Shilpa halfway across Otter's Reach and frightening the life out of her. Harriet was the one in the black dress, and Alison had a photo to confront her with.

'You're certain it was Harriet?' she asked.

'I didn't see her face exactly,' said the woman. 'But it was definitely her. I'd know her anywhere. She was almost my daughter-in-law, remember. That dark hair and scarf tied around her head. It was her.'

Shilpa thought back to what Lewis had said at the Drews' digital launch party. He was a friend of the Drews, and he had recognised Harriet at the airport with Finley, describing her wearing a scarf in the same way Finley's mother had.

'Have you told the police?' Shilpa asked.

'Pff. Why should I? They don't believe anything I say, and they have their man. One Drew is better than none, which is more than I got for my Finley.'

Shilpa nodded. Two women approached her, enquiring after a slice of the rose-and-pistachio cake. She told them the price and started to cut into the cake. When she looked up, Finley's mother had disappeared. She wondered if she should tell Theo. She could mention it to him. But Finley's mother was right. She wasn't a credible witness. She had a vendetta against the Drews. Shilpa pocketed the money for the cake and then pulled out her phone. She selected the photos she was after and sent them to Brijesh with a short message explaining what she was thinking. Then she put her phone away and drummed her fingers on the table. She surveyed what remained of her baked goods and decided it wouldn't be good for her bank balance if she just packed up her stall now. She would have to be patient.

～

Brijesh and Tanvi were out when she returned from the stall. It had been a particularly tough morning, and she still had a box of cashew-nut-and-caramel cupcakes left. Now they sat temptingly on a ceramic cake stand she had bought last month from the local flea market. She looked at her phone again. Brijesh had responded to her message with a simple two words. 'On it.' She hadn't received another message, so she assumed that he had either not found anything, or he had been called into work. She considered calling him but refrained. Maybe he was out with Tanvi before she headed back to London.

She thought about what Tanvi had said. It was only right that she should head back with her friend and visit her parents. It would be much better than if they came to see her. This way she could control how long she stayed with them, and it would be less emotional telling them the real reason for Dipesh's death if they weren't in his house. She didn't have long. Theo had mentioned that it was likely the Crown Prosecution Service would make contact with Dipesh's next of kin quite quickly. This morning they had been in touch to tell her Graham and John had been found and arrested in Deauville.

Theo… he was an enigma. Their relationship had started so well, but it had been marred by murder, which seemed to surround them. She hadn't seen him in the last twenty-four hours, and his phone calls and messages were becoming a novelty. She liked him. She was sure they had a connection, and he had good reason to be so absent. They were closing in on the killer of Mason and Alison.

Earlier, as she had been packing up her stall, Olivia had bounded over to talk to her. She had heard from Danny about Steven Drew's release. Nothing, it seemed, stayed quiet for long in Otter's Reach, although she hadn't mentioned John and Graham. Was Olivia just being polite, or had word not spread that she had been letting her uncle's murderers use her mooring?

'So, who d'you think did it?' Olivia asked as she bit into a cupcake Shilpa had offered her. They both agreed that it wasn't Steven Drew. Shilpa's main suspect was Harriet after what she had heard from Finley's mother, but Olivia surprised her by putting her money on Evan, which was a change of tune after she had categorically said the man she knew was incapable of killing someone.

'I can change my mind, can't I?' Olivia said. 'It's not a crime.'

'But what made you change your mind?' Shilpa asked.

'I was thinking back to our school days. Evan was always getting into trouble. Nothing violent, but still, he never listened to the rules. If a teacher said not to do something, he would be the first to do it.'

'Like most rebellious boys, I would imagine.'

'Being a mum of three, I should know,' Olivia said. 'But he's always had a thing for Harriet. Everyone knows that. So, what if this thing turned into an obsession and he just, you know, snapped. People can do things out of character.'

'Remind me never to call on you for a character reference,' Shilpa said with a smile. She wondered if people developed obsessions as they got older or if it was a trait you displayed from a young age.

'Perhaps they did it together,' Olivia had said.

Shilpa slumped into her sofa. Alison knew who had killed Mason. Alison's photos, once discovered, would tell them exactly who it was.

Shilpa heard a key in the front door. She looked up and waited.

Chapter Forty-Six

'So?' Shilpa asked, as Tanvi and Brijesh walked through the front door.

'Charming,' Tanvi said. 'That's a nice greeting for your oldest and dearest friend.'

'I managed to get in,' Brijesh said, walking down the stairs. 'I didn't message you because I didn't want to get your hopes up.'

'What do you mean?'

'Alison Bishop had two photo accounts with Herring Photos. It wasn't hard to access with those emails and passwords you sent me. But honestly, I couldn't see any incriminating pictures.'

Shilpa looked expectantly at Tanvi, who was admiring her nails. 'Don't look at me. I was having a shower.'

'Can you get back in?' Shilpa asked. Brijesh padded over to her laptop. He opened the machine and started tapping away. She was going to miss him when he moved out next week. Her house would be empty without his presence and of course, Tanvi's; her friend always knew what to say to make her forget her worries.

'I'm in,' he said in a matter of minutes. She passed him a cupcake and stood behind him.

'I'm looking for photos of the engagement party,' she said. 'The 10th of August.'

'Brij said there was one of you,' Tanvi said as she filled the kettle from the kitchen tap and put it on to boil.

'Of me?' Shilpa said.

'Just in the background,' Brijesh said, navigating the webpage he was on and simultaneously biting into the cupcake Shilpa had handed him.

'Any more of me I should know about?'

Brijesh turned to look at her. 'I think you know about the rest.'

'I do?'

Brijesh swiftly opened a file on her desktop that he had previously downloaded. There were several of her with Danny in the town centre which made her cringe. There were also several of her house: Graham coming and going from her garage and then tampering with her car. Even though she had seen this last picture before, it sent a shiver down her spine.

'You're right,' Shilpa said. 'Let's move on from these.'

'So, the party,' Brijesh said excitedly. Tanvi made three cups of tea and put them on the kitchen island. She helped herself to a cupcake then stood next to Shilpa.

Brijesh opened another folder. 'I'm downloading these,' he said.

'There,' Shilpa shouted as a pixelated photo came into focus.

'What?' Tanvi said with a mouthful of frosting.

'A woman in a black dress.'

'But it's only her backside,' Tanvi said. 'A slim backside it is. She carries that dress well. Large hat, gloves. Ten out of ten for effort.'

'There must be another picture of her,' Shilpa said. 'She's

entering the house in this one. She must have just been arriving when Alison was outside taking photos.'

'Thank goodness for stalkers,' Tanvi chipped in.

'She is carrying a bag. A large paper bag.'

'Looks like an expensive present. The killer has good taste,' Tanvi said.

'Exactly,' Shilpa said. 'That's what she wanted people to think. That she was just another guest with a lovely gift in that big bag. A bag that no one would have taken notice of because it was, after all, an engagement party.'

'So, what was in that bag?' Tanvi asked.

'A change of clothes and foundation. There was a smear left in the sink.'

'So, she's vain and used it to touch up, especially if there was a scuffle between her and Mason.'

'Theo said some of the guests noticed a woman in a black dress, but no one recalled who it was. The person didn't want to be recognised, so she was probably careful not to show her face. After she killed Mason, she must have changed. If the bag contained a change of clothes, then maybe Harriet isn't the killer. She wouldn't have needed a change of clothes. She could have just slipped back into her bedroom.'

'So, the killer does her thing, changes her outfit and then plants the bloodstained knife back in the knife block – odd choice, if you ask me. Why not throw it in the bushes, or wash it up? Explain that,' Tanvi said. 'And why not bring your own weapon?'

'I'm not a detective,' Shilpa said, although she wondered if DI Drayton and his team had got this far. 'I need to see more photos, Brij.'

'Maybe she didn't bring a knife to the party because she hadn't planned on murder that morning,' Brijesh said. 'And also it would be risky bringing a weapon to a party. Someone could have asked to see what was in the bag.' Brijesh started clicking though the photos.

Shilpa and Tanvi peered over Brijesh's shoulders as they carefully examined the party photos Alison had taken from her car and then from the front and back garden. The lady in the black dress appeared a few times, but in each shot her face was obscured – until they got to the last still.

'I know who that is,' Shilpa shouted, pointing to the screen. 'I know exactly who it is.'

'So, you followed him, then what?' Steven asked.

His wife was studying her hands. 'I'd seen him earlier with the flame-haired woman. One of his exes, no doubt. There were enough of them at the party.'

'She wasn't invited,' Steven said.

Margery looked up at her husband. 'I know,' she said. 'I've spoken to Harriet, but I already knew because I had control of the guest list.'

'Of course you did.'

Margery sneered at her husband. 'I wanted it to be just right.'

'Appearances are everything.'

She ignored this comment. 'But she turned up anyway, and I saw her screaming at him, accusing him of ruining her life.' Margery stared at Steven.

'You didn't want that to happen with Harriet.'

'I'd seen your photos; I wasn't going to let him ruin our family.'

'He went into the annex and the red-haired woman followed him?'

Margery shook her head. 'She left. But what does that

matter? She's dead. She won't be held responsible for his death. That option is out of the question.'

'But she didn't do it,' Steven said. The enormity of what his wife was saying hit him hard.

'No,' Margery said, as if Alison's innocence were irrelevant. 'I followed him to the annex. I let myself into the garage after he had stomped up the stairs. I was going to question him, ask him why he was doing what he was doing and also why his ex-lovers were just turning up at our house. Would that happen to Harriet in their marital home? I wanted to protect Harriet. I always wanted that mother-daughter bond, but I'm not sure we ever had that. She bonded with you well enough. I always felt like the spare wheel, and I shouldn't. I'm her mother. All that wedding planning in her life and she still turns to you when she's in trouble.'

That wasn't the case at all. Harriet hadn't spoken to him about Mason. She had just got on with life. He had assumed at the time she'd spoken to Margery, spent her grief with her. Now he wondered why Harriet hadn't said anything to either of them. Margery was looking at him expectantly.

'So, you didn't go upstairs to the annex?' he asked, his tone softening. 'You didn't take the kitchen kni–'

Margery didn't let her husband finish. 'Mason was going to the annex for a reason. He was going to meet someone,' she said conspiratorially. 'The red-haired harpy had left, so it wasn't her, and I was curious to see who it was.' Margery smiled for the first time. 'It could have been you who he was meeting. Pleading with him to forget what he had seen you do with his mother.' Margery gave Steven a disgusted look, but then her face softened. 'Or maybe it would be Harriet just wanting to catch up with her fiancé for ten minutes, just to have some time out together.' She looked at Steven. 'We did that at our wedding, remember?'

Steven nodded. Margery sneered again. 'Or was it some

over, ex, or current, wanting to fornicate while our daughter waited patiently in the marquee.'

'And? Who was it?' Steven asked.

Margery's face fell. She took on a sombre expression. 'And then I saw her,' she said. 'She had the knife.'

Steven stood up. He started to pace.

Margery looked at Steven. 'You're worried,' she said. 'You're worried about what our precious daughter has done.'

Steven stopped pacing and turned to his wife. 'Tell me,' he said in a soft voice.

Chapter Forty-Seven

'No, I'm not going to approach her. I'm going straight home to have a hot bath and then I'm going to sleep. I'll wait for news of your imminent arrest,' Shilpa had said to Theo just hours ago when she had hurried to the station with printouts of Alison's photos. She had told him that she had seen some pictures Alison had taken at the engagement party and that she recognised the woman in the black dress from these photographs. Admittedly there wasn't a clear one of the suspect's face, but she knew just who it was, and she was certain she was the killer.

Theo had asked her how she came about the photos, a question she didn't really want to answer. She left Brijesh's name out of it, along with the fact that she had broken into Alison's apartment. But she had confessed to having looked at Alison's private online photo accounts. Theo hadn't leapt for joy like she had expected; instead he had raised doubt as to whether evidence obtained like this would be admissible, given the way the account was accessed. Did anyone have to know that she got there first, she had asked. If the police knew that

Alison had a Herring Photo account, surely they could just ask Herring Photos to disclose the information required. Theo hadn't responded to that, and she wasn't sure whether it was an issue or whether Theo was making it into something just because she had a lead. It didn't matter if they managed to get a confession out of the killer, she reasoned, but she refrained from saying any of this.

She hadn't expected to see the suspect on her way home, although admittedly she hadn't gone straight back to Estuary Road like she had promised Theo. She had parked her car at home, but the night was pleasant, and she thought she would give Tanvi and Brijesh some time together on their last evening before Tanvi headed back to London. After parking, she had walked into town and stopped for a coffee at Leoni's before she closed up. After an Americano and a quick gossip on the possible fate of Graham and John, she had wandered up to the deli at the top of the High Street to get something nice to have with drinks for Tanvi's last night. Then she stopped to look at an art show on at the hub, a multi-purpose room that was often used for art exhibitions, ad hoc yoga sessions and pop-up concessions.

She had lost track of time as she looked at the various displays: ceramics and pottery that revealed the beauty of the ocean and paintings that exposed just how violent the sea could be. One particular painting with waves ravaging the shoreline and weather-beaten timber houses spoke to her, reflecting how she had felt in the last few days. She was still undecided as to whether or not to return to London with Tanvi. Of course, she could take a train at a later date – it was only London, not Borneo she needed to get to – but travelling with Tanvi would be so much more bearable. It was early days with Theo, but she wished she could take him home with her, just for the support. Her mother's reaction wouldn't be a pleasant sight and was probably best avoided. Just thinking of her parents and having to tell them about Dipesh made her want a large glass of Malbec, and so she stopped for exactly that at the wine bar on the High Street that had once been Dipesh's fishing store.

The bar had been busy with tourists, and she could barely hear herself think, but as she left, she made a decision. She would follow Tanvi back to London a couple of days later. She would have to speak to Leoni about her delivery of cakes. With the encouragement from the red wine, she decided she would ask Theo if he wanted to come with her. Why not? Neither of them was getting any younger, and they both liked each other. Would her parents scare him off? Highly likely, but then again, he had a big family. He knew what overbearing parents were like; he had said it himself. With a plan formulated, she found she had a spring in her step as she left the wine bar.

She realised then that she still hadn't told Theo about her run-in with Finley's mother and what the woman had said about Harriet. She was so taken aback by Alison's photos and the information they contained that she had completely forgotten that Harriet was seen with Alison the day she was brutally killed. She was sure that Theo didn't have that information either. Perhaps she would make a good detective.

She felt a warm glow in her cheeks. The Malbec had hit the right spot. She quickly sent Theo a message asking if they could meet, but he hadn't responded, and she didn't fancy the drive or the sitting around at the station waiting for him. Instead she had started the long walk home.

With a raffia bag on her shoulder containing a selection of continental meats and a nice camembert, she approached the estuary. It was a quiet walk back; most tourists with families had already made their way back to their cottages and apartments, and the young were holed up in one of the bars in town.

It was then that she spotted the woman in the black dress from Mason and Harriet's engagement party. She was sitting on a solitary bench, watching the curlew and little egrets find their supper as the tide came in and nightfall descended on Otter's Reach. She almost hadn't recognised the woman because of her scarf tied around her head, but it was that very same thing that also drew her attention. The woman seen talking to Alison the day she died was wearing a scarf tied in that way. What was she doing here? Shilpa doubted a woman of her social standing would just sit by the estuary on a public bench watching the local wildlife. She took a step back into the shadows of the tourist kiosk that was positioned just metres away from where her suspect was seated.

Shilpa watched the woman, who every now and again looked at her phone. She was waiting for someone. Her suspect stood up abruptly and looked around. Shilpa took another step back and held her breath. There was no reason to; she was well hidden thanks to the time of day and the shadow from the overhang of the kiosk roof.

'Are you the lady from the market stall?' a voice came from behind Shilpa just as a man started to approach her suspect. Shilpa reluctantly turned towards the voice and stepped away from the kiosk in fear of being spotted by her suspect.

'You are, aren't you, love. I've tried so many of your cakes now and they are all so delicious.'

Shilpa smiled at the older woman. She wanted to turn back to see who her suspect was meeting but she couldn't. The woman was looking intently at her waiting for a response.

'I am,' Shilpa managed. 'I'm glad you've enjoyed them.'

'My Agnes is turning forty the first week in November. Do you think you could do something small for her?' the woman enquired.

Shilpa nodded. She took out a business card from her

pocket and handed it to the lady. She could hear a couple talking and she was certain one of the parties was her suspect.

'Oh goody,' the old woman said. 'Let me find my number too. It's best you have mine as well in case I lose yours. Then we can be sure to make the arrangements.' As the customer rummaged through her bag, Shilpa furtively glanced over at the couple who were deep in conversation, but the old woman said something and she turned back without having taken a good look at the man. She took a step back and craned her neck to hear what they were saying.

'I can't see you like this in public, especially here; you know that,' the man said. 'Not now.'

'I know,' she hissed. 'But after you called, I had to see you. You said you had it under control. You said that you had *her* under control.'

'I do,' said the man.

'It doesn't look like it to me. She knows. You said it yourself, and if she knows, who else knows? It's only a matter of time.' She paused. 'Fat lot of good you are.' Shilpa's heart skipped a beat. She knew that voice. She was desperate to turn around now.

'I'm protecting you,' the man said. 'This isn't my doing, so don't blame me.'

'Here you go, love,' the woman said, reeling off a number from a little pink diary. Shilpa swiftly added the number to her phone and said goodbye to the woman before she had a chance to ask anything further. She turned back to the couple.

'You told her too much.'

'I had to give her something. She was getting too close. What is it they say... keep your enemies close? I know what I'm doing. Do you think I'd risk my career for this?'

'You always think you know what you're doing. You never learn, do you? It may be just a game to you, but this is my life.'

'That was different.'

'You slept with a suspect. You're lucky you didn't get caught. No wonder you hot-footed it down to Devon. But that's all it was – luck, not scheming on your part. You're inept at that.' The woman shook her head. 'Did you really think that feeding her a few lies mixed with the truth would satisfy her?' She shook her head. 'Unless…'

'Unless what?'

'You actually like her. She's pathetic and you're no better. You're never the one in control. You think you are, that you can play at being God. That's why you gave her information about the case. You're on some kind of power trip. You're like your father – weak. No wonder Mama left him to be with mine,' she said, turning away from him. 'I'm not going down for this. I won't, because if I go down, I'm taking you with me, brother dearest.'

The man turned towards her. He reached out and put his hand on her shoulder. 'Ismene, I'm not going to let that happen,' he said. 'I promised you, and I promised Mama I wouldn't let anything bad happen to you.' As he spoke, he looked up towards the moon. His face was visible. Shilpa took a step forward, holding her hand to her mouth to stop herself from screaming.

Theo looked towards her. She took another step back and held her breath. He squinted. Satisfied that he was not being watched, he turned back to Izzy. How had she not seen the resemblance between them before, the dark hair and olive complexion? Admittedly, she had only seen Izzy a couple of times. They had different surnames, different fathers, as Izzy had just alluded, but standing together it was glaringly obvious that the two were related.

Shilpa recalled the family photograph she had seen in

Theo's house. He had talked about his half-sister who was missing from the photo, saying she was used to getting her way, but he had been quick to change the topic. Now she knew why.

Shilpa wanted to scream. She had been played. Theo and his sister had been talking about her. He had been feeding her lies from the start. There never was a girlfriend who had moved to Costa Rica like he had told her. He moved to Devon to get away from what he had done. His superiors clearly didn't know about it, because he was still a detective sergeant, but then what did she expect? He was a first-class liar. He had been telling her half-truths all along, like the foundation found in the sink. And it made sense now how she had found Alison's emails and passwords so easily. Theo had been supervising the officers searching Alison's apartment. He would have told his men that he had already searched Alison's desk to avoid them finding the evidence that incriminated his sister. But it would have been too risky to remove something from the scene of the crime without someone noticing. Had he planned to return to Alison's apartment later to remove and destroy it? Or had he hoped that once her apartment was searched there would be no further examination of the place? He had tricked her. He had sabotaged the investigation.

Izzy, dressed in an emerald-green pussy-bow blouse and black trousers, crossed her arms over her chest and sighed. 'I've done nothing wrong,' she said. Her eyes were steely, like she was readying herself for a fight.

Theo took a step closer to his sister. 'You killed Mason and Alison,' he hissed. Shilpa closed her eyes. She had been foolish to even suspect Harriet for Alison's murder.

Harriet had worn a scarf around her head the day that she was seen with Finley at the airport. That fateful trip that would cost poor Finley his life. But Harriet wasn't the only woman who wore a scarf like that. Izzy had adopted the same technique to hide herself from the public when she approached Alison outside her home.

Alison invited Izzy into her home knowing that she had photos of her in the black dress. She felt a stab of guilt. She had let Alison down and ridiculed the photo she had of Harriet and Mason with Izzy in the background. Alison was right: she was the killer, and yet Shilpa had dismissed her so easily. No wonder she didn't tell Shilpa immediately when she realised she had photos of Izzy in the black dress. Instead she had turned to the killer to confront her.

'They got what they deserved,' Izzy said. 'Mason didn't keep his promise, and so he had to pay. I suppose you could say it was my fault for believing him when he told me he loved me and that he was going to leave Harriet.'

'That isn't an excuse for what you did,' Theo said.

Izzy looked nonplussed. 'Did you know he was with me the whole time he was with her? Harriet thought he was still interested in Alison, and I may have done something to fan that fire. I played the perfect mistress. It was quite enjoyable, but one can't be a mistress forever, can one? Do you know he pleaded for his life at the end? He said I was the only woman he'd ever loved, but of course it was too late then. I wasn't going to be taken in again.' Izzy laughed, then she stopped abruptly.

Shilpa took a breath. It explained why Harriet hated Alison, and it stood to reason that Alison hadn't been invited to the engagement party. But it was Izzy who had been sleeping with Mason. Izzy had remained friends with Harriet only to deceive her. Leoni had said that Izzy's relationship with Mason was brief and that Izzy had been the one to break it off. Leoni had been misinformed, but then she had confessed that her intelligence wasn't up to date, as Izzy had moved away a couple of years ago. It also explained why Leoni didn't know that Izzy was Theo's half-sister, given that he had only moved to Devon after Izzy had moved away from Otter's Reach.

Theo shook his head. 'You're crazy, you know that? I can't help you. You say that I like playing games; that I play God. But what were you doing? You killed Mason at a party where there were witnesses, not to mention cameras. You even put the murder weapon back in the kitchen. How could you be that stupid?'

Izzy scowled. 'You have to help me. I'm family. Imagine Mama's grief if I were to go down for this. And anyway, killing Mason at the party was a stroke of genius. I mean, there may have been witnesses, but that also meant there were suspects. I asked Mason to meet me in the annex. I wanted to confront him about his marriage to Harriet as he had previously refused to meet me alone. He didn't have a choice at the party because he was worried I would make a scene if he didn't meet my demands. I took the knife from the kitchen as I was passing through. Just in case.'

Theo shook his head.

'Alison nearly ruined it by approaching Mason and screaming at him for a good five minutes before he could get there. I followed him. After I told Mason what I thought of him and pulled the knife out of his chest – I underestimated how difficult it was to do that – my black dress was completely ruined, so I had to change, but that was the plan if things got a little out of hand, which they did. Black suits me, but it isn't really my signature colour, so I thought it was a good decoy. I changed, put my clothes in the bag and walked out to my car, put the bag in the boot and went back to the party in my fabulous green Matthew Williamson number.

'I suppose I was a little foolish with the knife. I should've taken it with me as well, but I panicked a little. I thought it would be better washed up and put back in its place. But that girlfriend of yours ruined that for me. She was faffing in the kitchen with that cake, and there were too many people. I guess

I didn't really think that part through. I should have washed the knife in the annex kitchen.'

'Why didn't you?' Theo asked.

'I just needed to get out of that room quickly. There was so much blood. After I changed, I took the knife out of the bag and popped it back in its place as I walked through the kitchen and out to the car to deposit my bloodstained clothes. I didn't want to keep the murder weapon in my car,' Izzy said, as if keeping her distance from the murder weapon would absolve her from her crimes.

'I'd assumed some minion of the Drews would have found it and cleaned it long before Mason was found,' she continued. 'I'd worn some lovely silk gloves when I touched the knife, so I wasn't too worried.'

Theo shoved his hands in his pockets. He closed his eyes. 'And Alison?' he asked.

'Oh Theo, stop being such a drama queen. I didn't want to kill her but she gave me no choice. She called me, the fool, saying she knew I was the woman in black at the party that some guests recalled seeing but couldn't identify. She said she had evidence. She was thrilled that some of her photos were finally going to be of use. I killed her to protect us,' Izzy said, like she had done Theo a favour.

Theo took his hands out of his pockets and rubbed his temples. 'We need a better plan. I have an idea, because I can't hide the evidence–' he started to say, but he stopped. He looked in Shilpa's direction.

Shilpa took another step back and bumped into a metal bin fixed to the outside of the kiosk. The sound of the clanging metal was deafening. She froze as Theo started walking towards her. She looked behind her and momentarily thought about running. It was no use though. She knew Theo; she had felt the strength in his arms, his legs. He could easily outrun her, and once he caught up with her, what would he do? Would he silence her, or would Izzy do that for him?

She had to think, and fast. She had two options. She could smile her brightest smile and tell him that she was just walking past, pretend she hadn't heard what she had. It was unlikely he would believe her. Her other option was to simply tell the truth; to confront this man she had been falling for, this man she was just hours ago considering taking home to introduce to her parents. But before she had a chance to make up her mind, Theo was upon her.

'You need to go home,' he said. 'Get out of here.'

Shilpa could have nodded, taken his advice and removed herself from this situation, but something stopped her. Theo wouldn't let her go that easily, would he? Not after what she had heard. He would come after her. She wasn't sure of it, but the thought filled her with fear, and she found she couldn't move. Izzy was walking towards them.

Theo turned. 'We need to go,' he said to his sister.

'And leave her here? No way. She knows.' Izzy stared at Shilpa with cold, dark eyes.

'She doesn't know anything, Ismene.'

Shilpa was silent. Theo was trying to protect her; at least that was something. But when she looked up at him, there was something menacing in his eyes. The knot in her stomach tightened. She would phone Drayton immediately. He had given her his number when she had been interviewed after finding the knife. She just had to get away.

'Stop calling me that. It's Izzy now,' Izzy said. She hadn't taken her eyes off Shilpa. 'We can't let her talk.' She took a step towards Shilpa and in one deft move yanked her hair. 'It's dark and sheltered from view over there,' Izzy said, pointing to a part of the estuary close to town that was shielded by a wall.

'Oww,' Shilpa screamed. Izzy hadn't let go of the hair in her hand. She pulled again and then started to drag her owards the estuary. Shilpa's raffia bag fell to the ground, the contents spilling onto the pavement. Her old Mulberry dragged along as Izzy pulled her. Shilpa tried to overpower her, tried slumping to the ground and even tried to kick, but it was all in vain.

'A little trip over the side of the estuary and you could bump your head really badly,' Izzy said. Theo looked around and then grabbed hold of Shilpa's legs.

'That metal handrail of the ladder down to the mudflats,' Izzy said. She looked at Shilpa. 'You could fall and hit your head on it. You'd pass out and drown in the incoming tide, and they'd find you in the morning, wouldn't they, Theo?' She looked back at him. Her lips, painted a bright red, formed a smile. 'He'd be devastated, heartbroken. You really thought that she was the one.'

In another quick movement, Izzy pulled something out of her bag and hit her over the head. She opened her eyes to see a small crowbar in Izzy's hand.

'What the—' Theo started.

'Oh, shut up,' she said. 'We have to finish this.'

'Yes,' Theo sneered, 'but not like this.'

Shilpa groaned. Her vision was blurred and she gasped for breath. She must have momentarily blacked out because her attackers had swapped positions. Her arms were being held by Theo, and Izzy was holding her feet. It was as if they were about to give her the bumps at a birthday party, but this was no party. They were going to knock her out and throw her into the estuary. The tide was coming in fast now.

'I could tell Drayton that I've found evidence at her home,' Theo said. 'Her prints were on the knife used to kill Mason, and she had an altercation with Alison before she was murdered.'

Izzy seemed to consider this. 'No,' she said after a minute. 'My idea is better.' She smiled at Shilpa. 'Another swing of this is needed,' she said, looking at the blunt metal instrument in her right hand along with Shilpa's left leg.

Warm liquid trickled down Shilpa's neck from the throbbing pain above her left eye. She assumed it was blood. She could barely see straight and her head was aching. She wasn't sure if Theo was holding her up or just trying to restrain her. She felt him squeeze her wrists a couple of times as if to reassure her, but she couldn't trust her own judgement, not through the pain.

Shilpa must have passed out, she wasn't sure for how long, but when she opened her eyes again and came to, she heard Izzy ask her if she was ready for the final blow. 'The estuary has filled up nicely and is suitably high for you to drown,' Izzy said.

Izzy tightened her grip on the crowbar, her hand shaking with anger. Shilpa opened her mouth to say something, but nothing came. She felt nauseated. Eventually she heard some words leave her mouth, but they were incomprehensible. She tried again.

'The photos,' she said, struggling for breath. 'You took... Alison's phone, but I've seen... all her photos. My friends... have too.'

Izzy was silent. Shilpa didn't know for how long, but she had to finish what she wanted to say. It was the only way she could possibly save herself.

'You were seen... outside Alison's apartment... the evening she died,' Shilpa said, taking deep breaths, which sent pains shooting down her spine. 'You can get rid of me... but what about the real witness?' Her words seemed to have the desired effect. Izzy hesitated and at the same time Theo let go of Shilpa's hands. Despite her poor vision and the excruciating pain, she managed to scrabble to her feet. She stumbled past Theo and found her last ounce of strength to run towards the nearest house.

'You idiot,' Izzy shouted to Theo as she started to chase after Shilpa, but Theo caught up with her and held her back.

'No,' he said. 'It's over.'

Izzy kicked and screamed as he held her, his arms locked around hers until Shilpa entered the house whose door she had been banging on.

'It's over,' Theo said, letting go of his sister. Izzy turned, slapped him across his face and fled.

Chapter Forty-Eight

Tanvi kissed the top of Shilpa's head where the white gauze was taped with micropore to her shaved skin. She put her arm around her friend and gave her a squeeze as the train pulled out of Totnes Station.

'Well, that was a different kind of holiday,' she said. 'Definitely more exciting than Marbella.'

Shilpa tried a smile, but she couldn't really manage it. It was all behind her, yet the memories of last weekend were still so vivid in her mind she had trouble sleeping at night. The therapist the police had asked her to see soon after her ordeal had told her to keep a journal, to write down and rationalise her fears. She hoped that in time she would heal. Talking was another therapy that she discovered was starting to help, and Tanvi had turned out to be a good listener. Brijesh bringing out the best in her.

'Thank you for extending your holiday,' Shilpa said to her friend.

Tanvi waved away her gratitude. 'So, it was Izzy after all. *Ismene*,' Tanvi said. She pressed her lips together.

'You can say it,' Shilpa said.

'Theo's half-sister. Did Danny find out anything?'

'Izzy was determined to make Mason hers. He had promised to marry her. In fact, he had already asked her and then one day he called it off and proposed to Harriet.'

'I've seen a picture of him; he wasn't all that good-looking to have three pretty women running after him like that,' Tanvi said.

'Alison was infatuated. She wasn't used to getting attention. Mason gave her some and she became obsessed. Izzy was just after his money by the sounds of it, and like Theo said, she was just used to getting her way.'

'So Harriet was the real deal?' Tanvi asked as they pulled up to the Exeter station. 'She wasn't the one who went to Alison's house that day then, the day Alison was killed?' Tanvi asked.

Shilpa shook her head as the train started again, pulling out of the station. 'Finley's mother saw what she wanted to. She was convinced the Drews were behind her son's death, so when she saw a woman with a scarf tied around her head talking to Alison the day she died, she was convinced that the woman was Harriet.'

'Ah, so she only put two and two together once she found out Alison was dead.'

'Exactly. I believed her though. It seemed too coincidental that both Harriet's fiancés had died under suspicious circumstances and that she or her dad were not to blame. But it turns out that Finley's death was purely accidental. A journalist looking at the Connolly case dug up the coroner's report and associated investigation notes in Crete. She contacted me after my name was mentioned in the blog. The journo didn't believe there was any foul play involved.'

'Harriet was just a bit heartless getting engaged to Mason so soon after.'

'It's not a crime,' Shilpa said.

'It should be. Look at Jason,' Tanvi said, pulling out her phone. 'Phoebe sent me this.' She showed Shilpa a picture on her phone of Jason with his arms around another woman.

'Molly?' Shilpa asked.

'The same.'

'I'm sorry, Tanvi,' Shilpa said.

'I'm not,' Tanvi said, putting her arm around her friend's shoulders again.

'Izzy was the one seen speaking to Alison outside her apartment building the day she died. Danny told Olivia that the neighbour opposite, who was away at the time, had a camera outside her door. She thought someone was tampering with her hanging baskets, so she wanted to catch them.'

Tanvi laughed. 'Only in Devon.'

'They had clear footage of Izzy and Alison talking right before Alison was killed. She confessed to the crime when questioned. She could hardly deny it when they found Alison's phone at her apartment.'

'She didn't get rid of it?'

'She had hung on to the thing, and Margery Drew finally came forward saying she had seen Izzy follow Mason to the annex with the kitchen knife.'

'Why didn't she say anything sooner?'

'Turns out she was glad Izzy killed him off for some reason or another.'

'What a strange lady.'

'Indeed.'

'So it was all Izzy.'

'Theo's half-sister,' Shilpa said with a distant look in her eye.

'What a creep,' Tanvi said. 'You're better off without him.'

'He wasn't all that bad,' Shilpa said. 'He saved me at the end. If he hadn't let go of my arms, I wouldn't have been able o escape. I'd have drowned in the estuary that night.' Shilpa touched her bandage and looked out towards the green fields.

Tanvi pulled away slightly and looked at her friend. 'Don't take up for him, Shilpa. He tried to cover up what his sister had done. He prevented his officers from finding vital evidence in Alison's apartment and made up the stuff about the foundation on the sink just to confuse you. He was a detective sergeant. That's so unethical.'

'He did tell me about the black dress. Although I don't think for a minute he expected me to meet Alison and tell her.'

'And look what trouble that bit of information caused. He should never have disclosed that, especially in his position. They have rules about that.'

There was a silence between the two friends.

'Anyway, when have you been concerned with ethics?' Shilpa said. 'You know what it's like with family. And don't worry about Theo. According to Danny, it's over for him. I don't think he'll be on the beat anytime soon.'

'I should think so,' Tanvi said.

'He handed himself in soon after the incident on Saturday night. They found Izzy at her house, packing. She was pretty confident that she had time to pack! She was so delusional.'

'I don't suppose she'll need much where she's going now. And you need to stop defending Theo.'

'I'm not defending him,' Shilpa said, shrugging off her friend's arm. 'I'm just saying he could have been worse.'

Tanvi laughed. 'I can hardly talk; it turns out I'm dating a hacker!'

'You're pretty happy about that, aren't you?' Shilpa said.

Tanvi gave her friend a wry smile. 'Like I said, it's more exciting than dating someone who fixes smashed phone screens.'

Brijesh walked down the aisle towards them carrying a tray of hot drinks. 'Sorry, got stuck chatting to someone. Here you go,' he said as he reached them. He handed Shilpa and Tanvi a cup each and sat down in the seat across the aisle from them. Shilpa watched as he put in his earphones and tapped something into his phone. He had insisted on accompanying them back to London, and Shilpa had to admit she was glad of his presence.

'You ready to tell all to the olds?' Tanvi asked.

Shilpa leaned back into her seat. Her parents already knew about Dipesh. The CPS had got to them before she had the chance. The investigation into Dipesh's death was being revisited. John and Graham had been arrested. Her parents were angry at the initial injustice, but they were worried too, for Shilpa's safety, wondering what kind of community she was living in. She hadn't yet told them about Mason and Alison, Izzy and Theo.

Had she made the right decision leaving everyone and everything she knew in London to move to a small estuary town in Devon? She stared out of the window as Tanvi busied herself with a glossy magazine she had bought at the station.

Devon was so far from what she knew, from her old friends and family. But her uncle had left her his house, and she felt a duty to make a life for herself there. It felt right to be there, especially after the circumstances Dipesh had died under. If she hadn't moved into his home, she never would have discovered the truth about his death. And murder aside, she was making a name for herself in Devon. Sweet Treats was gaining popularity in the short time she had lived in Otter's Reach, and it was all her doing. For the first time in her life, she felt like she was achieving something, something good. She most definitely hadn't found love, but she was making friends. Olivia and Danny had called on her every day since finding out about Theo and Izzy, Olivia wrongly blaming herself for introducing them. Leoni had come over with coffee more than once and for more than just a gossip. Even her neighbour Elaine Alden had ventured out of her home to visit her with the largest bouquet of flowers she had ever seen.

Shilpa Solanki looked out of the window and smiled. Devon, against all odds, was beginning to feel like home.

THE END

Acknowledgements

I was introduced to South Devon by my husband, whose parents have a beautiful house on the Kingsbridge estuary. Having spent time at this idyllic retreat, it was difficult not to want to set my next novel there. The changing landscape of the estuary is extraordinary. In summer the coming and going of the tide calms the soul. In winter the scene is raw but invigorating. The ever-changing landscape of the estuary never fails to amaze me on every visit.

Otter's Reach, Glass Bay and Mermaid Point are fictitious locations, but they are largely influenced by Kingsbridge and its surrounds.

My in-laws have been kind enough to share their home with me and provide me with anecdotes and fodder for my novels. Thank you, Jan and Bruce, to whom this book is dedicated, for sharing your home with me.

Thanks also goes to Neha for her cake baking wisdom, allowing me to check the pairing of flavours at any time of the day and night. Shilpa's cakes wouldn't be the same without you. Thank you to Anna and Dad for your unwavering support; Maggie Newton for coming up with the title and the usual suspects, Urmi, Subrina, Jigna, Gemma, Claire, Becky and Sigrid, for allowing me to bounce ideas off you and for listening to my wild plotting.

A big thank you to my writers' group: Abingdon Writers' Fiction Adult's Group. Thank you for your insight and brutal, but much needed, critique. And to Emily Nemchick who did an initial edit of my manuscript. Your support and guidance has made this a better book.

A massive thank you to the whole team Bloodhound Books. In particular, Betsy and Fred for taking a chance on me, Clare for her constructive insight and attention to detail and Tara for her guidance, support and all her work behind the scenes.

Finally, a big thanks goes to my husband James for putting up with my constant tapping at the laptop at all hours and my children Sophie and Nathan for occasionally napping, therefore allowing me to write this book!

A note from the publisher

Thank you for reading this book. If you enjoyed it please do consider leaving a review on Amazon to help others find it too.

We hate typos. All of our books have been rigorously edited and proofread, but sometimes mistakes do slip through. If you have spotted a typo, please do let us know and we can get it amended within hours.

info@bloodhoundbooks.com

Printed in Great Britain
by Amazon

82938091R00174